# BAWAAJIGAN

### STORIES OF POWER

# BAWAAJIGAN
## STORIES OF POWER

THE EXILE BOOK OF ANTHOLOGY SERIES
NUMBER EIGHTEEN

EDITED AND WITH INTRODUCTION AND AFTERWORD BY
## NATHAN NIIGAN NOODIN ADLER
## CHRISTINE MISKONOODINKWE SMITH

Publishers of singular
Fiction, Poetry, Nonfiction, Translation, Drama and Graphic Books

Library and Archives Canada Cataloguing in Publication

Title: Bawaajigan : stories of power / edited and with an introduction and afterword
by Nathan Niigan Noodin Adler, Christine Miskonoodinkwe Smith.
Names: Adler, Nathan Niigan Noodin, editor. | Smith, Christine
Miskonoodinkwe, 1973- editor.
Series: Exile book of anthology series (Exile editions Ltd.) ; no. 18.
Description: Series statement: The Exile book of anthology series ; number eighteen
Identifiers: Canadiana (print) 20190134917 | Canadiana (ebook) 20190140887 |
ISBN 9781550968415 (softcover) | ISBN 9781550968422 (EPUB) |
ISBN 9781550968439 (Kindle) | ISBN 9781550968446 (PDF)
Subjects: LCSH: Dreams — Fiction. | LCSH: Canadian literature — Indian authors. |
LCSH: American literature — Indian authors. | LCSH: Short stories. |
CSH: Canadian literature (English) — Native authors.
Classification: LCC PN6120.95.D67 B5 2019 | DDC 813/.0109353 — dc23

Second printing, 2022
Copyright © Nathan Niigan Noodin Adler, Christine Miskonoodinkwe Smith, 2019
Copyrights © to the stories rest with the authors, 2019
Cover art by Nalakwsis
Text and cover design by Michael Callaghan
Typeset in Fairfield, Cambria, and Gill Sans fonts at Moons of Jupiter Studios
Published by Exile Editions Ltd ~ www.ExileEditions.com
144483 Southgate Road 14 – GD, Holstein, Ontario, N0G 2A0
Printed and Bound in Canada by Imprimerie Gauvin

We gratefully acknowledge the Canada Council for the Arts, the Government of Canada,
the Ontario Arts Council, and Ontario Creates for their support toward our publishing
activities.

 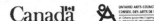  

Canadian sales representation: The Canadian Manda Group,
664 Annette Street, Toronto ON M6S 2C8. www.mandagroup.com 416 516 0911

North American and international distribution, and U.S. sales:
Independent Publishers Group, 814 North Franklin Street,
Chicago IL 60610. www.ipgbook.com toll free: 1 800 888 4741

*This book is dedicated to our Elders and trailblazers
who led the way so our stories could be heard.*

# Contents

# BOOZHOO! BIINDIIGEN!

## INTRODUCTION

Welcome to the *Bawaajigan* anthology, named for the Anishinaabemoowin word for *dream,* or *vision.* When I was thinking of how to bring stories together for this anthology, I researched what themed anthologies had been done in the past. A quick search revealed few themed anthologies of works by Indigenous writers.

I knew that I wanted to create a space to showcase the voices of Indigenous writers, and to sample the range of talent across Turtle Island, but I wasn't sure what theme could tie it all together. I enlisted the assistance of fellow writer Christine Miskonoodinkwe Smith, and we mulled over possibilities. In the end we turned to our Elders for advice: "Why don't you do it on *dreams?*" my mom, Mae, suggested. "What a great idea!" I agreed. "It's narrow enough to provide a focus and broad enough that many different types of stories can fit under this umbrella." A search confirmed that this idea hadn't been done before. *Sweet!*

This initial spark made me reflect on my own relationship to the dream-world: I have two spirit-names, one of which I received in a dream instructing me to follow my heart. Shki-Ode'jiiman. *New Heart Canoe.* Following your dreams, literally and figuratively, is for me a central part of what it means to be Anishinaabe. Wherever they may lead, however difficult the path, our dreams and visions are there to provide advice and guidance. I think of the time my grandmother started going to church because her sister, who had passed on, came to her in a dream and instructed her to go to church – a very Anishinaabe reason for attending to her spiritual life – even if it was by joining a Western church. Although dreams are often dismissed because they "aren't real," you ignore advice and revelations from such quarters, at your own peril. With this in mind, Christine and I set about curating this collection – and we're super excited to share with you the range and diversity of stories by these Indigenous writers.

Christine mused on the *power* of our stories and dreams, and it became the subtitle for the anthology: "Stories of Power." In this collection, dreams play a powerful role in how they shape the destiny of characters; blurring the edges of reality; blurring dream-world and spirit-world; blurring past, present, and future; offering dream-magic power and a glimpse beyond what we think reality is. The dreams in these stories come in the form of visions, hallucinations, hypnosis, and the surreal; conjuring a phantasmagoria of imagery – from wizards and talking eagles, to ghosts walking the hallways of a Residential School. They are stories that have the power to reveal, illuminate, and heal.

Here and there you will encounter an Indigenous word, and where writers didn't provide a translation, we chose not to include an additional Glossary. Please don't let this phase you, for in this world we are surrounded by a diversity of languages and cultures, and we hope this will encourage you to appreciate the beauty of this expansive land.

In many ways, how we "fall" into sleep, the way we fall into our dreams, is akin to our experience of stories. When we read, we allow ourselves to get swept up in a plot, the crises, dilemmas, and barriers the characters have to overcome – which is similar to the arena of our sleep, and the screen on which our unconscious projects its narrative medicine, working out quirks, and processing images and experiences. In this way, when we read stories, we are living a communal sort of dream, offered as a gift, a vision, a peak into the throb of a dream shared.

Sweet Dreams,
Nathan Niigan Noodin Adler

# IPAPAINO ~ WHITE BUFFALO WOMYN

## Katie-Jo Rabbit

People are always saying that you need eight hours of sleep. I think in all actuality you only really need maybe five. Lately I've been taking sleeping pills, but it doesn't help, I stay awake through the fuzz of medication and feel like I'm in between worlds. I wonder if this is how Granny felt, before her journey to the happy hunting grounds. I sometimes wonder if I will drift off one night and wake up in another world where I will have to find my way across the Milky Way. Or if I will wake up at the base of the Cypress Hills where the journey to the happy hunting grounds is supposed to start.

I used to think that when you die, your family and animals would be waiting to help you travel to the other side, but I also heard that if you're not a good person you end up lost, wandering around in the sand hills for the rest of eternity, or until creator thinks you've had enough.

I wonder, in the moments before I drift off to sleep, if this is the last time I will be able to exist in my reality. Part of me welcomes death. I know when I do face it, I will face it in an honorable way, I will sing my Blackfoot death song and stand proud as my grandmothers did when it was their time to die. Please, creator, don't let me end up in an old folks' home, unaware of what is going on around me; legs lost to the diabetus; sitting alone in a Pampers, while my non-existent children don't visit. I guess it's too late now to have kids, I mean I am over 35 years old, besides I don't want to have kids only to have them grow up wanting to be Kardashians.

*Paging Katie Fox. Paging Katie Fox. Please come to the front desk. Phone call.*

Huh, I'm being paged to the front desk. Who would know that I'm at the YWCA? No one knows that I'm home yet, and here I am getting calls.

"Hi, Katie, how are you feeling?"

"I'm tired from the day, wasn't able to sleep, but how are you?"

"You know the same, overworked and underpaid. There is a Deirdre on the phone for you. Are you able to take the call?"

"Yes, thanks, but can we take a message the next time?"

Being a former shelter worker, I know this is a FOIP issue; why the hell would she be allowing me to use the phone like I work here? The process should be that she takes a message and I will call people back when I can.

"It's okay, I know I shouldn't be letting you use the phone but the person sounds like they need someone to talk to."

Strange. How would she even know what I was thinking? I feel like I'm missing something. I pick up the phone and hear breathing on the other side of the receiver.

"Oki, hello?"

"Hey, it's me."

I knew the voice immediately, my crazy cousin, Deirdre.

"Heard you were back and the first place I knew you would go is the Y. How is the cook? You okay? Who did you say was the abuser this time? Which cousin of ours has their name on the list as your fake abusive boyfriend from

Browning. [Laughs] I just know your roll. I'm bored, I'm going to come pick you up. Be waiting outside in like 15 minutes, but don't get jumped, I have so much to tell you."

Always the clever girl, Deirdre knows me too well. I guess I really had no choice in the matter. I hang up the phone and the young worker is looking at me like she wants me to disclose what the phone call was about. Instead, I look at her like she should mind her own business and she looks away.

Just because you let me use the phone doesn't mean I am going to like you any more than I already don't. I feel like she wants to be my friend because she knows I'm not like the rest of the Native girls here. Plus she mentioned it when I arrived after speaking with me for not even 10 minutes and derived that I am not like the others. The others who are twitchy and jittery from the drugs leaving their system. The others who are packing three to six kids with them. The others who are all starving and poorly dressed.

I am here alone, I showed up with only a Pendleton blanket, a backpack and bag full of summer shoes. My drug is my homeland, this area which I've come to. It is the closest I can get to the reserve without really being on the Rez. Don't get me wrong, I love the Rez but ever since my granny died, I really have nowhere to go. Her house is not the sanctuary that it once was. I cannot go there now and serve myself a bowl of short rib soup and eat jam and bannock and lie on the couch like I normally would when home for a visit.

I head back to my room and decide to try to rest for a few minutes, for some reason, this has been the only thing I want to do. When I first arrived, the worker who did my intake and assessment led me to my room with what belongings I had, after she searched them, of course, and then encouraged me to sleep.

"Try get some rest, you need to relax." With kindness wrinkling the corner of her eyes, and a gentle voice, she folded back the blankets on my bed and fluffed up the pillows, then pulled the curtains to block out the light.

I thought this was a funny comment to make, because rest and relaxation were the last things on my mind. I just finished walking a gauntlet of girls sizing me up, speculating who I was or where I was from. Girls that I would be sharing this "safe space" with. They were also probably trying to weigh out what I had in my bag. Stealing is a big issue here, or so I was told.

It's been a long time since I had a good sleep. But really, what is the purpose of sleep? To drift softly in the realm of the third eye, maybe to vision? Most would say to restore health, but lately I feel something when I sleep. I think that's why the insomnia started. I feel vulnerable like there's someone in the room, or that behind my eyes there is a truth waiting to be discovered.

I am only here because it was the thing to do. Everyone knew that in the city there were sad places like this one that would provide you, if eligible, a place to sleep. A place to wait out the mandatory waiting periods to be able to access other housing services so that you would not have to rely on these services, with the end result being that you would be able to function in a system that wasn't set up for you anyway.

I was only home to make sure that whatever was about to happen wouldn't. I didn't know what exactly was going to happen, but a part of me felt an urge to be here. Part of me also wanted everything to be the way it used to be. But nothing good for me has ever been easy, plus I was heading toward a shot liver and a head full of angry thoughts about who owed me and who wasn't there when I needed them the most.

Too many stories of Native women end that way and I want my own lonely tribute to be the song of a warrior womyn. I know my mediocre life isn't going to be the end-all or be-all, but maybe something will happen in the universe and my name will fling into the limelight. But I also know that being in these types of situations also gives me character and tests my resilience. That is really the only way I am able to justify this. Or maybe by a twist of fate I will become the person I am intended to be, and I'll inherit my dad's land.

Back in my room, well, if you can call it a room, more like a bed in the corner of a dorm that is separated by sheets hooked into the ceiling like the kind you find in emergency rooms. Preoccupied with my own thoughts, I didn't realize I rode the elevator, or even walked myself into the room, but the smell of sanitizer and tears for sure could wake someone from a daydream. I feel as if I have done this before. I look around the room, my blanket is on the bed. I remember lying down and trying to sleep before Deidre called. I also realize I need to be outside in a few minutes.

Part of me knows how it is going to be.

I will be asked a few open-ended questions, because Deidre is trying to find some dirt. I know she is digging for information as to where I was; what I had been up to; if I had been drinking; or if I was on the straight and narrow. If I had come home to die. The last rumour I heard is that I am living with cirrhosis in Montana. In all actuality I'm not living with cirrhosis although getting close to it, working in a dead-end job and just trying to find someone to go home with. I always do better in domesticated situations. I feel like Deirdre doesn't take me seriously because I don't have kids. Even though I am taking care of myself and sending money to family, even though I need it more. I also know that I will never be taken seriously until I have a child.

"Oki, cousin, gee, you're skinny! You eating enough? Sleeping? Still having visions? Make sure and tell me about your dreams so they don't come true." Laughs. "Gee, you look good." Deirdre gives me an up and down, something that really bothers me. Is she judging me or is she sizing me up?

"Ahh, oki, cousin. Well, you know me, never really had an appetite, unless it's for wild meat. Thanks for stopping by just too quick to pick me up. I just crossed the border." I smile with my eyes so she knows I am happy to see her.

"Well, you know our other cousin is going out with a meth head from Browning? He told us you were coming this way 'cause he seen you by the river. Still waiting or wondering what happened to your lost lover? Well, guess what, you guys only snagged when he was drunk. He was at that river with someone else. Jokes, just kidding, don't get mad. It's been so long, you talk to anyone yet? How are your sisters?"

Her white truck is covered with dust and dried mud and just screams First Nation owned vehicle, come and stop me. It is a total heat score. It concerns me as I have been prescribed some Ativan and I'm carrying the pills with me; I didn't want to leave them in my stuff. One: they might get confiscated, and two: the girls sharing space with me were probably going through my things as we spoke.

I'd met with a doctor to help me through this transition. He told me to medicate and see a counselor. The Ativan helps me calm down enough to function, and the sleeping pills are to help me start a good sleep pattern.

Maybe I should confess all my pains and secrets to my cousin? She would be able to help me. She could tell everyone else what I am going through, and she could get me back in good with the family. But I know I can't trust her with my secrets. She told several people things that were meant only for her to know and wouldn't admit it when I spoke to her about it. She was the gossip, and I know that now. But in the moment; her kind oval face, her curly hair, her chipped nail polish with glitter painted over – I want her to know everything. I feel like crying and throwing up at the same time. I have no clue what I am going to do but I know I have to meet with an Elder, it's the logical thing to do. When you have an issue you seek out the words of the wise, and I have to try to convince my father he is going to make a mistake; something in my being is telling me to warn my father, of what I'm not sure. Maybe the Elder can help me make sense of it all.

"I haven't been up to much, too sick, this one; I loved him, he loved me, he's a good one, he just doesn't know it. Not like the one who kidnapped me to his reserve. I knew that if I could just be with him, that we would've worked out. Drunk or not, I know it was love. Besides, he was the best I ever had. But I just had to come home and be around family, even though no one knows I'm around, yet, I still wanted to be home. Don't tell anyone I'm here until I get my shit together okay?"

Deidre nods in agreeance, but I know she's already called and texted some people by the way she nods in silence.

"I always knew he was cheating on me, I just never had anyone I truly love die on me before. I convinced Cole he was a good guy, but he didn't want to believe it. It was his first year of death anniversary and I wanted to make a tobacco offering to his spirit where he died, that's why I was at the river that day."

Deirdre told her mom, (my aunt), that I lived with a man who beat me and was taken to his reserve to raise children that were not my own. She told our family that my trip to college was really a kidnapping, that I missed my last semester, and that I failed out of journalism school. She also said it was all because the guy I met didn't want me to be smarter than him, so he took me to his reserve to be his wifey.

It was the first time I'd fallen in love. I'd been with the guy three years and during the trip back to his reserve up North I found out he was abusive. And that he had two children his mother was raising but wanted me to take care of. Deirdre made sure that if anyone was ever proud of me, by the end of that year they all knew what was going on. So much for being like a sister to my cousin.

"Always the romantic. So what should we do, you hungry? You want to come over and visit? No one's home now, they're all over at the gym. David showed the kids a Karate Kid movie and now they're all into karate, even David. He looks right crazy in those small white robes."

It felt good to laugh, but it made me think of David. The absentee father of Deidre's kids. He's part Dutch, I'm pretty sure he's a Mennonite. But Deidre would never admit it. I say he is absentee because he works up North on the rigs, but I'm pretty sure he goes back to his real wife in the winter months. I know this because Deirdre let me go to her house a few times. No one else in our family is allowed to visit. And there was a wicked load of Mennonite pastries. Almond puff. Once, I even caught her untwisting her hair. David left his travel bag in the closet and she found pictures of another family, bus tickets for November and every November since he left to work on the rigs. But still he sends money back to care for his kids.

"That's cute. He's such a good dad. So what are we going to do? Cruise? Or are we going to your place?"

She thumbed the wheel and looked over her arm at me. I could feel my eyelids burning from lack of sleep, but I knew that I would never hear the end of it if I denied her offer to pick me up. Plus, she was one of the few cousins that could drive me around and lend me money, so I didn't want to screw that up just yet. I needed her truck if I was going to move into my own place eventually.

"Let's go visiting. The old crew I'm sure is still lurking around, people will want to see you."

As we drove away from the Y, out of the corner of my eye, I saw the shadow of a person standing at the end of the box of the truck. When I looked over my shoulder, there was no one standing there. But I knew in my gut. I'd seen something.

"Sooooo, tell me what were you up to? Where were you going when you came back? What's your plan? Are you sticking around?"

"I'm pretty tired, but take me to the north side quick, I want to go to my storage." When we get to the storage I go into the office to check in. The old guy there is fond of me because I paid a year's worth of storage fees in advance. When I left here it wasn't on good terms, but I wasn't going to live in the past or try and live up to people's expectations. This time I am here on my own account. I am no longer expected to perform. I left a black sheep, I would return the person everyone said I was – The Troublemaker, the crazy one, the one that would never amount to anything.

"Hello, SIR!"

His glasses are half off his nose, he can barely look up. But when he does, he is happy to see me. I can see it in his eyes. Broke my heart to see how much he's aged. Has it been that long since I've been home?

"My sweetie, the older the berry, the sweeter the juice!"

"As if, Rob, you're too old and not my type. I keep telling you I want to be with your grandson."

This comment annoyed him, I could tell in the way his body stiffened, but it also reminded him that sometimes he's inappropriate. But he is a harmless old man, plus if he did ever try anything I would kick him in his old balls and steal his petty cash. Of course, I wouldn't ever dare, but thoughts like this and thoughts of death linger in my mind. Funny how this gloom always seems to crowd me when I'm in the homeland. Maybe it's the air, the coulees, or reminders of the failure I endured when I was young and naïve.

Maybe it is the fact that I am no longer that young girl; I am no longer the scared girl who covers her insecurity with dark eyeliner and Goth clothing. I am now a womyn who is not scared to fight or raise her voice.

I rummage through my stuff while Deidre parks toward the small enclosure. I'm looking for a bag of clothes. I smell winter in the air. The same smell that reminds everyone school is starting, soon summer will be over and it would be a return to routine.

"Do you think you will ever settle down?" Deidre watched as I put on a couple layers of sweaters before putting my jacket back on.

"Gee, this one, do you ever stop with the questions?"

Deirdre didn't offer to help me but was on her cell phone while I searched for a decent jacket to wear. The night was long, we cruised around the city and made a few appearances at places where people-who-wouldn't-mind-if you-stopped-by-sober-or-not lived. The kind of places that, if you weren't careful, you would end up living in.

Deirdre brought me into a townhouse. She knew Nicki, the girl that lived there, would smoke a joint with us because she was always bored and having to take care of her five kids. She sublet a room in a basement apartment from one of her friends on a rent subsidy. Whenever workers came by, she was told to leave and make it look like the room she rented was a toy room.

The basement apartment itself is spacious, or at least it feels that way with the high ceilings and the dimly lit shared space of the big dining room and small kitchen area. I could see plastic mattresses folded up in the closet as we walked in. The smell of soup in the air and the heat blasting on full so I immediately regret putting on my heavy coat. My stomach growls, I am so hungry. There is a huge, silver, water-stained pot on the stove. But by the amount of the kids in the place I don't want to ask, so I tag along quietly trying not to look around in case they felt weird about me being in their home staring around. The aroma of fresh hamburger soup is nostalgic. It is the kind of soup that can feed everyone in the house and keep them full. It is the kind of soup that heals souls and reminds men of their humanity. The kind of soup you had to wait to be offered.

Deirdre walked into a different room to see her friend and I sat down at the table. I saw bowls on the counter with spoons laid out. Basically an invitation, but I didn't help myself until Deirdre yelled from the other room, "Katie, she said you can have some soup if you want. Help yourself."

Funny how every family has their own version of hamburger soup. It is basically tomato soup with hamburger and whatever extras you have in the house. Good hamburger soup is boiled for hours so it thickens. It is mandatory that it be served with bannock. Which there is, cut up and stored in large butter containers. This hamburger soup has corn and macaroni, just how I like it. Other soups had noodles or rice for filler, and sometimes tripe which is used for ceremony. I don't like tripe but this version looks and smells amazing.

The dining room is connected to the living room, the TV is on, and sitting around the coffee table are three kids. They are all eating quickly, like the soup is so good they want to eat fast to get another serving.

Deirdre returned from the other room and served herself from the industrial-sized pot simmering on the oven. The other two kids are eating on the floor in front of the TV. The room is quiet, and in the dim of the television glow I can see the kids hungrily dipping pieces of buttered bannock into their soups.

There are several mismatched bowls set out on the counter, the kind of serving bowls that fit perfectly into the palm of your hand, deep enough to get a good serving, and thick enough to keep the heat from transferring.

I hear the kids slurping their food. Deidre is talking to her friend about someone who was selling pills and had been caught by the tribal police. Nicki has her back to me as she scolds her kids.

As I serve myself, I watch this happen and wonder if I will ever have a family of my own to cook for. I dip the ladle deep,

I can feel how hearty it is, it's difficult to swirl the ladle around. The ladle disappears into the reddish broth, the steam and bubbles entice me. I am starving. I haven't eaten in a long time, I actually can't remember when I last ate.

One of the kids comes up from behind and asks for another bowl. Again I swirl the ladle in the soup. I take out a large serving. I hear my cousin talking about me.

"She was in Browning, I don't know where she came from, she looks good though. I guess she hitch-hiked but she won't tell me." Deirdre forgets to mention that I was brought here by some friends I made at the horse races.

I sit down at the table and butter a piece of bannock. I dip a spoon into my soup and notice a dark swirl of something in the broth. I add some pepper from a shaker and lean forward, lips puckered, blowing on a spoonful to cool it down. As I'm ready to eat, I notice again something long and dark in my bowl. My first reaction is to think it is a hair, but I look at the woman who cooked the soup. She has short hair. I lift the bowl closer to my face and see that it is dark and wispy. I think it's some sort of veggie, but when I lift out my spoon I pull out a long gob of hair covered in a greasy film.

I look around. Everyone is eating fast, they aren't looking at me, it feels like I'm not even in the room. I instinctively reach for the back of my head as I am the only one in the room with long hair. I feel a bald spot on the back of my head. It dawns on me that they are eating my hair – but how did they even get it when I was with my cousin? Did Deirdre cut my hair? Was I asleep? Was I dreaming or having a nightmare?

Back at the YWCA, I am lying on the bed in my room. I don't know how I got back to my room or when I got into my pajamas. I immediately feel the back of my head and a bald prickly spot where my hair used to be. I shudder and try to remember what happened the night before. I rationalize. Was I sleeping and dreamed I went with Deirdre? Could I be malnutritioned? Was this a reaction to the medication I was given? Maybe I've just been putting my hair up in a messy bun too much and I gave myself a small bald spot?

A pleasant voice on the intercom announces:

*"Good morning, ladies. Just a reminder that we have group this morning."*

All the girls living in the safe home need to join in talking circles, to provide some relief from boredom and an understanding of the triangle of abuse. I want to confess that I'm not really here fleeing abuse, I just didn't have anywhere else to go, and that the man I said was abusing me is really my cousin. Who, by the way, is known to be abusive – but not to me – to his actual wives who are desperate enough to stick around long enough to get abused.

I want to tell them that real womyn who experience abuse would not be caught dead here. This isn't really the place that womyn went when they were fleeing abuse. They'd find lonely older men, or a family member, to take care of them and their children so they wouldn't have to go back to their abusive situations. Some would just take a break, and then go back to the abusers to give it another college try. At least this is how it was for me and my family.

I sit close to another Native girl in the group. She tells us she is looking for her daughter whom she lost to the opioid crisis. I'm pretty sure this is the same womyn that was dealing drugs herself. She looks gaunt and lost. I can tell she hasn't slept; she is wearing the same clothes she wore yesterday; her hairspray is flaking off from not washing; and because I seen her hanging outside when I left last night.

I can't look into her eyes because she might see judgement from me and, really, who am I to judge? Like her, I am abusing the system.

My stomach gurgles. It usually does that when I'm going to have some major diarrhea, but I haven't eaten anything since last night. I can't bring myself to eat anything. I check my hair again and feel the bald spot. I am wearing my hair down to cover it. I can't bring myself to look in a mirror to see what I really look like. The gurgles from my stomach get louder. I excuse myself as some of the girls start to giggle. I go into what looks like a jail or dormitory bathroom, because both are similar, just different institutes.

I bend over to check under the stalls and see if there is anyone else in the bathroom. I have this thing where I'm self-conscience about farting, even though this is the most appropriate place to do it. I always hear my granny's voice telling me that ladies should never fart or burp in the company of others.

A gut-wrenching pain comes from my lower abdomen. I haven't eaten anything, maybe a few packages of crackers that I had in my bag, but I couldn't be suffering from that. This pain is like the time I got food poisoned after I ate crab legs. I should have known when I turned over the crab leg and green slimy water spilled out of it. I feel nauseous.

I pull my pants down to do my business. When I do, blood, nothing but blood, in my panties, on my pants, dripping from my inner thighs. I sit down and feel the cold of the toilet seat. Then I see a white gob of oozy fur poking out from my pee hole. I frantically pull at the toilet paper roll but there's none left. I start to push, to pee, and feel the sack start to exit my body. My eyes are watering and through the blur I see this white fur coming from my body part. My hand is shaking as I reach down to touch it. It is soft.

I hear someone come into the bathroom. "Hello?" my voice quivers.

"Uh, yeah?" The voice is not one I recognize.

"Sorry, can you pass me a roll of toilet paper? This stall is out."

A white hand pokes in from under the stall and hands me a roll. Soon after I hear the bathroom door close, and I pray for strength. I reach down and feel the soft fur again. I spread my legs wider and see that the white fur is streaked with blood and hanging halfway out of my body. I think I'm in shock, because then I just pull at it. It feels exactly like taking out a tampon.

I let it plop into the toilet bowl water. When I stand up I'm a little dizzy. I turn to look into the bowl and see through the tears. It is a fetus. Partly pink and covered in white fuzz. It floats in the toilet water and is covered with blood and slime. It looks dead; the eyes are closed.

There are sticky strings of blood still hanging from my body. I wipe away the blood and check myself out. I am no longer bleeding, but the thing in the toilet is a baby buffalo. It is a white buffalo. I immediately think of my father, who started his buffalo herd in the hopes that he would be able to one day say his herd had birthed a rare and good omen, the white buffalo.

I am drained, completely. I pull up my pants after rolling up half the roll of toilet paper to use as a makeshift pad. I will take a shower, but for now I need to flush this evidence. I stare down at the vulnerable little buffalo fetus and I can't bring myself to flush it. Instead, I go back to my room and cut a piece of my Pendleton blanket to wrap the body in. How could this be happening? Could it be that I am sick? Was I bringing a bad omen? How could I even be pregnant – let alone with a buffalo?

As I walk back to my room I hold the bundle close to my chest. No one is around and I make a plan to show this to my father, maybe he will understand. In the distance I can hear a buzzing, the noise of it slowly increasing in volume. As I get closer to my room, it gets even louder. Why is there no one around? Is this a fire alarm and everyone has been evacuated? I walk faster, and the bundle in my arms shifts and wriggles. Through the blanket I can feel the warmth of life, and the beating of a small heart. I choke back the urge to scream.

# BEAD DREAMERS

## Autumn Bernhardt

"The only ones dying today will be them." Rounds of machine-gun fire were met with rounds of machine-gun fire. "Who writes this shit?" Clarence murmured, glancing up from his empire of beads to the TV screen.

It was the second martial arts movie he'd watched that day, or rather listened to. Heroes looking for redemption and revenge through roundhouse kicks, arm bars, and superman punches. While the snappy comeback lines and bad guys flew across the TV screen, the instruments of Clarence's trade slowly orbited around him like the moons of Uranus. Shades of blue, from the lightest baby to the deepest indigo resting in upturned Frisbees on the plastic picnic table where he sat. Each Frisbee was organized by bead color, and each bead color was organized by approximate bead count. The plan for the day was to make headway on a pair of moccasins commissioned by the family of a young man. Clarence was feeling behind schedule, but a little action never hurt anyone.

Something about *Kung Fu* movies was good for beading. The plots were comfortably predictable and the formula set. Some guy with a complicated past (sometimes ex-Marine) returns home to save a damsel in distress (tragic beauty… sometimes blonde or sometimes Asian) that has been kidnapped by the yakuza (or the Chinese triads, or the Russian mob, or the Mexican cartel). Our tortured hero must fight the law, his own demons, and rack up a pile of bodies with no ramifications except the sexual gratitude of the damsel that he just delivered from defilement by the sadistic villain (usually with a facial scar). Every once in a blue moon there were permutations to this script but the story was classic.

These movies offered many hidden gifts. His projects crept one seed bead at a time and looking up to frequent explosions kept away eye strain and evening headaches. They also kept Clarence from getting too absorbed in what he was working on, and they kept him awake. Today, Clarence needed all the help he could get staying awake. Sunlight poured in the south-facing window, and Clarence felt more like a sleepy cat on a windowsill than a man with a deadline.

A dream about Eddy had put him at odds with sleep for the last two nights. Sometimes, you can tell when a dream is a dream, even mold it while you are dreaming it, and other times you wonder if you have any control over anything that goes on in your head. It had been so visceral. He had all the physical responses you would expect during an experience like that. And they still hadn't entirely passed. The shortness of breath, the dilated eyes, the heart quickening, the hands shaking, the blood pouring into lower extremities. Waking up with the urge to hit something or run away made delicate beadwork difficult. Maybe the badasses on screen would take care of the fight or flight response while he got some work done.

Even on days without the post-traumatic stress of an Eddy Dream, martial arts films with their thin plots and gratuitous everything, were an essential part of the Indigenous arts of North America. Men in Sweetgrass, Saskatchewan, filled up pickups wearing hatbands created while Clarence listened to

*The Chinese Connection*, and women in Mission, South Dakota, danced on the bare earth wearing leggings Clarence crafted while listening to a dubbed version of *Ong-Bak: The Thai Warrior*. Clarence would look up to watch a fight scene where the hero single-handedly takes out a herd of nun-chakus-wielding goons, all while his slender fingers worked on the latest masterpiece. Clarence had clothed and adorned folks from reserve to reservation, from powwows to Indian rodeos, and from Sun Dance to Sun Rise ceremonies.

Clarence beaded steadily. He had finally found a good rhythm, his hands, dancing from leather to Frisbee and back again, spurred on by the tune of car chases, heavy artillery, and bone cracking. But then there was another sound; almost like a knocking. Clarence looked up and saw the face of his cousin, Tryphena, staring back at him through the window.

She must have come from work because she was wearing her standard uniform. Blazer with button-up shirt tucked into a pair of dark washed jeans. She'd blown on the glass and drawn a heart with "Let me in" written inside. In cursive. He calculated how long she spent writing in reverse and how much trouble he might be in.

He got up slowly, making certain he didn't upset the Frisbees full of beads resting on the plastic picnic table. Once clear of the beads, he scurried in old white socks that drooped at the end of the toes. It was only a few steps from living room to the door in the kitchen. Tryphena kicked off her loafers at the threshold and sidled past, the cabin greeting her with the smell of woodsmoke. Gently she lowered two canvas bags onto the wooden table. "I brought you some odds and ends. Some of the old ladies came to tribal headquarters with coolers and camp dresses selling their wares."

Clarence raised an eyebrow, a smile peeking out the side of his mouth. He was envisioning the little reservation entrepreneurs in homemade dresses taking wadded up dollar bills into their clawed hands and shoving them into fanny packs. "Hmm…sounds interesting. Tell me more about these ladies. Did they make me any bread?" He rifled like a little kid going through Santa's bag, unpacking mysterious shapes. There were a couple of Apache steak sandwiches wrapped in foil, lime Jell-O with pineapples in snap-lid containers…and just as he hoped, bread imprinted with distinctive hatch marks. Bread that the old ladies still dried on tennis racquets.

Tryphena grabbed paper towels. Napkins would make this meal official. The bottom hem of her jeans normally hovered a few inches above her ankle but crept higher as she walked. She bent, pinched a layer of jean on both thighs between thumb and forefingers and shimmed the pants back down closer to her ankles. It wasn't like Tryphena didn't try, it was just hard to find things to fit a six-foot tall woman. The only clothing options were Walmart two towns off the reservation, or having your auntie make you something. She palmed the paper towel roll, looked back to the kitchen table, hesitating, her right eye squinting.

Clarence looked pretty good today; or at least better. He had shaved off the winter beard but kept a moustache. The hair on his head was heavy with thick tufts waiting to be tucked behind his ears, and he wore his usual turquoise earrings.

Unaware he was an ant under a magnifying glass, Clarence glided across the wood floor retrieving spoons and forks. His old patched Wranglers hung from his waist as he moved. Clarence had gotten gaunt in recent months. Tryphena knew he'd taken to jogging through a section of forest near the reservation boundary. A section known to be haunted. There were beautiful clearings where sunlight danced on the forest floor but most tribal members avoided it. "Doesn't even know which ghosts he's running from," Tryphena thought to herself.

Clarence pulled out a chair that creaked against the battered old floor. "What's with the strange looks, Try?" Tryphena folded herself into the chair on the opposite side of the table.

"I got you the yellow tea you like but you'll have to warm it up...not that that would make it any better. I put it in a urine specimen jar because the lid screws on tight." And anticipating the consternation bound to follow any urine reference, she also offered explanation. "They administered drug tests to tribal employees last week and there were some unused containers."

When Clarence made a strange look himself, she added, "What you should really be concerned about is that Theresa and her gang of ladies pick the weed for that tea right along the highway."

"Well," Clarence puffed out his chest. "I like drinking car-exhaust-tea because it makes me feel traditional. How do you say the name of this stuff in Apache? You should know these things because you work for Tip-po."

Life was full of acronyms for government workers, even tribal government workers. Tip-po or THPO was an abbreviation for Tribal Historic Preservation Office. It was the office tasked with remembering words, stories, practices, and anything else cultural just in case other folks forgot them. Tryphena and her team were the official archive of collective tribal memory.

"I think they call that tea disgusting in all languages" Tryphena offered. "Maybe the car fumes make it taste like that. I don't want to believe our people were drinking that swill in 1492 before Columbus sailed the ocean blue."

Tryphena would tell him exactly how she felt, regardless of whether he asked. He felt a little warmth in his chest when she said, "our people." He appreciated that. Inclusive language. Some folks around here treated him like some sort of alien being just because he didn't have 100% magical Apache blood. Not certain if Tryphena meant it exactly that way but he would take it anyway.

They feasted on the Apache steak sandwiches. In between chewing and sopping up juices that leaked out of the bread encasement, they talked tribal politics and her job. Too much money spent where it shouldn't, not enough where it should. Too much BIA involvement, except when it was actually needed. Somebody was getting fresh with somebody else and somebody said they liked it. From under her sternly cut bangs, Tryphena read off the local chidee like an old school newscaster.

At one point, Tryphena was talking about teaching a night class for young mothers wanting to improve their Apache. It was nice to see her glow with enthusiasm – though it was hard to tell. The Walmart only stocked makeup for non-Apache women. If a woman looked like she just walked out of kabuki theater, you generally knew she had a meeting at tribal headquarters. Tryphena definitely had a meeting today.

In Clarence's cabin, you could pretty much stand anywhere and see everything except the bathroom and bedroom. The kitchen opened directly into the living room with worktable, bookshelves, TV, leather recliner with worn patina, and a pot-bellied stove with metal engravings like smiling cheeks.

Tryphena scooped a wiggling mound of green Jell-O between her lips and nodded at the TV. Clarence had turned off the sound but the screen still flickered. A fight scene in an alley where someone had just taken a dumpster to the chest. "Who's your boyfriend today? He keeping you too distracted to answer your door? Last week, it was Jet Li…small but powerful, I imagine." She gave a closed mouth smile as if suggesting something carnal and forbidden.

He shrugged in subtle protest. "I'm switching it up and keeping it interesting. I watched one by some Kenpo Karate guy named Jeff Speakman. Not too bad," Meaning not Oscarworthy or critically acclaimed but good enough to keep him awake and beading.

Tryphena's eyes found the picnic table, the partially completed moccasins, and the Frisbees. She nodded again. "Wow, those are something. Who are they for?"

Most Apaches and other Athabaskans Clarence knew learned not to point, especially at a person. It could be interpreted as a witch directing a curse. Outsiders that came to work for the tribe, and who wanted to avoid rumors, learned the same lesson. Demonstrating with your head worked within the confines of his living room, but he had been out scouting elk with some of his other cousins last weekend, and it was anybody's guess what was being gestured to. You could follow the general direction of nodding but it was your responsibility to scan the landscape and detect the subject of discussion. Sometimes you just had to pretend to understand and wait for a clue to come along in the conversation to figure it out.

Tryphena was right about the moccasins, they were stunning. White square U's moving across a blue background fading into deep purple, as if a horse was walking through a dusky sky. White beads interspersed among navy and indigo like stars and far-off planets.

"I'm near done, but the family requested zigzags on the soles. Kind of like an Indian running-shoe tread." Tryphena waited further explanation. Clarence's stories were often expansive; he loved explaining the whys and hows of what he did and why. Very few people, even some of the really good beaders, could follow what he was talking about when it came to style and technique. Tryphena had grown up in a house full of beaders. It was always expected that she would bead but for her it was pure tedium. Because she understood the process of making something beautiful little bit by little bit with little beads, she could happily talk for hours about beading so long as she never had to do any herself.

Clarence's description of the moccasins quickly spiraled into a broader lecture on beading methodology but he offered nothing further about the soles. He stopped mid-sentence while making a point about spot stitch and cheerily exclaimed "SPECTACULAR SUNSET ALERT." Abandoning half-eaten Jell-O, he covered the distance to the door in a few easy steps. The elegance of his gait made him look like he was wearing Persian slippers rather than old white socks that drooped in the toes.

Clarence picked up the expression "spectacular sunrise alert" during his off-reservation sabbatical. Tryphena had been raised with Clarence, just a room down the hall. She had only left the reservation once in her life and beaten a path back as soon as the master's degree was in her hand. Clarence, on the other hand, ended up in a dreary government office in Tucson for four years. Sometimes in the late afternoons, one of Clarence's co-workers would send him an email titled "Spectacular Sunset Alert." Clarence would slip over to his co-worker's west facing window, and they would sit on the edge of the desk in ties and slacks watching pink, red, and orange clouds explode and fade.

Tryphena trundled over to the door. Clarence pulled on his work boots and handed her his gray plaid jacket. When they got outside, they propped up Tryphena's phone on the west windowsill and positioned themselves in front where trees met meadow. As the sunset slid down their backs, they held broad smiles until the timer went off and they heard the picture snap.

Back inside, Clarence started busing the table. Tryphena snatched what was left of her sandwich and the remaining bites of Jell-O before he carried them off and tried to pick up the detoured conversation. "What's the story on the moccasins? Why are you beading them like that?"

"The man I'm beading them for was a horse dreamer. His aunt said he was a pretty decent saddle bronc rider too, he rarely got bucked off and never got hurt. I guess the broncs just took care of him and kept settling him back down to the dirt on a cloud." Clarence opened his mouth to add more but curiosity had swollen up thick in Tryphena's throat. "Don't you think beaded soles are a bit strange?"

Clarence stood up from behind the fridge door, "Try, he won't walk on the soles. He'll be buried with 'em on. Car accident...not a rodeo. I'm on the clock so gonna use some lazy stitch to show texture...there's no chance the stitches will pull. Should make things go a little quicker."

Tryphena's eyebrows lowered half mast. "Oh, I see."

The moccasins with horse tracks across the night sky would only be worn once. "You said he was a horse dreamer? Is that one of the great mysteries from your buffalo side?" Tryphena always referred to Clarence's conspicuously un-Apache, Lakota heritage as his buffalo side. That part of him was indeed mysterious, not just because he grew up with Apaches, but because of his famously absent father, Franklin Peroux. Clarence had only met him once when he was 28. A friend had introduced them at a powwow in Colorado as if they were strangers.

The momentous occasion went something like:

"Clarence, you don't know Frank, but he's the Head Northern Drum Judge." Probably only Clarence knew who he really was, and he wasn't going to mention anything then, now, or ever. Why stir up the dust of an entire lifetime?

The funny thing was that he didn't remember his father's face or anything about him as a person. All Clarence focused on during the brief greeting with the Drum Judge was the polished cowboy boots he wore, and the beaded vest with whirlwinds, tipis, and morning star designs covering its entirety. He eyed the vest, memorizing colors and stitches. The designs were old – not the stylized bling that dancers wore now. "The Flash is Cash" had become the refrain to justify departure from tradition. It certainly was for Clarence. He made plenty of neon-sign pieces for online powwow customers. Nowadays, you might even catch a young kid sporting a beaded Pokemon, Hello Kitty, or Teenage Mutant Ninja Turtle instead of an elk or bear.

The modern designs Clarence beaded were seldom like his father's vest. The whole time that he was with the prodigal father Clarence kept thinking that maybe his grandmother or his great-grandmother or maybe even his great-great-grandmother had dreamt those designs, perhaps before there were highways or reservations or treaties or Holiday Inn-dians that went to powwows. Those designs were part of who he was, and it might be the only chance he was going to have to learn about them.

What Clarence understood of his buffalo side was hard won. He cased powwows, markets, and weddings to study bead designs; which tribes used what colors, and what their styles were back in the day when the first beads were irregular and imported. Some of his knowledge came from books. He was an academic traditionalist you could say. His shelves, unsteadily comprised of Walmart plywood, were crammed full of Plains beading designs and techniques. He even had a number of anthropological papers with black and white images of museum collections. The pictures in these books haunted his dreams. Museum pieces stolen by anthropologists and priests, extorted from food deprived families as curiosities for people interested in "primitive" cultures. Some of the pieces were even taken from corpses, but the books had what he wanted to learn. He wanted to know everything he could about beading.

His interest in everything old, new, and beaded came in handy for the tribe. He was pouring over museum collections in a book when he saw items that were distinctively Western Apache. Now, Tryphena, the Tribal Historic Preservation Office, the tribal attorneys, and several of the Elders were on the case. They were sending letters to repatriate the objects, and hopefully they would be returned so their power did not upset the natural balance of things.

What Clarence couldn't learn from books about his buffalo side, he learned from his cousin Tashina – she did the best quillwork. Quillwork predated beadwork, which was only introduced with European beads, so he sort of regarded Tashina as the Renaissance painter to his preschool finger painter. Someday, he would learn her secrets. Tashina was his cousin, to some degree in the universe that only Indians understood, where aunts are regarded as mothers, and friends of mothers are regarded as aunts, so essentially every woman is your mother and the entire universe is connected until some dogmatic Indian says that it is not.

On one of their long-distance phone calls, Tashina told him that classic geometric patterns came to beaders in dream, and they could be passed down within a family. Maybe Clarence was an inheritor of those dreams, those designs, that bead talent that he saw on Franklin Peroux's vest.

"Clarence...Clarence...I asked what a horse dreamer is? You said you are beading moccasins for a horse dreamer?" Tryphena spoke gently as if waking up a sleepy child. She had migrated to the bookshelves in the living room and was examining the titles.

"Sorry, Try." Clarence leaned back against the fridge. "I have some things on my mind." Mostly, what he had on his mind was charming, blue-eyed, and running for Tribal Council. Eddy.

"Horse dreamers are folks that have dreams or visions of horses. Best I know, they have a kinship and embody some of their characteristics like loyalty, simplicity, or agility. They communicate and that animal nation protects them. There are also snake dreamers, and hawk dreamers, and deer dreamers, and elk dreamers, and duck dreamers, and thunder dreamers, and buffalo dreamers, and you-name-it dreamers. Pretty much every special ability is dreamt."

"Duck dreamers!" Tryphena hooted. "That sounds 'bout as traditional as your interstate-tea. I bet the guy that hangs around the slushie machine at the gas station is a skunk dreamer."

Clarence let out a short puff of air, recalling the aromatic skunk dreamer who lurked around the slushie maker. "He must have had a real potent skunk dream. Maybe skunk told him not to wash it off for lifelong luck and unlimited slushies. Dreamers sometimes dream elements or people. Tashina told me that a Double Woman came to Lakota Woman in a dream and taught her quillwork. She was the first one to work with quills. Old school story."

Tryphena balanced a book against her sternum, a warrior sporting a red painted face and Mohawk on the cover. "North American Indians" visible in the title. Tryphena slapped the book shut and tried to shove it back on the shelf. Given the ridiculous size and heft, it took a couple of tries to negotiate its return.

Tashina and Clarence were cousins on his buffalo side. Tryphena knew all about the legendary Tashina even though they'd only met once when she came through Arizona for her son's basketball tournament. Tashina was infectiously likeable. Chubby cheeks, asymmetrical dimples, the way she matched outfits to the vibrant quill earrings she made. Purple stirrup pants with purple themed hoops. Yellow sundress with yellow teardrop dangles. Red stirrup pants with red medicine wheels. Tryphena had heard endless stories from Clarence about Tashina. She even knew how Tashina complimented all her customers after they bought a set of earrings by saying: "Those are my favorite pair. They look pretty on you."

Tryphena pursed her lips, "Did Tashina dream of this double woman?" Clarence inspected the watchband on her wrist. He'd made it for her birthday last year. A hummingbird reaching for a flower, every bead was tight and in place still. Not linear like the Apache designs the old ladies in camp dresses put on their moccasins. Something more akin to the what you would see in the Great Lakes region up North where Indians referred to themselves by strange terms like Aboriginal and First Nations. Lush leaves, beautiful flowers, and inspired spirals. Clarence's favorite beadwork style of them all.

"Not sure if Tashina dreamt of her. Always been too shy to ask. Stylish fellas like me are supposed to dream of a double-faced woman. It's the reason we're good at beading and making useful things." Clarence rocked back and forth pretending to fluff his unkept hair in a bouffant style.

"Uhh, by *stylish fella* you mean 'known homosexual'? Are you saying you dreamed yourself gay? What about Delbert in accounting?" She ran a hand along book spines, inspecting titles, then peered back at him. Everyone knew about Delbert in accounting. He wore flip-flops and capris pants, even though there was no beach or asphalt for miles around – not even in the tribal headquarters parking lot where Rez dogs slept under cars and trucks.

"Indeed. According to the old stories, we dream ourselves wíŋkte, and a beader, and a good listener, and probably a lot of stuff. You dream all those things, and they become your path. You chose them before you were born and then dream of them when you get here."

Tryphena folded her arms across her button up. "You've never gone on a vision quest, you've never even been to the Black Hills, you spend all your time with us Apaches. When did you have time to dream of this double-faced woman?"

"To be honest, I don't remember. But do you remember when I got strep in fifth grade. I had a fever and I slept for two days straight? I kept having dreams of Mr. Ellis, our teacher. Different scenarios over and over again. Stuff I haven't even tried out to this day. Stuff that might not work with earth's gravity but you kind of wish it would."

Typhena searched Clarence's face. Placid like he had told her some banal fact like, "Oh, incidentally, there is tea on the stove."

They had always been close, but they were still siblings. The saying about good fences making good neighbors applies to all relations, especially close ones. This level of disclosure wasn't typical for Clarence, but sleep deprivation and heart-break redefined typical. Tryphena wasn't certain if she was up for all this disclosure so early in the late afternoon.

"Mr. Ellis is no double-faced woman, but I suppose your fever lust counts as your own sweat lodge of sorts. Very tradi-tional like your tea. Mr. Ellis wore suspenders every day with a belt. Safety first! Probably because he knew little perverts like you were dreaming yourself into a state of beading ecstasy while he was up at the chalkboard and shit knows what else."

Clarence had her up against the ropes. This kind of advan-tage was rare, he must make use of this momentum before it was lost, startle her with more honesty. He must…

Tryphena went to turn on the faucet in the kitchen. She always wanted to wash her hands after touching the museum books. "Speaking of dreamy bucks, local chidee has been buzzing with stories of you and Eddy...our future tribal chairman." By the time she reached the sink, Tryphena had flipped the thrust of the conversation. "Supposedly, you two have been running all over the reservation in nothing but moccasins and thongs. At least, that's what I hear. What did you call Eddy? An elk man? Does that mean he's an elk dreamer?"

"Not necessarily. It's like they're born with an elk spirit. They tear the tribe apart. Charismatic, seductive, and power-ful like a bull that calls in a harem of cows, they call in fools like me, and well – like everyone. Maybe I'm not explaining this right. Uh, it's all mind plays and power games."

Clarence sunk into Tryphena's chair and sighed: "He'll fit right in on tribal council. I hope that's over now – whatever it was. With Eddy everything is on hopeless repeat, nothing goes nowhere. When I treat him as a friend he insults me in front of people, he steals my pajamas, and when we get romantic he pushes me away and tells me I got it all wrong. Two nights ago, I dreamed I was walking down to get the mail and he met me at the edge of the forest. A wolf with blue eyes. I knew it was him, and that he would never stop hunt-ing me. I haven't slept since. I'm too scared of what's on the back of my eyelids."

Tryphena walked over and rested a hand on his shoulder, speaking in a serious tone. "I better get you a dreamcatcher so you don't lose your pajamas. They're a Lakota thing so your buffalo side will like that, even if they've been appropriated by drowsy drivers. Maybe I can car-jack a white guy on the inter-state and snatch the dreamcatcher from his rear-view mirror. Harvest some wild tea while I'm at it."

She glanced down at the beaded watch Clarence had made for her. "Oh no, I've got to pick up Shawny." Clarence thought of his little niece waiting at the neighbor's.

Shawny and Tashina had never met, but they had the same life philosophy – when you wear blue, you wear all blue, and when you wear purple, you wear all purple. The only difference was that Shawny dressed it up with a pair of kicks that lit up every time she put her foot down. Truly classic. Clarence couldn't wait to bead more stuff for her as she got older. She'd already outgrown the necklace he'd made for her.

Clarence handed Tryphena her canvas bags, escorted her two steps, and held the door open. "I'll be looking forward to the carjacked dreamcatcher you promised. Also, could you send the sunset pic when you get to a place where there's a signal?" Tryphena grinned.

Later that evening, Tryphena was ready for bed. Teeth brushed, little ones tucked away, and two hours spent reading files from work. Her hair still smelled of woodsmoke from the cabin. She hadn't sent Clarence his spectacular sunset, so she opened the photo on her phone.

The sunset in the picture was on-fire-gorgeous. They were a little less so. Clarence's hair had a mind of its own and there were dark circles under his eyes. Still, he looked happy to be having his picture taken. She was older than she remembered herself to be and her face was a bit washed out. Perhaps, it was the lighting? Exhausted but not ready to get up from the couch, Tryphena continued to study the picture. Two glowing blue orbs seemed to emerge from the tree line behind Clarence. Perhaps light reflected from the sun? And the subtle outline of a large wolf came into focus.

It wasn't uncommon to see a wolf on the reservation. There were rumors that wolves were running with the Rez dogs. The tribe's wildlife program had reintroduced wolves and their numbers had exploded. Tryphena had seen one cross the highway on her way to work, and she always heard them howling near the high mountain lakes at night. Still, it was one thing to know wolves were about and a whole other thing to be standing next to one. This might be something best kept to herself for now. Besides, cell service was better at tribal headquarters.

As soon as Tryphena departed from his cabin, Clarence returned to the plastic picnic table and his orbiting Frisbees. He popped in an ancient but much loved tape of *Big Trouble in Little China*, beaded until 1:00 in the morning, then tucked himself between flannel sheets.

He didn't dream of blue-eyed wolves this night. Instead, he dreamt of a young man in a black cowboy hat riding a buckskin horse. North to an area heavy with the scent of pine. There, he met a woman, beautiful and oddly familiar. Every so often, she put her hand on the horse's cheek or gently touched the war bridle to keep him on the right path to a place where the stars twinkled blue. There, she turned over her charges to a grandmother who lived in the stars. Even though the young man journeyed far, along the Big Dipper, and the Milky Way, his feet never touched the ground, and every bead on his moccasins stayed just where Clarence had put them.

# FLIGHT

## Brittany Johnson

How old were you when you first learned how to fly? The first time you felt your soul leave your body because your body just couldn't hold all of that emotion or bullshit inside at once, and so you flew away?

Hunter's first time was sitting in church when Laura Fitzgerald bent over a little too far and his eyes lingered a little too long and he knew God would strike him dead for the thoughts in his head. He needed to get away to keep himself pure. The second time was after he and Laura got it on in the backseat of his dad's old beater with the custom velvet seat cushions. His dad loved those seat cushions. They spilled ice cream cones all over each other and the seat and it mixed with sweat and cum and tears. Hunter's dad noticed, put his hand on his belt, and Hunter knew he had to vacate his body. The third time was when Laura left him for Joey, that dumbass from the basketball team who was missing one front tooth. Hunter needed a break from the pain so he smoked a joint and sailed away. Every time after was because he didn't want to feel anything. It's gotten pretty easy over the years. Maybe that's why She came for him. Maybe not.

Being 22 and pissed off at the world, Hunter listened to a lot of metal. Made a ceremony of blasting Slayer in his truck when he drove into town. *God hates us all!* Mom hated when he listened to shit like that. "You're gonna become a psycho or invite evil spirits!" she would say; chewing-tobacco making her bottom lip fatter than it already was. Hunter liked to think it made him a better driver on winter roads.

He pulled into the Shell and gassed up, paying at the pump. He needed smokes though, so he went inside. Jimmy worked there and knew his cigarette preference. They'd gone to high school together. At one point they were friends, but Jimmy was a narc so Hunter stopped hanging out with him after realizing he was the dumbass who sold him out to Mr. Isaac over two lousy grams. Jimmy had two packs out already, his feminine hands swatting the packs toward Hunter before he even made it up to the counter. Hunter noticed his pale pink nail polish and overly tweezed eyebrows framing deep brown eyes.

Jimmy looked at his nails, then sighed. "Two today?"

"Yup." Hunter tried to look tough.

"You know these things are gonna kill you."

"Good." He stuck his chin up a little. He wanted Jimmy to think that death didn't freak his shit.

"Whatever, dude. Pay up." Jimmy rolled his eyes.

Hunter pulled a bill out of his wallet and handed it over. Jimmy counted out the change and tossed it on the counter instead of into Hunter's open hand. Hunter felt his nostrils flare and his fist tightened in his hoodie pocket. Hunter nodded and scooped up the change. He instead now turned and walked out, barely missing a cute brunette walking in. She scowled at him. Hunter opted not to flirt with her.

It was snowing lightly. He hopped in the truck and started the engine, speakers blasting to life at full volume. "Fuck!" He quickly turned it down. He'd forgotten how loud he had the music up before he went in. He opened a pack of smokes and lit one up, throwing the cellophane onto the floor. There were already several wrappers on the floor, some A&W bags, two Tim's cups, and an empty can of Pilsner. Hunter remembered a post his buddy Mick made on Facebook about how chicks keep their vehicles filthy and dudes keep theirs clean and how houses are the opposite. Both of his had garbage all over the place. Maybe today he would empty it. Maybe not.

He pulled into the A&W drive-thru, turned down the Slayer a bit more, and ordered a Mozza Burger Combo with onion rings and a root beer. When he pulled up to the window, he threw the butt on the ground and exhaled the smoke just as the girl opened the window to take his money. The windshield wipers left streaks of melted snow that froze in the cold.

"That'll be – dude, what the hell?" She had a severe buck-toothed overbite and her black hair looked like it hadn't been washed in a while.

"Sorry," Hunter offered. He wasn't really sorry.

"People like you are why I hate this job." She handed him the debit machine without asking how he would like to pay and closed the window. He fished his debit card out of his wallet, inserted it, put in the PIN, and waited for her to take the machine back. After about a minute of waiting, he turned the music up and placed the machine on the edge of the window. She opened the window and took the machine back inside with a look. Shortly after, she handed his food out with that same look and a glare down to the still smoking cigarette butt. *The crippled youth try in dismay to sabotage the carcass Earth!* He hadn't seen her working here before. He wondered where she came from but didn't ask.

Hunter drove a little way down the road and parked. He was a good winter driver, but he didn't like to eat while driving. Back in the winter of 1998 his dad had gotten into a bender when the pickles from his burger exploded out onto his shirt. He rear-ended an old lady in a brown GMC. They ended up having to pay out of pocket for the damages to avoid another insurance claim and the power got shut off for a couple days. Mom had to haul all their frozen food over to Auntie Helen's and she was super mad.

"Classic," Hunter grumbled when he bit into a semi-warm onion ring. It was really hit and miss with their rings. More hits than misses, usually. He tore open a packet of ketchup with his teeth, spitting the foil onto the floor and licking the red condiment off his lips. He slathered the ring in his hand before eating it. Sometimes ketchup made shitty food taste better, and today was one of those days.

After scarfing down the tepid food, Hunter drove down the road to the library. It was usually better than sitting at home doing nothing. Mick made fun of him for being a nerd whenever he saw him parked out front, but he didn't care. The realities in books were so much better than his lame reality at home. He parked around the corner, grabbing his leather gloves from the seat next to him. Hunter thought they made him look like a serial killer. Not that he was one. But they made him feel like he could take on anything.

The door to the library opened and the smell of old books and dust assaulted his nostrils. Hunter loved it. Ms. Hobbs, the librarian, smiled at him and walked out from behind her desk. She looked exactly like a librarian should: oversized glasses, graying hair pulled back in a tight bun, pastel pink blouse with a tacky floral vest, light brown pants and tan loafers. She had bright pink lipstick on today that highlighted the cigarette lines around her mouth. Her skin was light brown in color, but Hunter never asked her what her ethnicity was. Maybe she was Native. Maybe not.

"Hey, Hunter. Got some new comics in on Monday. Wanna check 'em out?"

He smiled politely. "Sure."

"There is one with a Native kid in it. You might like that one."

He pretended he wasn't annoyed. "Cool."

She guided him over to the tiny section marked COMICS AND GRAPHIC NOVELS and pointed out the new additions. She was babbling about the artist being Native too, but he had tuned her out already. He nodded, grabbed a few of the more interesting looking ones, and went to sit in the reading area, if you can really call it that. It was basically just one super old recliner chair, a leather beanbag chair that probably didn't get wiped very often, and two desks with ancient Dell's and plastic chairs.

Hunter took off his gloves and jacket and settled in on the old recliner. He opened up the first book and flipped absent-mindedly through the pages. It had a Native guy as the main character. He was a superhero of some kind. There was another one who was a villain. He smiled. As he leafed through the pages, the door opened and cold air swirled around him. He looked up and saw Laura. Bleached blonde hair hanging wild around her chubby face, no makeup except a layer of pink lip gloss, and an oversized hoodie that enveloped her tiny frame. Why did she have to look so damn hot?

Hunter's heart raced. What was she doing here? She didn't like books. In all his years coming to the library to escape, he had never seen her here. She was laughing, loudly, and was accompanied by Joey (that piece of shit). Joey's long braid was hanging out of a too-small black toque, so long it was hitting the ass of his camo jeans. Hunter thought about cutting it off. Rage bubbled up inside him, but he slunk down in the chair, trying to be invisible.

"You're such a loser," Laura slurred. She cackled and pushed Joey.

"You mind your manners, woman," Joey said back. He started to laugh too.

Laura walked towards Ms. Hobbs, who looked thoroughly unimpressed.

"Hey, I'm just staying here 'til my ride gets here. Needed to warm up. It's colder than Satan's tits out there!"

"Miss, you need to keep it down. This is a library. You can wait over by the doors but if you keep carrying on like this, I am going to have to ask you to leave." Ms. Hobbs looked super pissed. Hunter had never heard her use that tone of voice before.

"Holy, just real bitchy this one," Joey said.

Laura laughed. "Like why would we have to keep it down anyway, it's not like anyone ever comes to the library." She scanned the room and their eyes met. Hunter felt his face grow hot and he hated how just looking at her made him want her, even though she was making an ass out of herself and ruining his refuge. She looked sad for a moment then turned away. "Joey, let's wait outside. I don't wanna be in a loser place."

"It's fuckin' cold out there, woman!"

"I don't care, let's go!"

Joey looked angry but listened to her. He tripped over air as he walked out the door and fell to the ground. Laura laughed like crazy and helped him up. Hunter wished he would have smashed his face into the stairs.

Hunter could feel the familiar feeling of wanting to fly away. Not here, he told himself and he pinched his arm as hard as he could until he could feel himself settle back into his bones. It didn't draw blood, but it was going to leave a bruise.

He stood up and took the books back to the shelf. He never actually took books out because he didn't want to bring something that made him so happy into his messy house. The books would have felt out of place and scared. Ms. Hobbs didn't really care that he just came and read and never took things out because he was basically the only person who ever spent time in the library. Most people just came in to check their Facebook or take out a book and leave. Once, she taught Hunter how to play tile rummy when it was a particularly slow day and he didn't much feel like reading anyhow. He might have been the closest thing she had to a friend. Maybe. Maybe not.

He put on his jacket and slid on his serial killer gloves, preparing to face the cold and possibly Laura and Joey. As Hunter stepped out of the library, they were climbing into the back of Pim's minivan. Pim's real name is Pimihaw, but she's never went by that. As soon as they had closed the door Pim drove off. Hunter was glad he didn't have to deal with them.

"Why do you even care?" he asked himself.

Hunter hopped into his truck and started it. It reeked like A&W and musty cigarettes. While the truck warmed up, he lit a smoke. *I am the new Hell on Earth, the Lord of agony divine.* He rolled his eyes and switched from AUX input to radio and turned the music down. The local country station was the only one that ever came in with a good enough signal. Garth Brooks was singing about a rodeo. Hunter rolled his eyes and turned it down more.

He stopped in at the Tim's and took a leak, buying a double-double on his way out so he didn't look like one of those losers who just uses the bathroom in a restaurant and leaves. Not that he thought they would even care if that's all he was doing. But the guilt would have been too much for him to bear.

He burned his lip as he took a sip on the way back to the truck and cursed. Laura once made a big deal about him burning his tongue on some molten cheese from a pizza, and they made out to make it feel better. Hunter really wished she would just leave his brain. He lit up a smoke and pressed it into his upper lip as hard as he could without wrecking the filter. The pain was nice.

As he drove back out to the house, the snow really started to come down. It was so bad he couldn't even see where the road became the shoulder. He reached for his coffee and took another sip. Something darted across the road in front of him and Hunter drifted off the road to avoid hitting it but was able to maneuver back without tapping the brakes or spilling his coffee. He thanked driver training and not being a dumbass. He blinked quickly, scanning the side of the road and not seeing anything there. It had looked like some sort of owl.

He set his coffee down in the holder and switched back to AUX input, turned it up a bit, and set it to shuffle. Vaguely,

Hunter thought about turning around, but he was a good winter driver. He was getting close to the turn-off when he saw Pim's van sitting in the ditch. Skidding the whole way, Hunter came to a stop and popped the hazards on. *Radioactive people search for medicine, pray for shelter, kill for food.* He hopped out and made his way toward the van.

It was empty. Tim's cups sat steaming in cupholders and Pim's purse was sitting on the floor. They couldn't have been very far ahead, Hunter thought. He circled the van, checking for tracks as Dad taught him back when they went out hunting. No footsteps anywhere. Hunter looked around, out into the trees, not sure what was happening. It was then that he noticed the silence outside the van. Tanya Tucker was wailing through the stereo speakers, but everything else was completely silent. Hunter blinked several times and shook his head. The sound came back and once more he could hear the wind blowing and the distant horn of a train. It felt as though there were eyes on him. Maybe there were. Maybe not. He didn't want to sit around and find out.

Hunter ran back to his truck and slammed the door, catching his breath and trying to make sense of everything. He lit up a smoke and cracked the window a little to let the smoke blow out. His hands were shaking so bad he could barely light it, and he dropped it out of his mouth and burned the top of his hand on the cherry. He swore and picked it up, sucking it back faster than he'd ever done before. He could feel the headrush coming on but just lit up another smoke and reached for his cell phone to call 9-1-1. He didn't have any service out here usually and it was no surprise he didn't have any now. Hunter put the truck in drive and decided to head to the house and call from the landline.

He turned the radio down again. Slayer never failed to deliver sweet guitar riffs that go on forever, but he didn't need to rock out, he just wanted background noise. The turn he was looking for came up quicker than expected, and he had to slam on the brakes and pop it into reverse. Hunter looked over his right shoulder and reversed, then quickly popped it back into drive and turned, taking a big slurp from his coffee. It either tasted burnt or the cigarettes were making it taste worse than usual.

The way to the house was pretty simple. Two intersections, then hang a right and you're in the front yard. Hunter still lived with his mom and dad. He had the entire basement to himself. His dad worked away a lot and his mom was almost always over at Auntie Helen's, so most of the time it seemed like it was his own place. He crossed over the first intersection and suddenly was confused. Was this the first intersection? Or did he still need to keep going?

The snow was coming down heavier and thicker and Hunter decided he better keep driving. It was a straight shot to the house. He could drive there in his sleep it was so easy. The road began to curve to the left. "What the fuck?" He couldn't hit the brakes because the snow was so deep; he might get stuck. Hunter glanced down at the gas gauge. A quarter tank left.

"Didn't I just fill up?" *Cursed, black magic night, we've been struck down, down in this Hell.* He kept driving around the curve, completely confused. All of the roads around here were straight quarter section roads with no curves.

As he rounded the curve, Hunter saw something out of the corner of his eye. It looked like Laura standing out in the trees. He slammed on the brakes and scanned the treeline.

*The force of evil light.* She was nowhere to be seen. Hunter's heart was pounding. He put his foot down on the gas and the wheels spun but the truck didn't move. "Fuck!" He popped it in reverse, but it didn't budge. "FUCK!" He looked around for something to shovel the snow out from under the tires and found nothing. Hunter jumped out of the truck and began frantically scooping the snow out from around the tires with his gloved hands.

"Hunter."

A whisper floated along the wind toward him and Hunter jumped up and looked around. There was no one there. He started to dig even more frantically, looking over his shoulder with each scoop. No matter how much snow he removed, it kept filling back in. Panic crawled up his throat and he could hear a horrible sound, like a cross between a shriek and a growl. It took him a moment to realize it was coming from his own mouth. Hunter ran to jump back in the truck, put it in drive and floored it. *As demons come forth, Death takes my hand and captures my soul.* The engine sputtered, empty of gas.

"How is this even possible?"

"Hunter."

It came from inside the truck. Hunter whirled around but no one was there. He reached for his cell but there was no service, and the battery had drained to four per cent. He looked up the road ahead and thought he could make out a house. He decided to head to the house and call for help. He jumped out of the truck and started to run for it.

"Hunter."

It was then that he saw Her: tall, beautiful, eyes every color at once but never a color he could name. Her body was covered in hides and furs from various animals, their heads still attached to their skins. She smiled and Hunter wondered how She might feel wrapped around him. She lifted Her hand and gestured for him to come. Hunter nodded and began walking, knowing somewhere in his mind that he shouldn't be going with Her but he didn't care. Maybe he cared too much. They walked out into the forest for what seemed like seconds, but when Hunter glanced back over his shoulder, they were so far into the trees that he could no longer see the road.

"Do you want some tea?"

Hunter turned back and saw that they were standing next to a fire, over which hung a hunting kettle. He nodded. He was so cold. The fire began to thaw his arms and legs but the longer he stood there, the colder he felt. She handed him a mug of piping hot tea. He swallowed and could feel it burning him from the inside out. He kept drinking because the burning felt so good. Hunter could feel the familiar tingle of flight come over him. She grinned and Hunter ejected from his body, flying far above the fire with the tops of the trees. His body was on the ground next to a pitiful attempt at a fire, his serial killer gloves still on his frozen hands. Close by was his mangled truck, headlights on, a local country station playing, and the engine still coughing.

She took his icy hand and led him to the highway, the snow falling lightly and the cold wind oddly warm against his skin. Hunter saw Pim, Laura, and Joey. They were outside the van trying to push it up and out of the ditch. Hunter blinked and tried to make sense of what he was seeing. She placed a finger to Her lips, and shook Her head: "No." Hadn't they crashed before him? "They helped you learn to fly and now you need them no longer."

Hunter tried to run toward them, to warn them. But the closer he got, the farther away they felt, as though he didn't really know who they were anymore.

"Come," She grabbed his hand again. "Let's feast."

Hunter screamed, pushed against Her, and reached out to the van. He threw himself toward Laura, but it was too late. She had already put Her icy lips to Laura's, sucking and licking hungrily. Pim and Joey screamed but the snow blanketed the sound and they fell to the ground, seemingly unable to move. Hunter watched feeling sick yet euphoric as She drained Laura, then Pim, and finally Joey. Their bodies transformed into animal pelts and She wrapped them around Herself, and covered up Her tracks with fresh snow. Hunter felt like he should feel bad but he didn't. Steam rose from their coffees and floated up into the cool air.

She smiled and grabbed his face, blowing into his mouth to feed him, and he struggled for a moment until he tasted the sweet fleshy air. He dropped to His knees, satiated, yet growing hungrier as He feasted, their tongues twisting together, Her cold lips sucking on His cold bottom lip. He smiled back at Her. Together, They flew up into the trees, surrounded by snow and wind and hunger, their bodies swallowing one another until They became one.

# THE TRUTH BETWEEN US

## Richard Van Camp

She snuck past the men talking. Smoking. Holding rifles. The dogs wouldn't stop barking now. Their teeth bared at what was happening in the field. Were her dreams coming true? Lara crouched low as her breath caught.

There her aunties stood under the full moon: washing the stump of a hand. Washing the stump of a leg. Some of the women washed body parts and prayed as others smudged the body and each other with burning rat root.

They sang with grim faces a hymn into a washing song.

One of the fingers on the gnarled hand twitched and her Auntie Zelda dropped the hand on the ground. The hand coiled and reclaimed itself as a fist. It opened and closed. Opened and closed.

The other hand did the same. The hand looked like a thick spider walking on the table. It turned and locked itself to the stump of a wrist.

The toes on the foot moved slowly, as if remembering earth.

"Lara," Granny Saw called to her. "Come."

The aunties looked at her with the whites of their eyes. Still they kept singing. As she approached her aunties, Lara felt the back of her mouth touch her front. Vomit rose. Her stomach rolled. The body had been spread out on the tables usually reserved for processing meat and fish. The dismembered shapes slowly rolled, trying to pull, trying to reach each of its parts.

Someone was being born again.

The women sang

Granny Saw reached her hand out and Lara, wide-eyed, slowly reached to her, grateful for her grandmother's warmth.

"Shhhhh," Grandma said. "Watch, my girl."

Lara did. The torso sat up and the head flipped over, catching itself.

The old eyes opened in their sockets and looked around.

It was a Dene woman's face. This was a woman now.

Her jaw started clicking, working itself back.

"Cahhhhhhhhh," she called. "Caccccccchhhhhh."

Mannee's voice scraped Lara's brain. She flinched back but her grandma held her tight. "You wanted to sneak past the men," Grandma said to her. "You wanted to see what we were doing, so now you watch."

Grandma's grip lightened as Lara focused on the body, sitting up and looking around. Long stringy hair hung in clumps from the scalp of an ancient Dene woman. Dirt and flowers marred her hair. Old flowers, Lara wondered. Why had flowers been tucked into the hair of a monster?

"Cahhhhh," the woman said as she looked at her hands and flexed. "Aminay?"

"*Ehtsi*," one of the women said. It was Peggy, Lara's second favorite auntie.

The old woman looked at Peggy. "Heh eh." Her face twisted causing more wrinkles, as if being born again was both exhausting and painful.

"Mannee," Peggy announced with a shaking voice. "We are sorry to call you back from your dark sleep. We are sorry to pull you from your rest."

"What?" the creature said through spit and clay. "What do you want?" It sounded like she was speaking through a hole in her throat.

Peggy looked to her sisters and then their mom before speaking. They all urged her to continue. "You turned whee-tago after you were bit," Peggy said loudly. "We lost you far too soon."

Mannee looked up and sniffed the air. Her eyes glowed yellow.

"Auntie," Peggy said. "We need your help. The world has changed. We can no longer count on our men to help us. We can no longer count on anyone but you to help us."

"What do you need?" the great-grandmother asked.

"In our town," Peggy said, as she looked to her sisters, "we have men who steal our girls, our women, and sell them."

"To do what?"

"To do what men want them to do."

Mannee tilted her head and squinted to look at Lara, her great-great-granddaughter. "Go on."

"We need you to hunt them. We need you to help kill those men. Eat them. Free those girls."

The old woman listened.

Granny Saw spoke. "Our leaders bought a buffalo farm. We have 67 buffalo. You can have them all. I know you're hungry."

The old woman nodded.

"But when you're fed. We need you to eat the slave makers too, okay?"

Peggy held up a list. "These are the names of those who are stealing our relations."

The old woman pulled her foot on and listed.

"After we kill every single one of them," Peggy said, "we will return you to the earth, okay?"

"No," the being said. "Not put me back. Let me hunt."

The women looked at each other and smiled. They thought of their cousins across the borders. They would welcome the old woman, they would feed her, they would feast her with names, addresses.

"Okay, Mannee," Peggy said. "I made you moccasins."

"I made you a shawl," Petra called out.

They dressed her while Granny Saw combed her hair.

They sang.

The being looked at Lara and held out her hand. "My girl," she said, "come."

Lara froze. The breath stilled in her chest and her heart beat loudly in her ears. Did she reach out and touch the being that would eat the men who stole women, or would she run?

"Go to her," Grandma Saw said with a heavy voice. "Nah. They always pick one to help."

Lara was always brave. Always breaking rules. Not listening.

"You are her helper now, my girl."

She decided, for once, to listen.

Lara held out her hand and walked to the old woman who looked younger, stronger.

"It was a girl becoming a woman who stole me to the dark sleep," the old woman said before turning to look at Lara. "I heard you praying for me. You called me back."

Lara thought of her two aunties and cousin who were stolen. She remembered praying over Mannee's grave, praying for her ancestor to come back and help hunt who was doing this to her family and people.

"*Ehtsi*," Lara bowed. "Grandma."

She took the old woman's hand as the old woman's hand took hers. It was cold and strong now with the girl's life and wish.

"Take me to the buffalo," Mannee ordered.

Mannee looked so dignified in her moccasins, her shawl. Her hair was growing long. Soon it would drag in the snow behind her as she hunted and fed.

Mannee turned. She could smell the fear in the buffalo downwind. She could taste the fear in the spit of the barking dogs. She looked into the eyes of the young girl they called Lara, and Ehtsi could see her reflection. Her granddaughter was just as starving as she was.

# HOW MOSQUITO GOT HIS NAME

## Gord Grisenthwaite

Nłeʔkepmxcín (IngKLAkapmookcheen): the language of
the Nleʔkepmx people
séme? (shaMEH): white person
yéye? (yahYEH): grandmother
sínci? (shinGHI): grandson / little brother

I was eight years old, and so short for my age that my grand-pa used to say I needed a ladder to reach a footstool and laugh until Yéye? made him stop.

My father was drunk. He was drunk a lot, maybe even most nights.

"What are you doing in my house?" he asked.

"Dad. It's me, Darryll."

"Dad? I'm not your father, you thieving séme? Get out or I'll kill you."

A rat trapped in a snake's gaze. I was unable to move when he came at me. His hard, black eyes reflected the kitchen light. This wasn't the first time he said that he'd kill me, but this time I believed him. Sometimes his mouth said words that were the opposite of what he was doing. "I love you" was usually the music just before the monster crashed through the door. This was one of those times his words and actions didn't lie to each other.

I thought, This time he's really going to kill me.

Drunk or sober, he wore the same look. He stood over me like a tree on hearing "timber." Soon his fists or belt would snap against me like branches crashing to the ground.

"You got no right to be in my house, white boy. Time for you to go." He grabbed me by the throat with one hand, lifting me off the floor, choking me. My tiny hands pulled uselessly at his huge one as it closed around my throat. Unable to find the floor or wall, or anything else solid, my feet kicked and hit him in the crotch. He yanked open the basement door with his other hand. My apologies caught in the hand around my throat.

Thirteen steps from the kitchen floor to the basement landing, not counting the top one. I could run up them in three seconds, taking two at a time. I could get down them in six seconds, no faster.

My body folded on the first bounce. Lightning lit my brain, followed by thunder. A sharp crack echoed through my body. I held my breath, and waited for the pain to scream through me, but I floated in the air, frozen, as if in a picture of me falling down the stairs.

"And that's you," Auntie said, "flying down them stairs again." She laughed like Yéye?. Her eyes danced and her body jiggled and it sounded as warm and smelled as sweet as fresh-baked bread. This picture of me bouncing down the stairs, looked like Auntie had popped through from the floor above to take it.

"Yes, Auntie," I said, stretching out my short little legs. "They made them stairs too long for my stubs, innit?" She wrapped her arms around me, held me close – a warm Sunday morning smelling like hard work. I looked up at her and smiled. She squeezed me a little tighter when Me-Who-Looks-At-Me appeared standing across from us, one hand on his chin. He had stolen my height and had hair as coarse as Auntie's. He never bruised up like I did. His black eyes never smiled. He only showed up when bad things happened.

"So," I said to Me-Who-Looks-At-Me, "this is what breaking a leg feels like."

I had stopped moving, hung in mid-air like Wile E. Coyote at the moment he realizes that there's no ground under his feet. I was about to fall, a little bit at a time, stretched like an old spring. And then, wham.

"Yes. That's a broken leg all right. If you make a turn right signal you would be a swastika." Me-Who-Looks-At-Me laughed.

"What?" he asked. "You look so funny right now. If you could only see what I do."

"Am I going to be dead when I hit the bottom?"

"Fucked if I know," he shrugged.

I hissed a whisper, "Don't say that word." I hated even thinking that word, coz it tasted like blood and fear.

"'Fuck?' You mean fuck, don't you?" Me-Who-Looks-At-Me laughed. "Why the fuck not? It's a fucking good word, fuck is. Fuck. Fuck. Fuck."

"I said stop it. You want him to hear us?"

"Listen. I'm not afraid of him," he shouted. "Here's some nursery rhymes for you: 'Jack and Jill fucked up the hill, just to make a baby.' Oh. Oh. This one's even better. 'Mary had a little fuck, little fuck, little fuck. Mary had a little fuck, she'd used to buy some bread.'"

And then Me-Who-Looks-At-Me stopped. The color ran from him and pooled at his feet.

I thought, O, great, the eff word really killed me, just like my father had said it would. If Me-Who-Looks-At-Me dies now, do I?

The fall should have killed me, not some ugly little word.

A woman's gentle laughter warmed the air around me. Lots and lots of warm. Warm and then furry warm, and I wished I was alive to enjoy it.

So, this is the Happy Hunting Ground, I thought. I had expected more, some color, at least. And puppies running after pine cones.

"You're not dead, sínci?." She called me by Yéye?'s word for me, "little brother." Her deep voice soothed like ice on a bruise.

"If I'm not dead, why does Me-Who-Looks-At-Me look like a ghost?"

"He sees me." She chuckled.

"Are you a ghost?" I still couldn't see a thing. *Blinded by the fall.* Hit my head so hard on them steps that my eyes rolled out like soggy marbles.

"No, I'm a bear."

She didn't smell like any bear I'd been near. She smelled good, like an early summer morning.

"Oh. Are we going to hit the bottom soon? I want to be done falling."

"We've stopped falling." She laughed. "I tried to catch you. H'i. You was a tricky line drive. But I got you on the first bounce."

"My father will shoot you. You should go."

"It's all right. Your father will be out awhile. We're safe."

"At home?"

"Yes, Grandson, at home."

Bear sat with me all night. She sang to me in Nłeʔkep-mxcín. I didn't know the song, but I knew almost none of our songs. Her words bandaged me. Me-Who-Looks-At-Me scowled and slunk off.

Bear let out a low growl. Her laugh. She rocked me and said, "Me-Who-Looks-At-Me's tongue is split from the soap he ate. Some words will leave a bad taste, sínciʔ. Remember that."

"Okay."

Then black nothing.

My father's feet hit the floor like two shotgun blasts right above me. He must have passed out on the couch again. The bear held me tightly.

"Do you remember what your grandfather said to do if you ever saw a bear?" she whispered.

"Yes. He said to drop to the ground and play dead."

"Do it now." One of her thick-clawed paws slid over my face, easing shut my eyes and she feathered me onto the cement floor, adjusting my left arm to look like I was signaling a right turn.

"Hmmm, he's right. With your arm like this you do look like a swastika."

She moved my arm onto my chest, patted my hand, and then disappeared, letting the cold from the cement floor grab ahold of me. Pain cut through me. I screamed from the top of a mountain, I screamed for the whole world to hear, I screamed but only a weak, little moan gurgled past my dry lips. The basement door opened, and light from Sunday spilled around my father and down the stairs, painting me with its dusty brush.

"Stop fucking around, you little prick with ears. Get ready for Sunday School."

Even my not-broken parts couldn't move.

"If you're not on your feet by the time I get down there, you'll join your mother." He wore his black nose pickers. They had clickers on the heels that sort of sounded like spurs when he walked. And the silver tips – Haida-style thunderbird crests worked by my uncle – kicked off shards of light. Uncle didn't want to make them, but almost no one could say "no" to my father, not say "no" and mean it, anyway.

Twenty-eight clicks. Slow steps on a dusty street, the spurs jangled my death song. He undid his belt, the one with the huge Ford truck buckle, the snake with a silver head. Whish! His belt hissed from his jeans. Leather end or buckle? I couldn't see his anger. I couldn't ready my body for the beating, coz my body refused to listen.

"You took a chunk outta my stairs. See what you did to the paint?"

He nudged me with the silver toe of his boot. His belt dangled over me like a noose.

"Hear me? Them repairs is coming out of your allowance. And no movies for a month.

"You bring this on yourself. Careless. Lazy. You just never learn, do you? You never listen. My belt's the only thing that gets through to you, innit?" He tapped my ear with the belt. Pain held me still as stone.

"You fucked up good, so I got no choice but to give you the beating of your life. Drop your drawers. Show me your bare ass."

His words rolled out like they were punched on a music box.

He pulled the belt, looped – leather today – up above his head. My mind flinched. My hands tried to reach my pants and failed. The rest of my body refused to move.

His belt dropped to his side, dangling like a dead garter snake in a cat's mouth.

"What the hell? You clumsy little shit."

He nudged my thigh with a silver-tipped toe and then wiped the blood smear off on my ribs.

"What a mess. Why didn't you say nothing? Don't go nowheres. I'll get some help."

And soon the Sunday sun washed over me again.

Somehow the doctor and my father sneaked up on me. It wasn't so much their words that made me notice them poking my chest and legs, but the brand-new thunder and lightning storm that raged through me.

"Yeah, Doc, I don't know what happened. I send him downstairs to get a jar of cherries for breakfast, and I hear this loud crash and wonder what he's doing down here. And this is how I found him."

"Looks like he's been here a while. Are you sure you came to get me straight away?"

"Doc. What are you saying?" When my father used that voice, he magically turned a "no" into a "yes."

"It's true, innit? What I said? Hey, Junior?"

Junior. Yeah, right. Junior, with a knife between the shoulder blades. I tried to laugh. It sounded like burbling blood. What I could've said… Instead, his words came out like I'd said them through a split tongue: "Yes, sir. Just like he said. I am short and clumsy. Not built for climbing stairs."

"Hey, you know us Indians. How fast we heal. Got that Great Spirit thing. That's why you Europeans didn't kill us off like you thought you would."

"I suppose," Doctor Brown said, "I need to call the volunteer fire department. We can't move your son. He needs a stretcher."

"What's it gonna cost me? I don't got much money, you know."

Blackness closed around me, muffling light and sound.

⟡

I got to spend more time in Saint Jude's Hospital than I had since my birth. Mostly old people ending their time, and newborns waiting for white welfare to put them in foster homes. They were the only ones spent any time at Saint Jude's. Us people in between birth and death went there to die or wait until they had room for us in a real hospital.

My grandmother and Auntie Violet sat with me every day. Some of the old people trapped inside Saint Jude's sat by my bed and told me stories, and some sat saying nothing until a nurse chased them off. Hazel Bob – no relation – walked with a stick, and pulled a clear, plastic bag on a wheeled pole. She spoke a jumbled mix of English and Nłeʔkepmxcín. I didn't understand her, except when she tapped her V'd fingers to her lips, "Smoke, sínciʔ? Got any tobacco?"

Auntie sometimes brought me a box of Cracker Jacks and said they were from my father, who would have come himself, except he hated the smell of hospitals.

I laughed. "Auntie, they can't be from him coz the prize is still in it."

She winked and laughed too.

Auntie dragged me outside every day and made me walk with her to the General Store, owned by a white family called Major. I don't know why they didn't call it Major's store. I don't know why they didn't leave it called Lum's Grocery and Sundry. Almost everyone still called it Lum's or the Chinaman's. The Majors would close your tab if they heard you call it that and wouldn't let you get anything else until you'd paid it off. I got myself barred for a full year – maybe longer – so my father had to get his own smokes and milk now. I rested on my crutches beside the old totem pole chained to the General's wall while Auntie got us Drumsticks. Two white guys, maybe in their 20s, and from someplace else, watched her walk in and the shreds of her clothes fell away as they gawked.

"Pretty good-looking for a squaw. I'd do 'er with your dick," one said. His bare legs were at least as white as a white ass, and the hairs on his legs glistened yellow in the sun, like an angel's shine. He elbowed his buddy's ribs and laughed.

"I'd do her with my dick, too." The other one laughed and grabbed his crotch. "A squaw that good-looking must have some white in her, eh? Let's grab a six-pack and take her back to the room. Put a little more white in her. What you think?"

The Angel nodded and laughed as Crotch Grab humped the air Auntie had stirred up.

My crutch broke against Crotch Grab's back and he lay on the ground, his arm twisted under his body. I landed on my belly, chin first, and scrambled to get up to take down the Angel.

"What the hell? What the hell!" said the Angel.

"No one talks about my auntie like that."

"You little shit," the Angel said.

I got to my feet with all of my weight on my good crutch. The Angel kicked it out from under me and I dropped. Dead weight. He kicked my cast. Kidneys. Ribs. He kicked like a baby. It didn't hurt nearly as much as I could take. I could have beaten the Angel if I could have gotten up, but that stupid cast weighed me down.

He stopped kicking. I started pulling myself up. Then he flew backward with a girly wail. He landed hard on the totem. Its chain rattled and the pole wobbled, hit the big front window. Cracked it but didn't shatter it. Old man Major would find a way to make it my fault, and I guess it was.

Auntie growled, "Pick on someone your own size, you."

She kicked the Angel in the ribs. Hard. He curled up like a baby and cried. The sidewalk, his white shirt and shorts began to stain red. The totem had broken skin on the Angel's forehead and Auntie had broken his nose. The guy I'd whacked hadn't moved much. He moaned on and on about how much I'd hurt him.

"Move again and I'll real hurt you," Auntie said. The Angel groaned and half-nodded. Auntie came to me and helped me up.

"What happened?"

"They was rude, Auntie."

She picked up the Drumsticks and pieces of the broken crutch, laughed and said, "Nephew, you're like a mosquito on a cow's ass."

In a town this small, we had nowhere to run, so we sat on the curb and enjoyed our ice cream and waited for the cops.

The judge wouldn't let me speak: "What does an eight-year-old boy know? Nothing I need to hear."

But he listened to them white guys from Big Town, those two big babies. They said they didn't know why my Auntie had ambushed them or why I, that crazy little cripple, had tried to kill them with my crutch. Old man Major said he had witnessed the unprovoked attack by my auntie and me on those poor men. He said he wanted us to pay for the damage to his totem pole and replace his big picture window. The judge nodded and looked sternly at Auntie and then painted me with a look that dried up my mouth. He told me how lucky I was to be only eight or he would have put charges on me, too. He said that I deserved to get spanked every day until Crotch Grab's arm healed. I knew it wasn't okay to laugh at a judge, and I put on my best carved-Indian face and bowed my head so he couldn't see me laughing through my eyes. Yéye? pinched my wrist all the time that judge spoke to me.

Auntie put a finger to her lips. "Shh, Mosquito."

I hid my face from the judge and smiled. The judge turned to Auntie and said that he knew her from way back, so she had to go to jail for six months and barred her from drinking in town for 18 months after that. Auntie drank only tea, so she asked him if that meant she was barred from drinking tea. The judge turned black as a thunder cloud and then sent her away for a year-and-a-half instead and barred her from drinking for three years.

We stood so the judge could leave the room. Auntie and I hugged for the last time in a long time. She kissed the top of my head. The Angel and Crotch Grab stood across the aisle from us, and didn't look at us. They were grown men and I was a worthless eight-year-old boy. They were men, and I stood taller than them both.

# PTARMIGAN

## Joanne Arnott

Patti began in a small way, completely at one with the Source, a turn in the wave.

Her mother sat up uncertainly as the nurse approached.

"Here you are, Mrs. Baker. Feed the baby."

Mrs. Baker swallowed the pain in her throat, and with hot tight breasts reached red-faced for the bottle. Nearly 30 and in shock from the process of birth. Who would have imagined? Hot tears pressed behind her eyes; she poked the plastic nipple at the small searching lips. When the babe turned its head and nuzzled up toward her cloth-covered breast, she jerked away from the invitation, flashing her dark guilty eyes at the empty doorway.

When Patti turned six, the air was dry and very bright, each mote a dazzle from daybreak to nightfall, leaving faces pinched and eyes exhausted. Inside the house Patti watched her mother in profile, seated across the room: a gray and white dress, one leg pulled up to rest against the other, her whole body tipping against the wall for a bit of support. For the birthday, the neighbor had come with berries and three tiny children, the smallest a quiet lump in her lap.

Patti's brothers played on the floor while the neighbor kids bit their lips, keeping one hand on the back of their mother's chair.

Patti wandered out of their orbit, peered for a while through the screen door, a grid of infinitely small boxes, then pushed the door open and walked out across the dusty yard.

Mr. Baker's legs were visible, from just above the cotton knee to the bottom of his heavy boots. Patti squatted on the grass, several feet away, listened to the metallic mutterings of the man and his car. She was moved by curiosity but reined in by cautious reserve. The man was at one with his God right now. Patti hated making mistakes. Automatically she became more still, more quiet in breathing.

Five days a week Patti got up at her mother's first call and put on her school clothes. Her brothers would need to be called at least twice, but at 12 Patti was older and tended to comply straight away, avoiding the inevitable struggles and combat around her.

She went into the kitchen, along its sloped floor to the table where her mother sat dazed, staring into the middle distance over a steaming mug of tea. Patti pulled out a chair across from her, took a bowl and spoon from the middle of the table, and stretched for the handle of the big spoon where it leaned in the pot of warm, stiff porridge.

"They're still in bed," she said.

Mrs. Baker looked at her daughter, taking several minutes to understand what the girl had said. Those kids, she thought. Then, yelling, "Hey! You guys! Get out of bed!"

Patti, startled by her mother's shout, regretted having spoken, tight with a feeling of blame. She mashed the porridge and milk along the inside of her bowl. When the boys came in, quarrelling, her mother leaped from the table to escape them.

Mrs. Baker said, "Shut up, you two, eat your porridge and just stop fighting."

At the age of 13, on a dry winter day, everything changed. Patti had her first period two weeks before, quelling her fears of possible abnormality – that for her it would never happen. She was helping her father in the yard, pulling away rotten straw and stacking fresh bales around the perimeter of the house. Despite all Patti's care and caution, attempting to mind read what her father might want from one moment to the next, Mr. Baker got angry. He shook the girl, pulled on her arm, and slapped her head.

That was all it took.

Mrs. Baker, hearing the sounds she was practised at ignoring, had her attention caught by an inhuman rustle, followed by a quiet, masculine gasp. She looked out into the yard.

Her husband stood; mouth open, unmoving. A flicker near the derelict barn told her where her rowdy sons were keeping. It was only by following her husband's wide-eyed gaze that she was able to locate her young daughter, Patti, as she turned into a ptarmigan. Transformed into a winter-plumed bird, Patti scuttled off into the bushes behind the house.

"Patti?" her mother, leaning against the cold window, breathed, fogging the glass.

Patti moved through a maze of light snow and stalks and dead bush, deep into the wood. She made a riffling call, plaintive, and found a shadowed place to lay down her feather-white breast. She swelled against the cold and blinked. All puffed up within, with an animal sadness.

# MISSING

## Délani Valin

Leesa convinced a white guy with a swollen lip to boot her a mickey of Fireball. She waited for him behind the liquor store with Shannon's dog, Harriet. Shannon's mom had asked Leesa to take Harriet for a walk. The springer spaniel whined incessantly since Shannon disappeared three months ago. Leesa shut her eyelids. There would be booze soon, something she craved more often since Shannon went missing.

Swollen Lip Guy jogged back with a brown paper bag.

"Thanks." Leesa held out her palm, a bill folded between her fingers.

He shrugged, handing her the bottle. "What's your deal, anyway? It's Tuesday morning, don't you go to school?"

Leesa unscrewed the cap and tossed it to the sidewalk. She drank deeply, eyes shut.

"I said thanks." Leesa wiped her mouth with the sleeve of her oversized sweatshirt. The man was still quizzing her as she turned and walked away.

Harriet tugged Leesa toward the town park. Here, other listless people dallied. Some drank, some smoked cigarettes. It felt like being in a clinic waiting room or a grocery store line. Leesa's mother told her never to come here at night. Williams Lake had a lot of crime, and the park was a good place to do it. Shannon had never been afraid of it though. Leesa took another gulp of liquor.

She'd been having odd dreams lately. Not the nightmares she would have expected, but then, her mind was active enough to conjure waking nightmares worse for their potential to be true: Shannon being hurt, Shannon being grabbed by a stranger, Shannon punched out for mouthing off like she did. Instead, she had hazy dreams of a squat blue house, with peeling paint and a black door. Perched on the ground in the middle of an overgrown yard strewn with trash, moulding newspapers and food wrappers. A large misshapen mound buzzed and throbbed. A hornets' nest.

"You look so glum, kiddo."

Two older women were tearing up bread from a bag and feeding the scraps to three fat ravens. They wore baggy winter jackets and scarves. One of them had on a baseball cap branded "Gary," by a local mechanic, and the other wore a bright yellow toque with a pink pompom. The words "Just Chillin" were embroidered in bold black letters. Harriet pulled closer to sniff at the bread, causing the birds to hop toward the bench.

"That's a nice dog," the woman with the baseball cap said. "Does he want a piece of bread too?"

"We're feeding our black chickens," the other smiled. "But we can share with him."

"Sure," Leesa said. "She'd like that."

The woman with the baseball cap tossed Harriet the heel of the loaf, and Harriet tugged so hard Leesa lost her balance and her grip of the leash. Leesa dropped the empty bottle of Fireball, and it landed with a clatter on the pavement. Harriet leapt past the bread and pounced on one of the ravens.

"Harriet!" Leesa screamed. Black wings whooshed before her, and Leesa winced at the screeching from the other birds as they flew for higher, safer ground. From a nearby birch, the two remaining ravens cawed and croaked at the pile of feathers, blood, and bones at Leesa's feet.

Leesa grabbed Harriet's collar, tugging her away from the dead bird. Frail legs bent at unnatural angles, a wing twitching reflexively in the breeze. A shiny silver house key glinted inside of the raven's carcass.

"Oh god." She gagged. She couldn't breathe. She crouched down, afraid she might throw up.

"It's okay." The woman with the baseball cap knelt beside her and placed a cold hand on her forehead. "It's okay. Look."

Leesa forced her gaze toward the dead bird, but there was no grizzly, shredded body. The three ravens hopped and pecked at their breadcrumbs.

"They're tricksters," the woman on the bench laughed.

"It's okay." The woman beside her pressed the key into Leesa's palm.

Leesa took Harriet home and didn't tell Shannon's mom about the incident in the park. But she knew she'd have to tell her own mother.

"Honey, do you realize how that sounds?" Her mom, Sylvia, a veteran day care worker, used the voice she used on the four-year-olds she gave apple juice boxes to from Monday to Friday. She turned down the volume on a news report about the economy that flicked off-and-on into a pulsating static. Leesa hated the news. They'd started showing Shannon's face, her deep brown eyes and that over-bleached smile with the slight overbite, along with all those other names and faces belonging to women and girls who never came home.

Leesa sighed and took in the mess of her mother's things scattered around the living room: an old treadmill that now served as a clothes horse, a long-dead ivy plant in a hand-painted terra cotta pot, a keyboard Sylvia had bought with the hope that Leesa might take an interest in music. She hadn't.

Leesa remained calm. "Yes, but that's what I saw. The bird was dead, and then it wasn't. And the women acted normal – they saw it too." She hadn't even gotten to the part about the key.

"I'm worried about you," her mom clicked the TV off. "I know we agreed you could take time off school, but now you're out walking all over town and seeing things…"

"You think I'm crazy," Leesa said.

"I didn't say that." Her mom's voice softened and shifted registers, as if she was talking to a small child. "But I don't think it would hurt to talk to someone. It's time to see a doctor."

"Fine." Leesa shrugged. If her mom got worked up, she'd call Leesa every hour, every day, just to check up.

"Good, let's go." Leesa's mom stood, stuck her feet into moccasins she'd worn since Leesa was 10. Some of the beads from the Métis floral design had popped off and the deerskin was blackened on the soles.

"What? Right now?" Leesa crossed her arms over her chest and her shoulders rose to meet her ears. Her back ached from tension.

"You just told me you hallucinated. Do you think I'm going to sleep on that?"

Leesa didn't mind the hospital. Apart from the smell of hand sanitizer and boiled vegetables.

The nurse came down from the psychiatric unit and sat Leesa and her mother in a quiet room. She introduced herself as Marie. She wore a pink polka-dotted uniform and asked Leesa questions, which Leesa's mother answered.

"It sounds like you've been going through a lot," Marie said.

"Isn't it unusual to hallucinate like that?" Sylvia perched herself on the edge of the faux leather chair.

"Stress and trauma can have all kinds of effects on people." The nurse kept her gaze on Leesa. "If you'd like to see our psychiatrist, he flies in from Vancouver next Monday. He has a practice in Vancouver and can't spread himself too thin with the hour-long flights. We can keep you until he arrives."

"What do you think, Leesa?" Her mother lapsed into day care sing-song, her brown eyes round with concern.

"I just don't want you to worry about me," She doubted a psychiatrist could help her. Finding Shannon was the only way Leesa could think of to make all of this go away.

"You should know that our ward is voluntary, and only locked from the inside. People can't get in, but we can't keep you in, either. Does that make you feel any better?"

Leesa stared at her ragged fingernails. Shannon was gone. Nothing made her feel better.

"Leesa?" her mom asked. At least, it sounded like a question. The narrowing of Sylvia's eyes made Leesa think that if she were to refuse, there would be an endless debate once the nurse was out of sight.

"Sure." Leesa toggled the zipper on her gray hoodie, then zipped it all the way up to her neck. "I'll go."

Her mom squeezed her in a tight hug, breathing in the scent of the off-brand, fake floral conditioner her mom swore by. Sylvia stood back and braced Leesa's shoulders. "I'm proud of you. I know it isn't easy to do this."

Three storeys up, the nurse led them through a locked door. The ward was small, with six, single sleeping rooms, a nurse's station, a kitchen, a common area, and a shared bathroom.

"You'll be staying here." Marie gestured to the bed inside of a well-lit room. A wide window gave a view of the town. Third Street, the library, the Catholic school and, in the distance, the lumberyards.

Once the nurse checked her in, Leesa's mother went home. Alone, Leesa pulled the silver key from her pocket. It was lightly tarnished but unremarkable, a key she could have gotten cut at the hardware store in the valley. But it felt oddly jagged, like it might bite into her hand if she squeezed too hard. Even as the metal was warmed by her fingers, she wondered if it was real. Her throat burned for liquor but she needed sleep. Leesa placed the key beneath her pillow and dreamed about the house. Peeling paint. A stained sheet tacked over the front window. A red scarf wavering in the weeds surrounding the porch.

In the morning, she ambled past the nursing station and into the kitchen. She'd been told last night that she could make her own breakfast: there was toast or cereal.

"Hey." A young, tall white man in sweatpants nodded to her. He looked tired, with concave cheeks and an eyebrow piercing. The spiked barbell was held by such a thin layer of skin, the jewellery seemed in danger of dropping off into his bowl of Cheerios.

"Hi." She reached for the box of Honey Nut.

"Those are mine," he pointed. "I mean, I brought them from home. But you can have some."

"That's okay." Leesa opened the box of Shreddies instead.

"You got here last night," the man said. He smoothed his patchy goatee with a tattooed index finger like a statement of superiority. Asserting his few short years over her. "I'm Jeremy. I've been here for a couple days. Detoxing. You?"

"Leesa," she said, spilling milk into her bowl. "I might be crazy."

"Fair enough," Jeremy shrugged. "'Nother lady in here and she's batshit."

"How many people are here?"

"Just us three, unless someone else came in last night?" Jeremy mopped his forehead with the sleeve of his hoodie. "I'm fucking boiling."

Leesa sat down at the table across from him and ate quietly. Jeremy toyed with his phone.

"They didn't let me keep mine," Leesa said.

"No shit." Jeremy snorted. "Not if they think you're crazy, you might call the FBI or something. I'm just in here to stay away from 'H'. I get to use mine for like, a couple hours a day. Mind if I turn on the radio?"

"Go ahead." Leesa downed the last few soggy squares of cereal in a gulp.

Jeremy crossed to the living area and clicked on a sturdy radio. It was an old-fashioned thing four times the width of slim Jeremy. He tuned it to the local classic rock station. Returned with a cup of coloring pencils and a stack of blank paper.

"Better get to work," he said, dropping them on the table.

"What do you mean?" Leesa asked.

"There's nothing else to do in here." He pulled a red pencil from the cup and began to doodle.

"Good morning, Jeremy." A woman in plaid pajamas strolled into the kitchen. "Oh, and good morning to you, newbie."

Leesa offered the woman a brief wave. "Leesa."

"I'm Betty," the woman said. "And I'm going to make some coffee *tout de suite*."

Leesa smiled. "Can I have a cup?"

"Of course," Betty said. "I see you've got the coloring out already."

Jeremy nodded. "Beats the hell out of watching another educational video."

Betty sat down with them. She drew stars and flowers and cat faces.

"Go ahead and draw, dear," Betty said. "It really does help pass the time."

Leesa shrugged and stared at her sheet of paper.

She found it hard to think of anything but Shannon, the drugstore vanilla body spray she half-believed was a love spell. Too strong and too sweet. Shannon spritzed it on before parties, flashing her bleached teeth, and the sparks in her gray eyes. Leesa felt her intestines coil tight in her gut. If she tried to draw her friend she would truly lose it.

"What brings you here?" Betty spoke with a voice like molasses. Grandmotherly and reassuring, though she couldn't be older than her mid-30s. Perhaps Betty had been moving at a slower pace since she was 12.

"I guess I'm nuts." Leesa focused on connecting blue lines on paper.

"That makes two of us." Betty nodded.

Leesa looked up. "But you seem fine."

"I work retail, dear. I know how to hide my feelings." Betty laughed.

Leesa smiled, and they continued working on their drawings, silence punctured only by Jeremy's complaints. "Damn hot in here."

Leesa's paper was filled with dark blues, blacks, and greens.

"That's a nice drawing," Betty remarked.

Jeremy lifted his head from the lion he was working on.

"Hey." He laughed. "That looks just like my buddy's old house. I used to score pills there."

Leesa stared at the page, trying to determine whether her familiarity with it came from reality or from her dreams. She had been to some strange houses with Shannon. She asked, "This house looks like your friend's house?"

"Yeah, well, he doesn't live there anymore. He—"

Without thinking, Leesa slapped her hand down over Jeremy's wrist. "Where is it?"

"It's up before the airport," he said. "Man, maybe you are crazy."

"Don't listen to him," Betty said. "I mean, maybe you are. But it's not up to him."

Leesa stared at the house she'd drawn. Probably a lot of houses looked like this one – blue with a black door and a scruffy yard. She wasn't the best artist, after all.

At lunch, a nurse came in and turned the TV on. Like the radio, it was an old square thing. Leesa faintly recalled having one in her living room as a child. A rectangular box underneath swallowed bulky VCR tapes.

"Okay, now you get to fight over what to watch for an hour," the nurse said smiling. "But remember, if anything upsets you, either change the channel or leave the room. We want it nice and peaceful in here."

"Cool, I'll grab the *Jurassic Park* tape." Jeremy stood.

"The hell you are," Betty scoffed. "I don't need dinosaurs getting me down. We're watching *Wheel of Fortune*." Betty tucked barrel-curled, highlighted hair behind her left ear. The lobe sagged a bit, perhaps from daily use of heavy, dangly earrings.

"Wheel of Fuck-my-life," Jeremy muttered.

Leesa joined Betty on the worn couch in front of the television. She watched the spokes of the big wheel turn, but she couldn't focus on the puzzles.

Betty solved them all ahead of the contestants. "Buttermilk biscuits, dipshit!"

Leesa smiled, but her smile fell when the television reception briefly turned to static. A familiar black door appeared through the fuzz. The door opened and the camera panned into the living room toward a large bookshelf against a yellow wall.

"Bet...Betty are you seeing this?" Leesa stammered.

"Oh, I am. I can't believe they haven't guessed it yet."

The image on the screen disappeared behind white static. Then the yellow wall came back into focus, but the bookcase was gone. Instead, there was a large, dark hole where the shelves had been. The hole looked as if it had been created by a sledgehammer. Bits of drywall clung to the ragged edges and white dust littered the floor.

"We've got two 'L's!" *Wheel of Fortune* was back. Leesa blinked, her eyes watering from staring transfixed.

There was a hole in the wall. What was down there?

"I have to go," she said.

"I told you *Wheel of Fortune* was a bummer," Jeremy said as she rushed past him.

Leesa rushed into her room. Grabbed the key, her oversized sweatshirt, and stuffed her feet into runners. She darted back past the nursing station toward the big locked door.

"Leesa, is everything okay?" called a nurse.

"Yes, I'm fine," she said. "I have to go."

"If you leave now you might end up at One South," the nurse warned, "You won't be able to leave that place—"

But Leesa was quickly out of earshot and barreling down the hospital corridor. She left the building, jogged up the street and hesitated in front of the Liquor Depot. She wanted a drink badly but didn't want to take time to stop.

She dodged traffic and stuck her thumb out on the other side of the highway. As she waited, adrenaline coursed through her veins. Her palms itched, and her heartbeat throbbed in her temples. She needed to move. Hitchhiking was stupid, but walking on the side of the highway for an hour wouldn't be smart, either.

Finally, a gray pickup truck pulled up ahead of her.

"Heading to Prince George?" the driver asked. He was a husky man with big cheeks and tacky sunglasses that likely came as free promotion with a purchase of a 24-pack of beer.

"No," Leesa climbed in. "A house near the airport. That okay?"

"Sure," the man said. "But you know, you really shouldn't be hitchhiking. No judgement, but lots of girls 've been disappearing."

Leesa's stomach sank, "I know."

"Even mixed-blood girls like you aren't safe."

Leesa frowned, "I get it."

The man shook his head and pulled into the right lane.

She watched as he took his hand from the steering wheel to the gear stick, and back. Could she fight if the hand landed on her left thigh?

But the man made no move to touch her, and he turned off the highway when she asked. Houses lined the streets in a row on either side of the neighborhood.

"Which one is it?" he breathed heavily, impatient to get back on the road.

Leesa scoped the streets. There were trailers and shabby houses with overgrown yards. Then she spotted the one she dreamt of: blue with chipped paint, a black door, and a yard covered in weeds.

Except the yard was strewn with toys, an empty kiddie pool, and a tricycle. There was a dog in the yard. It looked just like Harriet but with different coloring. There were three ravens perched on the roof. There was no hornets' nest, no red scarf flowing from the porch.

"Right here," she told the driver. "Thank you so much."

"Don't mention it," he said. "Stay safe, kid."

The driveway was empty, so Leesa opened the gate, and subdued the dog by petting it. She urged herself forward to the front door, whispering to herself the house can't be that bad if there are children here. The silver doorknob matched her silver key. She turned it once to the left and it creaked open.

The hallway looked just like it had on the staticky screen, except there were stuffed animals scattered about. She turned right and found the bookshelf she had seen. It was mostly filled with DVDs. It didn't look too heavy. With a groan, she shoved the bookcase away from the wall. There it was: the gaping black hole she'd seen. It was pretty big – she could fit her whole body through it if she sucked in her stomach and went in sideways.

Thankfully it didn't smell bad. She'd half expected to be assaulted by the smell of rot, but the whole house smelled like soup stock, nothing sinister was seeping from the hole. She stuck her arm through and felt nothing. If she'd got her phone back from the nurses she could have shone a light in.

Maybe she could step into it? Leesa braced herself on the bookcase and stepped through the hole. Her left foot fumbled for purchase, but there was no solid ground, and worse, her hand slid from the bookcase and she lost her balance. She teetered forward and fell. Leesa flapped her arms in a panic. It occurred to her to try to protect her head, right before she landed on her side with a thud on a cold concrete floor. She held her breath for the shockwaves of pain, the throbbing of her head, or the ache of a cracked rib, but nothing came.

She peeled herself from the ground, and examined herself, stretching her arms out in front of her and pulling up her pant legs to check the skin. After such a fall, she would have expected to get a fractured wrist, a serious scrape or, at the very least, the breath knocked out of her. But she had a surprising lack of injuries. Light streamed in from a small window. The basement was empty: no furniture, no boxes.

She climbed a flight of wooden stairs back to the main floor. The hallway was now devoid of toys. Another hallucination?

She abandoned this line of thinking when she opened the front door.

A dark-haired girl sat in the yard with two other young women. They were bundling sage and laughing. Leesa recognized the girl immediately.

"Shannon," she called.

The girl turned, and Leesa registered the silky brown hair and hematite eyes. The blue-white teeth. Over-bleached.

"Hey, loser," Shannon laughed. "You kept me waiting."

"I'm sorry," Leesa said. Sorry for being late, as usual. Sorry for leaving early from those houses all those times without knowing how Shannon would get home.

"You're here now." Shannon pulled her friend into a tight hug. Leesa had never felt anything more real.

# MEDICINE WALK

## Cathy Smith

It was Damien Rathschild's dream to be a master magician, and he hoped that Atotorah the Haudenosaunee wizard could help him fulfill his dream. It was torture to be told he had to wait.

"Your apprenticeship will begin in 10 days, do not come back before then," Atotorah told Damien when he was sent into town to pay his final respects to his former master, Asa Norman.

Damien wished he could escape the convention, but at least mourning was only 10 days on the frontier. It would've been a full year back in the Old World, but the ruggedness of this country bred a certain practicality into its natives and settlers. They couldn't put the business of living on hold for a year when it took so much work to live off the land.

Yet there was a certain sentimentality to these folk that wanted to mark the passing of friends and family. Asa Norman was supposed to be his uncle and people would talk if he didn't show him respect. So, Damien wore black for 10 days, but refused to shed tears for the man. It was all he could do not to smirk; he'd outlived the master who kept him trapped in a bad contract.

It was a good thing Atotorah gave him a generous supply of tobacco for the funeral.

"I don't smoke," he'd said.

"You'll need it for smudging to get rid of the bad energy."

Damien didn't know what he meant until the cremation. He'd ordered it to make sure Asa was dead. Thick, black smoke emerged from the incinerator, it tried to smother him and the funeral director.

"May I?" he asked Mr. Bart between coughs.

"Keep your pinch for the living."

"He would've wanted it," Damien murmured while he pointed at the corpse in the pine box.

Mr. Bart nodded, "Yes."

Damien threw the tobacco bundle on the fire and the smoke became gray and ascended the chimney.

"Hmm, maybe you're right! I've seen nothing like that," Mr. Bart frowned.

Damien took the precaution of smudging the effects he inherited from Asa with tobacco smoke too, because it was likely Asa only bequeathed them if they had hexes attached. For a moment, the smoke turned black when he wafted it over the goods; he stopped fanning the smoke over them when it became white.

He never thought he'd ever use light magics, but it was best to cleanse his new tools from their past owner's bale influence. Indian Medicine had proven its strength to him again.

By the time he was done it was time to head to Atotorah's cabin to start his training. He arrived at dusk and was shown to bed.

Atotorah's frame and choice of apparel made him look as tough as any woodsman, but his strength came from Indian Medicine. "You must get up early tomorrow for your first medicine walk," Atotorah told his new apprentice.

Damien nodded as more admonitions came from the Haudenosaunee wizard, "Pay attention to your dreams tonight."

"Divination isn't one of my gifts, so I'm not sure your people's vision quests will be useful," he sniffed.

"Keep tabs on your dreamlife and you won't need vision quests," Atotorah said.

◢▲◣

Damien hoped he wasn't expected to report on his dreams because his night was uneventful. The scent of woodsmoke woke Damien at dawn. Black magicians were touchy, and he assumed Atotorah would be insulted if he worked while Damien slumbered. He took this as his cue to get up. The banked wood stove warmed pots full of mush, boiled eggs, a skillet of crisp bacon, and toast on a rack. He only had time to scoop out some hard-boiled eggs when he heard heavy footsteps. The front door stood open and he was alone in the cabin.

Had Atotorah stepped out for an errand? He followed the sound of footsteps, which led him down a path he could barely make out in the dawn light.

New World forests were wilder than any Damien had seen before. There was a high canopy formed of pines, and a lower canopy formed of shorter ash, birch, chestnut, hickory, oak and walnut. Closer to the ground were woody shrubs and a fine layer of herbs and grass. The only break in vegetation came from trails trodden down by beasts and men.

There were dark corners along the path Damien found enticing but he ignored them to keep up with the footfalls. A glint of light caught his eye and the footfalls stopped. There was a pile of silver underneath a silver bracelet.

"Ah!" Damien sighed.

Atotorah wasn't trying to cheat him like his last master, he probably only wanted to check his private hoard. A bracelet writhed and he jumped back; it revealed itself to be a snake with glossy scales and ruby red eyes. Damien stared at the creature. He didn't fear snakes, and the creature was far more attractive than it had any right to be. Then again, the same could be said about himself. He was in the beginning of his prime, and a perfect specimen of the white race. This creature, in its own way, was his equal. Its eyes seemed far too intelligent to be that of a simple forest creature. It saw the eggs still in his hand and opened its mouth as if it were a baby chick. Damien wouldn't have cared usually, but the snake's shimmering beauty moved him. He ripped a hard-boiled egg in half and fed it.

The snake swallowed the half egg whole. It should've been disturbing, but the bulge caused by the egg gave the snake's body an entrancing shimmer. Its scales were so bright you'd think the bulge was a bead inset in a bracelet until the bead slid to the end and elongated its tail.

*What a trick.* Damien laughed like a child in delight, so he gave it the other half of the egg. The bulge, less noticeable this time, smoothed out into a longer tail. The silver snake was now the size of a necklace and he was tempted to place it around a woman's neck. The kind of women he preferred would delight in such a macabre adornment while his feminine adversaries would've been horrified when they realized the "necklace" was a snake.

It opened its mouth again, and Damien shivered, "No, let this be the end of this." The mouth closed and tears as bright as diamonds dropped from its eyes. He held up his hands to show they were empty, and it sniffed. It was hard to tell if the sniff was a sob or a snort of disgust…

Damien awoke to the smell of breakfast. It might've been a replay of his dream, but for the fact Atotorah stayed to serve him breakfast. There was a wood stove for cooking and heat. Atotorah's log cabin was like a settler's but with exotic additions. Dry corn cobs were braided by their husks and hung from the exposed rafters. Pelts hung from the walls, teeth and claws intact. Damien already knew the pelts were a part of Atotorah's magic-working or he would've assumed the man was a trapper. The wizard's most prized possession was a wolf skin that he used to become a wolf.

Breakfast was cornmeal mush with maple syrup and berries he couldn't identify. They ate off a dinner table. There were also eggs and bacon. Damien was given hot tea but paused after the first sip. "It's better for you than coffee or tea." Atotorah said. Damien drank the rest of what he hoped was an herbal tea without comment, knowing better than to object.

Damien supposed his discomfort was natural considering his former master turned into a different man once they were alone. But Atotorah had honored their agreements so far, so it was likely he'd continue to do so. "You said you already know some medicine?" Atotorah asked, ignorant of Damien's racing thoughts.

"Just enchantment. I want to expand my skills. Being an enchantress is fine for a woman but a man should live on more than his charms," Damien snorted, though it might've been best not to disparage a gift he was counting on to win Atotorah's preferred heir to their line of work. The recalcitrant nephew was a reluctant magician.

"It might be worth my while to see an enchantress," Atotorah said. "Have you ever seen one?"

Damien grimaced, "My mother: we've lived off the generosity of her admirers for as long as I can remember."

"She's able to practice her love medicine in the White Man's world?" Atotorah asked.

"People think she's an uncommonly successful actress, but her continued success becomes more and more suspicious as she gets older, though it's ungentlemanly for me to say so." Atotorah glanced at him and frowned. Damien remembered the Haudenosaunee were matrilineal so, after an awkward pause, he changed the subject. "I think your Great Horned Serpent inspired a dream last night."

The Haudenosaunee wizard had sent his familiar against Damien's former master. A massive serpent that dwarfed Asa Norman, a middle-aged man at the height of his physical and magical powers. It must've rattled Damien more than he thought if he was dreaming of a serpent, even if it was barely bigger than a bird.

Atotorah frowned, "He wouldn't do anything without my orders."

"I'm not accusing you of anything. I dreamed I met a snake luck charm, but it was smaller and prettier," Damien said.

"A small and pretty snake," Atotorah intoned slowly before asking, "Did it have silver scales?"

"Yes." Damien's brows drew together.

"Sounds like Onyare, the Pretty White Snake." Atotorah was still frowning.

Damien asked, "Is that bad?"

Atotorah let out a breath from the back of his throat. "Before the white men came, a hunter dreamt that he came across a pretty snake with silver scales. The snake was small and puny, so he felt sorry for it. He fed it every time he came back from a hunt. Onyare grew bigger and bigger and the hunter fed it larger and larger animals to satisfy its hunger. The hunter spent all his time hunting for Onyare. Finally, he thought it was big enough to hunt for itself, but it followed him back home and devoured the entire village.

"Soon after this dream; White Men appeared." The wizard rested his chin in his hands. "The Haudenosaunee consider it a bad omen to dream of Onyare, the Pretty White Snake."

"So, was this Onyare a dream or a luck charm?"

Atotorah pursed his lips and took a swallow of his tea before saying, "I always thought it was a dream, but luck charms come to the Haudenosaunee in dreams."

Damien grimaced and fiddled with a ring that acted as a ward. It was all he could do not to throw it into the fire since it'd proved useless. "Demons have to be summoned among my people. I wouldn't want one around without taking precautions."

Atotorah bit his lip. "It's traditional to go to a luck charm society when you seek a charm. My people treat it as a social occasion, but I suppose it's a precaution. Luck charms offer themselves to those who want one. They tend to act civil."

"So, they need an invitation." Damien let his eyes roam around the rafters checking for any signs of wards along the walls. "I didn't even know what a luck charm was until I saw you and Asa fighting."

Atotorah's stared at a turtle rattle hanging from a post. "You came to Turtle Island to learn medicine, didn't you?"

Damien's eyes narrowed. Was the turtle rattle supposed to be a passport to occult knowledge? "Turtle Island?"

"You call this land the New World." Atotorah spread his arms, as if encompassing all their surroundings. "We Haudenosaunee call it Turtle Island."

Damien sighed; this wasn't the occult knowledge he was hoping for. "I had to come here so Asa would take me on as his apprentice." Damien held back from saying more. His journey hadn't been very productive; he hoped Atotorah could help salvage it.

"You entered Onyare's territory desiring medicine." It was Atotorah's turn to let his eyes roam, landing on a closet door that contained his tricks. "That must've been enough of an invitation."

Damien rubbed a fist along his jawline. "He'd offer himself to a white man?"

The wizard shrugged. "I've never heard of it happening before."

He motioned to the closet door. "I have a Hadoui mask packed away. I could take it out to keep Onyare away if you want."

Damien bit his lip. Should he accept the offer? He wasn't sure if it was worthwhile or not. "If your People's magic-users reject him as a bad omen, maybe he is desperate?"

Atotorah tilted his head as if listening to a sound in the distance. "Maybe, but even the most powerful luck charm won't do anything to you unless you agree to take them on."

Damien glanced at Atotorah. Luck charms were probably kept respectful when summoned within a group. The local magical practitioners could back each other up. Would it take more than two magicians to keep Onyare in line?

Damien moistened his dry lips with his tongue. "Is a luck charm that solicits a White Man playing by the rules?"

Atotorah sighed. Of course, a White Man wouldn't feel safe without a rigid protocol to govern the supernatural. "I don't think it's about honor, Damien." The wizard met his eyes. "Luck charms need to be empowered to act. Either by a witch cursing you, or by you agreeing to become their witch."

Damien's shoulders relaxed. Onyare had been small and pitiful. He wasn't powerful enough to ignore the rules. "I need not worry about this then."

"If you dream of the Pretty White Snake again, don't feed him."

Damien shivered. He'd already broken this rule, but at least Onyare was still small.

It was time for his first lesson. Damien wouldn't have objected if he'd been awoken at midnight. That was the regular time for occult rituals back home. Instead, he felt lazy and shiftless when Atotorah awoke him at dawn, as if they were to engage in a commonplace frontier chore. Damien obeyed, but had to restrain himself from snapping at the man for waking him at such an early hour.

"It's best to gather medicine plants early in the morning," Atotorah told him as they walked down a path to the forest.

Damien blinked, rubbing his eyes. "Plants?"

"Medicine comes from orenda. If you gather plants and use them right, you can use their orenda to increase your own.

But first, you have to learn how to read signs to gather safely."
He pointed to a tree with bark worn off. "We'll have to go
around to avoid the bear."

"Bear?" Damien couldn't keep his voice from rising an
octave.

Atotorah guided Damien down a different path, "I've
hunted bears, but since we have no weapons, we're better off
staying out of its path."

He paused to point at a plant with clusters of three
almond-shaped leaflets, small greenish-white flowers, and
grayish-white berries. "This plant is used for bad medicine.
But you're better off staying away from it too." Damien
reached out to touch it but Atotorah gripped his wrist. "It's
poison ivy." Atotorah shook his head. Damien flushed red.

Not far down the path they found a plant Atotorah didn't
want to avoid. It had small arrow-shaped leaves that were
green-white with a fine dusting of frizz on the underside.
Damien squinted one eye as Atotorah picked the plant, laid it
on a red handkerchief, and placed tobacco in the place where
he picked it. "This makes a good topical salve for skin irrita-
tions."

Damien tried to remain respectful but couldn't stay silent,
"You promised to teach me Indian Medicine in exchange for
helping convince your nephew to become a medicine worker.
I didn't come to the New World to gather weeds!"

"I am teaching you what I know, Damien." The words
were civil, but there was a hint of venom.

Damien spoke through gritted teeth "I saw you defeat a
black magician. Asa was hired by land developers to fight
against you. I want that kind of power. I want to be a master
magician, Atotorah. What good is gathering herbs?"

Atotorah continued gathering his plants. "Indian Medicine includes anything that promotes health, from herbal remedies for ailments to what you White Men call magic."

Damien made a fist and smashed it against his other hand. "You didn't improve Asa Norman's health." Damien snarled like a young wolf cub itching for his first kill. "You crushed him."

Atotorah sighed. Almost regretfully. "That was Bad Medicine," Atotorah said in the same calm tone he used while gathering herbs.

Damien reached out and gripped Atotorah's left arm. "Then teach me Bad Medicine."

Atotorah shrugged his grip off with a slow rise and drop of his big shoulders. "If you want to unbalance a man, you have to learn what creates balance first."

Damien threw his hands in the air. "I already know simple magic. I want to learn higher magics."

Atotorah looked Damien straight in the eye. "You may know White Man's magic, but you've never been taught Indian Medicine."

Damien composed his voice and features. "There should be no need for me to start from scratch considering my experience."

Atotorah turned toward the plants. "I won't teach you Indian Medicine unless you're willing to start from the beginning."

Damien shook his head as vigorously as a wet dog shaking off droplets of water

Atotorah frowned. "This is the way I teach Indian Medicine, Damien Rathschild. I won't teach you any other way. You're welcome to leave in the morning."

It was dusk when they made their way back to the cabin, so Damien was forced to impose on his host for another night. He headed out in the morning and regretted not asking Atotorah to guide him when he saw all the scratched tree trunks.

He wound up in a field of poison ivy. Onyare slithered out of the underbrush. Damien swerved to avoid stepping on him, tripped, and fell. The plants smothered him, but he thrashed away...

Searing pain woke Damien. Joints so swollen he couldn't move from his bed. Atotorah shook his head when he saw Damien's condition. "It looks like you didn't leave soon enough."

Between lucid moments Damien slipped in and out of the dreampaths over the next few days. He knew he was dreaming when he saw the pretty white snake, and was awake when he saw Atotorah. In dreams Damien tried to walk away from Onyare, but the snake followed him. Eventually, he became so tired he didn't have enough energy to walk. After an entire night in the snake's company, the luck charm finally spoke, "You're dying."

Damien believed the creature. "Can you help me?"

Onyare slid up to him, the dry scales of his body coiled softly around his arm, "I can tell you how you can be healed."

"What is the price?" Damien asked, as if he could bargain. They both knew he'd agree to anything.

"You will become my witch and I will become your luck charm."

"Will I have to spend the rest of my life here?" Damien looked around at the dense forest, the shadows of the pines creating a deep shade.

"You will be my witch wherever you go, White Man. You can leave Turtle Island once you've learned Indian Medicine. But you must take me with you."

"You're a snake,"– Damien gently stroked Onyare's arrow-shaped head with two fingers – "but I agree to your terms. Tell me what I need to know."

"Ask Atotorah to do a penance ceremony for you, to appease the medicine plants you slighted."

It was all Damien could do not to throttle the snake. "I slighted the medicine plants?"

"Indian Medicine will avenge itself for all slights," and the pretty white snake curled further up his arm so he could whisper in Damien's ear. His forked tongue delicately tickled his collar bone as he tasted the air.

Damien laughed hoarsely. "I've been cursed for insulting a bunch of weeds?"

"Sssss!" Onyare hissed. "Say nothing else or there will be no help for you!"

When Damien woke, he told Atotorah what the pretty white snake revealed in his dreams.

"I need to appease the medicine plants with a penance ceremony."

Atotorah wasted no time, he threw tobacco on the fire and spoke in his own tongue. Damien tried to pay attention but the words were a monotone and went on and on. He hoped the medicine plants didn't feel slighted again if he fell asleep during the ceremony.

When next he woke, the pain was gone but it took days for him to recover his strength. Atotorah burned tobacco on the wood stove every day during his recovery. When Damien could finally get out of bed and eat a solid meal, Atotorah made him burn a pinch of tobacco for Onyare, "It's a good idea to thank the medicine spirits when they help you."

"I already paid him. I agreed to be his witch so he'd help me," Damien said.

Atotorah sighed, a rumbling breath from the back of his throat. "All the more reason to burn tobacco as an offering. Give him his due, or he'll turn on you."

Damien stroked his chin. "If a simple medicine will avenge itself for being slighted, then I suppose the more powerful medicines are even more dangerous?"

"The medicine plants almost killed you, and you still want to learn Indian Medicine?" Atotorah wondered aloud, as if to himself more than Damien. He paid the high price of Indian Medicine's to help his people even if they disapproved. It was hard to imagine paying the price for nothing more than personal ambition.

"Indian Medicine impresses me. If the lesser medicine is strong enough to kill a man, then I want to learn it." Atotorah shook his head as Damien spoke. "I won't be foolish enough to insult the medicine again, but I needed to see this demonstration of power."

"We'll go on another medicine walk when you've recovered." Atotorah rubbed his knees, as if preparing himself for the walk. "I expect you to listen this time."

Damien nodded. "Indian Medicine wouldn't be worthy of respect if it didn't demand it."

With his left hand Atotorah gripped the leather pouch he wore around his neck. "You'll have to make your own medicine bundle now that you have your own luck charm,"

"How?"

"Onyare, the Pretty White Snake will tell you what he wants."

⋏

Onyare was waiting for Damien in his dreams that night. The snake had grown to the size of a small dog. A pattern of gold scales had emerged, so glossy he looked like living jewelry. Pretty White Snake did a writhing dance that was disturbingly sensual.

Damien gripped his tobacco pouch in a tight fist, hoping to break the spell. It was the strongest glamor he'd ever seen. Sweat formed on his brow, but he was unable to avert his eyes. The snake's scales shone with reflected light, and actually started to glow with an inner light as he emerged from his old skin, shedding layers of coins onto the pile he sat on.

Onyare slid off his nest to reveal discarded scales composed of silver and gold, "Fill your pockets. Use some of the scales to bead my likeness onto a fine, leather pouch. Fill the bag with the rest of my skin. That will be your medicine bundle."

The precious scales ranged from fine, round beads to flat sequins thick as silver dimes. He threw the tobacco pouch next to the pile and filled his pockets.

Onyare raised and lowered his head in a nod, "You need a guide on the dreampaths. You can't afford to insult medicine beings before we've built our strength. It's best to use diplomacy at this point in your training."

The dream melted away in a shower of glittering scales. Damien woke with salt encrusting his eyes and heavy pyjama pockets. The scales looked like silver beads and gold coins. "I must hide it so it doesn't get stolen by petty thieves."

When the bundle was complete, he and Atotorah went to a silversmith who verified the silver. A jeweler verified the gold. Damien held the bag in sweaty palms as he hefted the weight. More wealth than he'd ever had in his life! It would help him amass power. He could buy whatever instructions and tools and people he needed.

His hands shook. The medicine pouch was a self-filling money bag as long as Onyare, the Pretty White Snake was his luck charm. Damien realized he was also bound to Onyare for life. He'd never outgrow his need for silver and gold.

When they got back to the woods from the jeweler's, he opened the bag to study his hoard.

Atotorah smirked, casting a glance at Damien out of the corner of his eyes, "Medicine bundle owners may use the contents on an as-needed basis. If they feed their luck charm regularly."

# JUMPERS
# ON BOTH BRIDGES

### David Geary

Eagle was hungry. She spiraled above Moodyville searching. The black tar snake provided the odd snack – a squashed squirrel with a side of gravel to help grind in her gizzard. What is that? Eagle slowed her circular descent. Eyes glared up out of the patchwork snakeskin. She set her feathers, ready to swoop away.

A muffled scream and THUMP. Maybe the snake had swallowed someone? Back to those eyes. One square and blue with two white pupils, the other red with one white pupil.

Blank, blind eyes. Perhaps this was disease? And they were pus-filled boils? She banked and glided lower. Another scream, another THUMP. Something being crushed and slowly dissolved in stomach acid. Stop, check yourself, think again. Perhaps the great serpent was setting a trap? It was faster than her. Older. Wiser. It would lure her in, and then strike.

Eagle lifted her head, flapped hard, soared higher. She would consult the trees. They knew things. She perched on her favorite roost, closed her eyes to listen. Trees use vibrations to communicate, from their hearts out to roots, branches, and bark, but leaves are easiest to understand.

Leaves and feathers share the air. Eagle understood Tree language but it was not, obviously, her mother tongue. At first, all she could pick up was a chaotic clickety-clack static, but twisted whispers emerged:

—She looks good on the outside but is hollow in the middle.

—He's stealing my sunshine.

—He'd root anything with bark on it.

Trees love gossip. Eagle often tuned in to their daily sap operas for the entertainment value. She picked up the weather, the water, the water, the wind, the weather, wind, wind, water – all things dear to tree hearts. Then more gossip:

—Hummingbirds are more reliable than dragonfly-mail.

—I don't trust either of them. They can't sit still.

—See a hummingbird – change is coming and you know what it is. Hear a hummingbird – change is coming and it'll be a surprise.

—True that. I heard a hummingbird, and I didn't predict this traffic jam.

—A dragonfly told me it's because of jumpers on both bridges.

—I wish they'd all jump.

—No, it's daredevils! Crazy Kiwis who bungee out of the womb on umbilical cords.

—No, it's protesters.

—Not protesters – protectors.

—What are they protecting? Us? As if!

—Anyone tries to climb me; I break a branch. A broken leg five points. Fifty for a neck.

—You, Fir, are always going against the grain. Got a mean streak. Just like you, Eagle.

—Yes, Eagle, you're busted! Leavesdropping!

—Ha ha ha clack clack clack.

Like a lot of old things, trees have a terrible sense of humor.

"No, it was an accident," argued Eagle. "I was trying to listen to the rocks but—"

"Cut the crap," said Cedar. "They're not evil snake eyes. It's a 1-2 domino on top of a car delivering pizza."

"Oh, I love pizza!" exclaimed Eagle.

"And," interrupted Fir, "we've told you this before."

"You have?" queried Eagle. "Sorry, my eyes are still sharp, but my memory is a honeycomb."

"Really? Is that how you conveniently forgot to pay us for the last wisdom we gave," added Fir. "You were supposed to deliver messages."

"I'm not a carrier pigeon!" declared Eagle.

"It's okay," Cedar said to Fir, "Her feathers have lost their sheen. Her beak is blunt. Eggs dried up. Soon she will drop dead and repay us in fertilizer."

"But inside the snake sounds like murder," said Eagle.

"Oh, no," the trees chuckled. "That foolish pizza boy, he's just—"

A helicopter chop-chopped up the inlet, drowning out the trees. Eagle lost the feed. Frustrated, she RAAAARRRKed, and winged toward the evil-eyed pizza car.

Inside a hatchback, pizza-delivery boy Aaron was hammering the steering wheel, screaming through clenched teeth. Cross-legged, busting, he needed to piss bad. Real bad. He checked the inside of the car. Surely, he left a Starbucks cup somewhere. He dug deep under his seat. Found some old math homework he never finished. He hated fractions. Found something sticky. Found something sharp. Fuck! His finger bled. He sucked it tasting blood and whatever the sticky dusty furry shit was – Aaron spat out the window. A gruesome gob landed on the sidewalk beside a Norman Rockwell painting – the big sis and little bro selling lemonade to the traffic jam. The young entrepreneurs frowned. Aaron scowled back. He needed a Band-Aid.

HOONNNK! blared the bus up Aaron's ass.

RAAARKKKKK! Eagle corkscrewed back to her roost.

Aaron thrust a rude finger at the bus, then floored his hatchback forward five metres. They'd gone 20 metres in three and a half hours. 33°C degrees at 1:48pm on a Friday and climbing higher. Mirage light shimmered off the stacked-up vehicles. Steam coming off the occupants. Especially those close to the squashed skunk who were forced to have their windows rolled up.

The pizzas – 10 Meatlovers, three Hawaiian, and a Vego Supremo – had gone cold long ago. Fuck it! Aaron wrenched open the freezer bag with a customer's Coke Zero. Ripped out a can and guzzled it down in one giant gulp. Turned up AM 730 radio: All traffic! – All The Time! Hunched over. Unzipped. Took sweet relief into the can.

The NASCAR-Nut bus driver behind announced: "Sorry, folks, I just heard there's jumpers on both bridges. We're not going anywhere. Take a walk." He opened the doors of the 232 Phibbs Exchange. The passengers filed out prisoner-style. Slammed into the wall of heat.

Christian, an acne-riddled teenage God-botherer from a fundamentalist-splinter-group/polygamist-cult in Abbotsford, had come in early to "Lo-Lo," the hipster rebrand for Lower

Lonsdale. He'd come to witness at the Quay, push his Godlit on lost souls, and pray for conversions. Laboring under his bag of Bible-basher magazines, Christian spied someone collapsed over the wheel of a Domino's car.

"Help!" Christian shouted, "this man needs to be saved!" Passengers circled the hatchback. Aaron looked up in shock, and accidentally exhibited his pale pink salmon dick. What happens next isn't pretty, and doesn't make logical sense, but in his panic Aaron tried to hide his shame by ramming the can down on his tender little member. It thrust deep into the can. The razor-sharp rip-top sliced into the soft tissue and tendon, and…Ouchie.

Eagle saw people circling. The scream confirmed her suspicion that some dark ritual was being performed – humans had many that made no evolutionary sense.

The scream also aroused the Ghost of MacGyver who was lounging in a limo behind the bus. He was back in Moodyville, where he'd once been King of Eighties family television, to act in yet another remake. In this reboot, he was dead, but sending down advice from heaven to buff-as-hunk MacGyver Jr. The script sucked harder than an industrial vacuum, but it got the Ghost out of Phoenix where he'd retired due to allergies. Phoenix – where the crematorium baked bodies 24/7 into overpriced urns engraved with ranch scenes. Phoenix – where America went to die.

On the big screen in the limo, the Ghost of MacGyver watched the old REM video for "Everybody Hurts." If he pumped up the volume, stepped out of the limo, and lip-synced to Michael Stipe, would anyone get it? Or would it be too obscure a reference, proving he was the has-been he feared? The Ghost was riddled with fears. He feared he couldn't remember lines anymore. Feared he couldn't act. Feared he'd relied on cosmetic surgery, crash diets, and personal trainers to get him back in shape, but had lost touch with his true self. So far he'd resisted the urge to trawl fan sites for comments on his imminent return, but as he checked his Facebook Fan Page, the one with the blue badge of authenticity, there was clickbait in the sidebar: You'll Never Guess What MacGyver Looks Like Now!

The Ghost clicked. Oh God, Photoshop was a lethal weapon. They'd grafted his head onto the body of Jabba The Hutt. He fumbled to phone his agent, to lawyer up and get this removed. But then he heard a scream. Someone in trouble. Someone real. Maybe this was a job for MacGyver, the real MacGyver?

Eagle smelled fresh blood. She dipped wing and arced lower. People carried a bleeding boy into the bus. "Help! We need a doctor!"

Eagle flapped back to her tree roost. She might be hungry, but she loved a good show. She loved when humans acted like lost ants. The roost fir flexed – sending a splinter into Eagle's talon. RRAARRKK! She leapt up.

"Make yourself useful," said Fir, "find a doctor."

"Me? But there's a traffic jam."

"Well, at least get closer – be our eyes."

Eagle swooped down to observe more closely.

In the back of the bus, Aaron was wailing and flailing.

"He's bleeding out!" a passenger exclaimed gleefully while live-streaming.

"We need a helicopter!" another added, also live-streaming so those at home could cut between cameras for a more cinematic feel.

"We need painkillers." Felicia, a diminutive Filipino woman in her late 50s, was the voice of calm. Everyone had painkillers, sedatives, medications – enough for a pharmacy. Everyone was in pain. Everybody hurt. Felicia selected four pills. "Take these, son."

"No way!" Aaron objected. "You don't look like a doctor!"

"Well, I am." Felicia didn't reveal that she'd only been a vet's assistant, specializing in spaying and neutering the wild dogs of Manila. She felt she had some expertise in genitalia, though she had to settle for being a nanny here as her credentials meant nothing in Moodyville.

"What's your name, son?" asked Felicia, the mother he'd never had.

"Aaron."

Rita, a middle-aged woman of color, offered a fat joint, "Here's some medical marijuana. It works for my hip."

"I'll take it!" Aaron moaned, and toked hard.

"Hold him tight, everyone," ordered Felicia. The passengers pinned Aaron as he drew deep on the dope. Felicia turned to a man in overalls doing sudokus. "Roughrider, have you got tin snips?"

Felicia was referring to Ray the roofer in a Roughriders jersey. He'd played one pro game, got his bell rung, and never been the same since. Sudokus were supposed to keep his brain active, but they just made him feel dumber. He'd much rather work with his hands. Ray opened his tool bag, found his snips.

"I'm not sure about this…" started Ray.

"You can do it," said Felicia, "cut the can off."

Aaron saw the snips and howled, "Let me die!"

"You're not going to die," Felicia comforted.

"What about the blood?" yelled Christian, hysterical.

"Yes, find me as many O Rh D negative blood types as you can," said Felicia. "See if any are Universal Donors."

"Transfusions are transgressions against God!" declared Christian.

Ray flinched, "And what about AIDS?"

Felicia turned to Aaron. "Son, do you have HIV, hepatitis, or any other blood diseases?"

"No."

"Have you been to prison, had sex with a man even one time, and/or handled the fluids of monkeys?"

"No! No, I'm...I'm a virgin," blurted Aaron. "I'm going to die a virgin!"

The passengers tried not to smirk, held Aaron firm, he whimpered, and Ray snipped the can away. Blood and piss gushed everywhere. The passengers flinched. Felicia was unphased.

"Ray. Plyers. I need to clamp a vein. And I need a shoelace as a tourniquet."

The blood slowed and stopped. The crowd applauded. The scene streaming to over 30 countries now. They were going viral.

"What about the cut?" Ray asked.

"I have my beading kit," said Rita. "But I ain't touching no bloody white dick with my precious needles."

"Ray, do you have Crazy Glue?" asked Felicia. "It's what vets...surgeons, veteran surgeons use all the time. And a transected artery will often spasm and clamp off blood flow by itself. Blood-loss also causes the body to divert circulation away from extremities to vital organs, slowing bleeding and allowing it to clot. He's going to... "

The Ghost of MacGyver loomed in the door of the bus.

"Hi, folks! Can I help with anything?"

Was it? Could it be?

"MacGyver! Is that you?" exclaimed Ray.

"It's me. I have returned."

"Whoa...time has been cruel," said Rita.

The Ghost ignored her, asking "What happened?" And was hit by an avalanche of info. He had to invent something. "I know! We'll cauterize the...thing...the bleeding thing with tongs heated on a BBQ?"

"No, use my cigarette lighter," said Chew. The Cantonese can recycler offered his prized Zippo, and home-made vodka to use as antiseptic.

"I'll take the alcohol," said Felicia, "but there's no need to cauterize anything. The glue's got this. Aaron's going to be fine."

Which was the truth, but also an anticlimax. MacGyver felt like a spare prick at a wedding. "No, I got this! We'll use the cigarette lighter from my limo!" He sprinted off, followed by Hormozd, his Persian-Canadian chauffeur.

"Sir," panted Hormozd. "I have strict instructions to keep you in the limo."

"I know. But don't you see? I'm getting my mojo back!"

Rita couldn't stop laughing. Dumb white guys had been putting their dumb dicks into all the wrong places ever since they'd turned up. It was sweet justice to see one get it stuck in a can of Coke. Rita cackled like a mother hen and sucked her teriyaki wings from the Park Royal – no-tax-'cause-it's-on-a-Rez Deli clean to the bone.

"Aaron, don't go to sleep," commanded Felicia. "We need to get in touch with your family."

"No, please, let me die," Aaron mumbled through a haze.

"You're not going to die," said Felicia. "We've saved your…"

"Dick!" the crowd shouted, high-fiving as they ran back into the bus, led by MacGyver holding his red-hot cigarette lighter ready to brand a calf.

"You're going to have to name your babies after us, kid," joked MacGyver. "Because, buddy, it won't win any beauty contests but your little joystick will see other days and nights and backseats and…"

"Beezlabub! That's what any baby will be called!" shouted Christian.

"Okay, well, that was pretty random, so let's cut the chat and cauterize this…this…"

"DICK!" everyone shouted – the carnival atmosphere contagious.

"Go party somewhere else," ordered Felicia. "Now! I got this."

The Ghost wavered, stuttered. He'd lost his lines. Someone saved him. "Party at MacGyver's limo!" And they all sprinted off past Hormozd to raid the limo's well-stocked minibar, leaving the Ghost holding his cooling cigarette lighter.

"…Thank you," said the Ghost to Felicia, "I don't think I could have…"

"I know," said Felicia, and the Ghost slunk back to his limo. Rita leaned over to retrieve her joint from Aaron's hand, took a long slow drag, and offered it to Felicia.

"No, thanks, trying to give up…I'm not actually a doctor."

"But when duty calls, right?" said Rita. "Once a shapeshifter always a…"

"I live on the Rez," mumbled Aaron.

Rita got in his face.

"What's your name, dopey dick? Who you related to?"

"Aaron."

"Aaron who?"

"Aaron Harris."

"Oh, no! Not one of Izzy's tribe?"

"Izzy is my auntie…and now she'll, she'll know and…I want to die!"

Aaron erupted into tears. Rita wanted to join him. Just when she thought it was safe to laugh at someone, and the bunch of humans they belonged to, it turns out they're related. Blood is thicker than water, and nothing is thicker than most of her relations. Rita softened, moved in close to Aaron.

"Listen, we need every life-giving joystick dick to do their part for a better future for our people," said Rita, "so I'm going outside to lay down medicine and say a prayer for you. And for you…Doctor."

Rita stepped out of the bus to break open a cigarette and light some tobacco in a lost hubcap.

"Hold on, isn't there a fire ban?" asked Christian.

Eagle saw the smoke go up. Medicine being burnt was a sign the ritual had been a success. Damn, thought Eagle, no fast food after all. Then she saw people spill back out of the long white limo and surround the evil-eye car. They were all sharing pizza, her pizza, and heading back to the limo. Maybe they'd throw a crust for an old eagle?… Nope.

"You know, this is great story," The Ghost of MacGyver was holding court. "A community coming together over – we won't be able to tell it exactly how it happened…we'll change it to a bleeding…thumb."

"A thumb?" asked Ray, deflated. Already Hollywood had sucked the vital life force out of the story.

"And I'd like to use all your mobile phone footage. You'll get a credit." The Ghost announced plans for his new tele-movie *Blood Brothers*, where he – MacGyver – not Felicia – saved Aaron in a makeshift back-of-the-bus triage. Kimberley, a not-unattractive young woman sashayed up to the Ghost as he poured cocktails, and cooed, "Excuse me, but do you have a tattoo of Death Valley across your butt?"

"No!... Who told you that?" asked the Ghost, the pale showing through his fake tan.

"My mother."

Oh. Shit. Thought the Ghost. Never get out of the limo. Never get out of the limo. The Ghost raised his left eyebrow at Hormozd, who slipped his right hand under his left armpit to finger the holsters of pepper spray and his Glock.

"In fact," said Kimberley, "if you have that tattoo then you might be my father."

The mobile phones broadcasting live to the ether turned on the Ghost. His mouth worked but no sound came out. Lines, lines, he needed lines. Finally, he blurted, "Okay, con-fession, I'm not the real MacGyver, I'm just a very good look-alike. And I believe the original real MacGyver had a stunt double with a unique butt tattoo who often tricked people, like impressionable young women, into believing he was the real deal, but unfortunately, he died in a tragic pyrotechnics stunt and was charred beyond recognition. And, let me say, that I have the mojo of MacGyver, so for my next trick, I'll deal with that squashed skunk! Watch how I get rid of it with a fishing rod, duct tape, Ziploc bag and an aerosol flame-thrower."

The Ghost sprinted off with his entourage in hot pursuit, past the bus where Felicia and Christian were now in heated debate.

"Blood transfusions are Satan sucking at your veins like a vampire," vowed Christian.

Felicia had been brought up devout herself and quoted the Bible back at him. "Do not let any part of your body become an instrument of evil: Romans 6:13. So use your body as an instrument for the glory of God. And I would include blood donations in…" Felicia reeled around. "Where's Aaron?"

Aaron was no longer in the bus. He'd grabbed a Thomas the Tank Engine blanket from a baby stroller and made a run for it. Well, hobbled off, with his sore dick and stoned brain, down into the Moodyville forest. Aaron winced his way onto the Spirit Trail and found a second wind. He'd taken a left-over slice of Hawaiian with the malformed idea that he was meant to be the Unlikely/Reluctant Hero of the Day. And now it was his divine mission to save a jumper on the Ironworkers Memorial Second Narrows bridge with a slice of pizza.

"I mean, who doesn't like pizza?" Aaron argued with a Mountie guarding the foot of the bridge, a moustache on a motorbike.

"Listen, loser, no one is going up there. And I don't know why you're wearing a child's blanket, and I know it's legal now, but you need to stop smoking so much and go home. Plus, shouldn't you be at school?"

"I dropped out. I couldn't do fractions. I fucking hate fractions. And now I deliver pizza. Although I'll probably get fired for…if I could do fractions, I wouldn't be here – here with this piece of pizza, which is a fraction of the whole of pi something squared something…"

The Mountie reached for his RT, or his handcuffs, or his taser…so Aaron threw the pizza at the mustache and ran off, over the train tracks, past Coal Mountain, to the waterfront.

He heard Rita and other searchers calling his name. He crawled through a gap in the barbed wire under the bridge and lost them.

Eagle had followed Aaron's erratic path to where he sat under the bridge like a troll. He looked up but couldn't see the drama unfolding high above between jumper and negotiator. The world seemed far away. RAAAAAAAARRRKKKK! Eagle landed on a log nearby.

"Hi, there," said Eagle. Aaron ignored her, because... because eagles don't talk. She hopped closer and eagle-eyed him: "So you're going for a swim?"

Okay, thought Aaron, a talking Eagle – roll with it. Dick stuck in a can, operated on in the back of a bus, glued up, stoned, MacGyver – whoever he was – a talking eagle – why not? Join the party. Roll with it.

"I said, are you going for a swim?"

"None of your business," said Aaron, but suddenly it seemed like a good idea. So he took off his trainers. Placed them side by side on a rock. Folded his socks neatly inside.

"Who taught you that?" asked Eagle. "Your mother?"

"Don't talk about my mother."

Aaron dropped the blanket. He was naked except for his makeshift bandage and Domino's Pizza T-shirt. He bet they'd bill him for losing the shirt once his body was found. Aaron dipped his toes in the water. Recoiled.

"A bit cold for you?" asked Eagle.

"Don't try to save me," said Aaron.

"Oh, I'm not here for that."

"Why are you here?"

"For fast food. Us eagles are painted as noble birds of prey, when really we're super-chill scavengers, lazy mofos, no muss no fuss, give me squashed squirrel roadkill over chasing some-thing down any day of the week. Mmmm."

"Get away from me, you freaky...fucked-up bird," yelled Aaron.

"Oh, come on. You don't want your flesh anymore, let me take it."

"Oh, I get it – reverse psychology!"

"Ha, yeah – 'Don't throw me in the briar patch, Brer Fox. I can't stand briars.' You know I like that Brer Rabbit. I bet he tastes good, too."

"Who's that?"

"Look," said Eagle, puffing up her feathers, "you've been showing off your tasty little cocktail sausage all day, and now I've got a powerful hunger."

"I have not been..."

"You're a tease. Teasing my tail feathers with your..."

"Noooo! An Eagle can't say shit like that!"

"I can say whatever, do whatever, but first, as some form of grace before the meal, let me tell you a story about what came before. A cautionary tale about when good teasing goes bad."

"No," said Aaron. "All I ever get is old stories. 'I remember when...' 'You know when I was a kid...' Old stories about how things used to be...blah blah blah." Aaron folded the blanket to place on the seaweed. His life might have been a mess, but he'd leave a neat pile behind.

"I feel your pain," said Eagle, "but I'm telling you anyway."

The tall tale was a Tree story. The distant Trees strained to listen, to see how much of a mess Eagle made of it this time.

"When the white ghosts turned up, the Trees recognized their relations – masts – standing tall on the floating ships. Then the ghosts cut down all the trees to make more masts.

Some sailed away, but many stayed and cut down more trees to build houses and hotels. In fact, Aaron, right on this spot…"

"How do you know my name?"

"Oh, I've been watching you."

"Watching me?" Aaron's eyes shifted from side to side as if looking for an easy avenue of escape. "For how long?"

"To continue. On this spot, was one of the most notorious drinking holes. Drunks were chained to a Drunk Stump here. If you counted the rings they went past a thousand. So while it was a shame for a drunk to be chained to a stump, the trees saw the shame of a great-great-grandfather chained to a drunk. The drunks sobered up and were freed – if a Thunderbird didn't swoop down first, plunge its talons in – crack him open like a walnut – pluck out the still-beating heart – savor it, and swallow it whole, feeling it beat all the way down, gizzard to gullet. And that," whispered Eagle, "is what I'm going to do to you. All those dick jokes before? Smoke and mirage. It's your heart I'm after."

Aaron had fallen asleep on the soft seaweed. Eagle's tall tale backed by the gentle wash of the waves had been the lullaby he needed.

Eagle hopped closer. Checked the boy's lids. Deep sleep. Sweet dreams. She'd lift the boy up real gentle, then drop him on the rocks like cousin crows did with mussel shells. It had been a long day of circling and waiting. Young heart meat would replenish her old soul. Eagle cradled Aaron in her talons, flapped her wings and he murmured like a kitten. In Dreamtime, Aaron figured it was his Mama finally come back home to put him to bed after he'd fallen asleep on the sofa.

Aaron was heavier than Eagle thought. Tough to carry but that just meant he'd crack harder on the rocks. One…two…

"Are you sure about this?" asked the Trees.

"You! What do you want?"

"Well…while you've been watching him, we've been watching you."

Eagle tried not to lose her grip. "This is none of your beeswax."

"You know, you're not a Thunderbird, right?" Fir asked.

Eagle flew out over the ocean to escape judgement. That's the thing about Trees, they're very judgy. They might communicate with other creatures nearby, but they never travel. Travel expands the mind.

That's when Aaron woke up, dangling in mid-air, in the clutches of an eagle, suspended 50 feet above the ocean. He gasped and thrashed, and Eagle lost her grip. Aaron fell. Eagle swooped to save him, but Aaron hit the water – SMAACKK – in a beautiful belly flop. Salt water flooded into his lungs – filled him right up. He sank like a stone to the bottom, to the sludge and old shopping carts.

The Trees saw all that. Said nothing but…

"Okay, okay," and Eagle made like a pelican and dove down, found Aaron, and dragged him back to the surface. Spluttering, Aaron punched up at the Eagle.

"Okay, die, see if I care," rarked Eagle. "You'll taste too salty now anyway. I'm out. Good riddance to bad rubbish."

Eagle flapped hard and flew up the inlet to the other bridge, to the other jumper. Maybe she'd have more luck there. She reeled back for one parting shot. "You know, Aaron, you could have been something special, you could have been a part of me. We could have flown together. Been free. That's all you really wanted, right? To be free?"

"And then you would have shit me out!" spat Aaron.

"That, too! But what a ride."

Eagle flew into the sun setting over Lionsgate Bridge. Aaron thought he heard the Trees chuckle – clickety clack clickety clack.

"Better start swimming before the current gets you," said Cedar. The current slipped a rope around Aaron's feet. He felt the salt sting in his dick – sharp and deep. Aaron thrashed in a demented dog-paddle until he reached the shore. Collapsed back on his seaweed and blanket bed. He'd die here. Easy come, easy go – except then the mosquitoes came.

Aaron dragged himself up onto his bleeding knees, stood. His head hazy as a smokehouse. His dick throbbing like he'd stuck it in a blender.

"How come I can't kill myself?" he howled at the trees.

"Perhaps 'cause in some ways you were already dead," said Fir.

"Eh? And what, this was some dumb dream and now I woke up?"

"Maybe. Who's to say when dreams start and end, and what it is to be truly awake. Except now you got another problem – now you're talking to Trees," said Cedar, and all the Trees cracked up. Ha aha aha clak clackey clickety clack.

"…That's a problem?" asked Aaron. "That's a problem," he repeated, to himself. "Is it?"

The Trees retreated. No more translations.

Aaron wrapped the blanket around himself and stumbled slowly back up toward the road. Through the trees he could see the traffic hadn't budged. He turned back into the forest, back to the Spirit Trail. The Trees bent forward to show him the way, the way home.

# MELINDA IRENE AND MADAME BOUVÉ

## Yugcetun Anderson

Dear Madame Bouvé,

Bouvé because so many have diary how could it, if lost come back to me?

Besides my mom thinks I am really writing a letter.

I am so excited to start this super secret super cool ~~letter~~ JOURNAL.

Summer is so easy - I can sleep all day or bike to the pond! As long as I am out of sight no one thinks to look for me!

♡   Yours Truly & FOREVER

Melinda Irene
MAY 12

Madame Bouvé

I got sunburned yesterday
I walked out after my
afternoon nap. I ate a
biscuit - buttermilk, of course
and walked to the bridge.
I was so happy to be by
myself. My older sister
went to Saint Marys for
a couple of weeks. Why would
they let her go and I can't
even go up the road to my
BFF. ♡

It's because its farther
than I can walk. I think.
And DAD is too tired when he
comes home & its a waste of
gas money

Melinda IRENE
MAY 23

SUNBURNT
SUCKS!

Madame Bouvé

Just a quick note,

The River is high. My
Dad killed the Neighbor's
Dog. and ~~through~~ threw it
it the river.

Mom made me go check to
see that it floated away.

Oh He killed it with a
SKI POLE!! wow!!

He GOT THE SHAFT! 44 no

That will be the last time
that dog will kill our chickens

That dog was
scary anyways!!            Melinda IRENE
Growled all the time.
                        JUNE 4

POOR
CHICKENS

MADAME BOUVÉ

Am I bad? I don't know...
MA is Always yelling at me
DAD is Always spanking me.
I am not even sure why.

Melinda IRENE
JUN 10

MADAME BOUVÉ    MY TEARS

I am so so so SAD. My BFF
My nolonger friend said I lived
to far away and that I
need other friends

WHAT FRIEND? HOW? WHERE?
She knows I live out in the middle
of nowhere. OK
OK I can do this. I've been
alone before. I can do it again
I HATE HER! lonely Melinda IRENE
JUN. 17

MADAME BOUVÉ

Don't EVER name your goat Beauty! Beauty kicked the milk bucket over and I got blamed for it. No poop for me! :( at least I had a biscuit in my pocket. I should have left when I was 8.     Jun 18

MADAME BOUVÉ
Butter ▷ ◯      I saw a man today. He is a friend (I think) of my parents. He has a fat wife and two little kids. A boy and a girl. He is BLOND and has ~~piercing~~ ice blue eyes. Funny thing is is that he saw me. He actually stumbled when he saw me. I have to hide when I see people. At least until the bruises fade.   Melinda IRENE Jun 2

MADAME BOUVÉ - June 30

I saw him again today
the swelling on my lip had
gone down. and maybe he
saw the blue on my eyes as
eye shadow. My sister wears
a ton of it.

OOPS GOTTA GET THE COAL ¢
SOME WOOD. LATER.

OK BACK.

Why does everthing have to be
so bad, sad, painful. How can
I do what she wants, if I
don't know what it IS?

Bring in the
WOOD, COAL        Cut hooves - Goats
MILK the goats    Dump the Honeybucket
get the eggs      DO Dishes
Feed and water for goats & birds
Feed the Dogs     WASH the Floories
                  MAKE DINNER every day too

# HE SAW ME AGAIN

## MADAME BOUVÉ

He saw me again. We locked eyes. I was scared. I hid in the barn for the whole 3 HOURS they were here.

I think he was looking for me. I hid down the riverbank. MA says I am sleeping with him. BUT HE SEES ME. I'm scared of all adults. They hurt me. MA shook my hair so hard last week that I couldn't see straight for DAYs. LESSON learned! DONT go neer anyon.

👁 👁                Melinda IRENE

July 1

MADAME BOUVE

I want so much! I want to wear shorts but can't until the switch ~~marks~~ fade.

~~I saw~~

I was walking on the rode back from the bridge. I guess he was bringing milk for cheese He ACTUALLY STOPPED TO TALK TO ME! ME!

Not my DAD or my Mom or the neighbor. JUST ME!

He talked about building a barn. I talked about the Mountains I wish I could get eaten by a bear (My MA SAYS I am rotten to the core so the bare will prob ~~die~~ die. Alone
HAPPY & Alone
Melinda IRENE
July 5

MADAME BOUVÉ

What would happen if I
killed myself? Would they be
Sorry. I don't think so. I'd
would have do it ironically.
I don't have the energy to do
that. But there is a nice tree
in the back. I wish the goats
would attack me. The bucks are
too of calm. I could jump in
the river and float away to
the ocean. It's too cold tho.

LOVE ≠ Melinda                    July 7


AM I IN LOVE? I asked
him what that means. He
said he didn't know but
he thinks he loves me. Why
would ANYONE LOVE ME? I am
ugly and everybody hates me.
Why else do I have to comb the
spit out of my hair every night
after school?

## MADAME BOUVÉ

He came. I walked on the
road and he came. Okay
it was a long walk. 4 hours

I hate my life, but he is
the one bright spot. When
I grow up I hope I have
some one like him ~~~~~~~~~~
                    Melinda IRENE  July 25


## MADAME BOUVÉ

I don't think I want to
baby sit for them any more.
I didn't know it could
HURT SO MUCH. ☻ I
threw up afterwards. He
said it'd be better next time

        Melinda
        IRENE  July 27

## MADAME BOUVÉ

Neibergs got a knew dog. Chased our 150 ducks we just got. We can find 20 and 3 chickens good thing Dad owns the land we lost a lot of money. He broke into the nieghbors house and shot the dog.

My older sister went to see but I couldn't. too many chores. I think it's gross to dance in glee over the death of an animal. Poor stupid dog. I wish it was mine. But its not. So THERE,

Melinda Irene
July 28

MADAME BOUVÉ

I feel like a thing. And I
can't say no. It's the only
time I get to be touched.
The only time someone talks
to me. The only time I think
I might be ~~human~~ and not
an Ugly.

Melinda IRENE August 30

MADAME bouvé,

I think I might look for a rope. Everbody
hates me. at school, at home. even he gets
mad if I dont do it with him. Everyone cusses at me
or hits me or spit on me. why?

MADAME bouvé, can you come get me?

Melinda Irene
mi post 352 richardson hwy
Sept 23

Madame Bouvé

    When will you come? where are you? why
don't you come?

    Broken Heart →                Sept 24
                     Melinda Irene

MADAME BOUVÉ

    I know I MADE You up But could
you be real? Just this once? Like Peter
PAN was real for Wendy? ——→
                            SEPT 25
                       Melinda IRENE

Madame Bouvé

    I didn't hurt as much the
thirteen time. He says I'll like it more
later. I don't think I will. Oh! almost
forgot! I thought I saw a girl
with fire red hair today. 🍁
she didn't see me.          Fire the color of
                            her ha
My dad asked my why I was so bad
today. So... That happened. I dunno I
guess is not an answer. I don't care anymor
I'm gonna float up into the mountains & let
the wind take me to space Atleast I'y
be surrounded by lots of nothing.    SEPT 25 MI

MADAME BOUVÉ

Today I tried goin into the woods & losing myself. Too bad I have a ~~better~~ sense of direction. I think there was a lynx up there. Or a feral cat. (what does feral even mean? wild? I guess) It was howling the closer I got to the stream. The stream pops out of the ground and then a few feet later it disappears back into the ground. I never saw the cat but you can't mistake the YOWL!

Sept 26

Forever Doomed   Melinda Irene
to be ordinary & ugly   Bleh!

MADAME BOUVÉ

I met her today. The red haired girl. Her name is Vannesa Sarah Wallace. She goes by Sarah. If I was her I'd go by Vanessa. Oh. MA shot the cat. She said he crapped in the feed barrel & was gonna give the goats thread worms or hook or round worm. I dunt know what they look like but the cat (mouser so he'd be a good mouser — but he wasn't.)

continued
Mouzer (ôgô ← not actual tears). They say each animal
as enough brains to tan their hide. (not beat
hem,) to make a blanket. I don't think
ts supposed to have bone bits in it. "

Melinda Irene
Sept 17

## Madame Bovve

    I wish I could go to Paris
Or at least halfway across. I
read a book. Paniika And Her
Pet Polar Bear Pete. She rode her
friend Pete all over everywhere
They ate loads of Salmon!
    My dream is to ride a polar
bear and have the biggest mound
of SALMON, ever! And I'd share
it with ~~Pete~~ Pete and watch
the sun go down into the sea.

here's to wishes & dreams
Melinda Irene
Sept 28

MADAME BOUVÉ
     I am packing. I am going into
the mountains to find a polar bear. Or
something like that. I could probably
make it over in about two days.
Eklutna, is over there. I am
almost done.

Melinda IRENE
Sept 29.


Madame Bouvé


     I am so angry! Mom
found my pack! She took it,
and said I was hoarding!
She took ALL the food! And
ALL my blankets and camping
gear! I AM SO ANGRY!!!
and my Boy Scouts woodcrafting for Boys in

School will start soon. I guess I'm going.
I don't want to. it'll be more mean kids being
mean. ⊙ ← me sighing   Until next time
Melinda IRENE
Sept 10 30

MADAME BOUVÉ

High school isn't as bad as middle school. At least the library is bigger.

I think my ma found you. she is meaner I have to quit swimming - too many bruises to many questions. I want to go away and never be found.

Melinda Irene              Sept 30

Madame Bouvé

Good bye. I am sure MA FOUND You.

October 1

I hate to but I have to burn you. My hands are bloody Tomorrow if I can get out of my sleeping bag
October 2

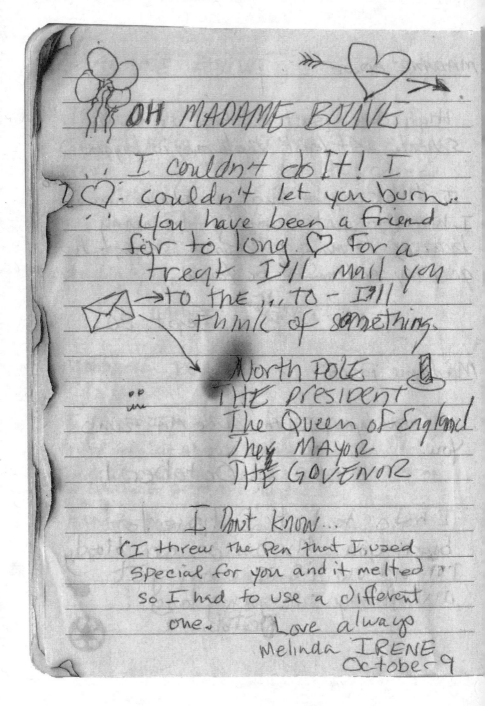

OH MADAME BOUVE

I couldn't do It! I couldn't let you burn. You have been a friend for to long. For a treat I'll mail you to the ... to – I'll think of something.

North POLE
THE PRESIDENT
The Queen of England
They MAYOR
THE GOVENOR

I Don't know...
(I threw the pen that I used special for you and it melted so I had to use a different one.         Love always
            Melinda IRENE
                October 9

ICE LAND Postmaster

You shall go to:
Postmaster
Helluhrauni 3
660 Myvatni
Iceland

and I will fly with you
on your journey happy
knowing you're gonna
raise HELL in HELLhrauni
I'll visit you one
Day & we'll raise HELL
TOGETHER AGAIN

Yours Truly & forever
Melinda Irene
Oct 10

# GHOST WALK

## Gerald Silliker Pisim Maskwa

Nokomis shines down on me. Her light falls like the gentlest touch. On a hill in the distance, the Residential School sits, like a rotten tooth pointing up at the night sky. My shoulders slope as if carrying a great weight.

"Why did I survive when others did not?" I ask. "What made me so special? Out of all the Native children, why am I still alive?"

Then I'm standing in a hallway. The walls are covered with blood, the ceiling is covered with blood, blood drips from ceiling to the floor. Wind moans down a bisecting passage. A thick fog moves along the corridor at floor level.

I groan. I'd sworn never again to set foot in this place, but here I am. I try walking toward an exit, but the hallways loop back on themselves in impossible circles. I know every inch of this place, and they aren't supposed to connect up in these ways.

I guess I'm not going to be able to leave until I accomplish whatever it is I'm here to do. Maybe not until I've faced the memories which anchored me down so many years, drowning.

"Jaaaiiirrrreeee." I hear my name being called. "Jaaaiiirrr-reeee. Jaaaiiirrrreeee." I step back and slip in a puddle of blood. I fall hard on my left shoulder and hear something pop. There's a sharp stab of pain. I hope I haven't broken something. I scrabble to my feet covered in blood. My jeans and my shirt are soaked.

A scream fills the hallway, so loud it hurts my ears. I take a breath. I slowly open my eyes, and see Tommy standing in the doorway of Miss Love's classroom. He is too pale, and there are dark circles under his eyes.

"You could have warned me. She hated Native children that spoke their language instead of English… Why didn't you help me?" Tears run down his cheeks.

"How could I help you when I couldn't even help myself? Other kids must have told you not to speak Ojibwe in front of those white people. Why didn't you listen?" My heart aches, but what can I do for him?

I edge past Tommy and continue down the hall past Mr. Jonathan's classroom. I can hear footsteps behind me. I turn to see little Roger. He also seems too pale and has dark circles under his eyes. He was known as the school's busybody. If you wanted everyone to know something, all you had to do was tell Roger.

"You could have told me! You knew what he was like…you knew he was no damn good…No damn good."

"What the hell are you talking about?" I ask.

"You knew what he liked to do with young boys."

I feel heat rush to my face. "You didn't care when it was happening to me! And now you accuse me? You knew what was happening and you didn't say anything!" Roger flinches.

I furiously walk away, leaving little Roger behind. I can't believe he blames me for not warning him! Everyone in our dorm knew what was happening. I am carrying enough guilt already; I don't need more.

I walk until I run into Jake. He looks dead. His eyes are sunk deep into his face like a prisoner of a Nazi concentration camp. He points a finger at me.

"You knew about the blankets…the blankets." His breath rattles in his chest, as if it were his last. "You knew what those people were really like."

A fire kindles deep inside me. "No! Damn it! I didn't know anything… What the hell are you talking about? What blankets?"

Jake grabs his stomach as if he's been punched. "The blankets came from…came from…" But before he can finish speaking, he fades into the thick fog. It seems to have a life of its own this fog, omnipresent, gathering and dispersing at will, swallowing entire walls, swallowing entire portions of the building, curling around at my feet.

Why the hell is Jake talking about blankets as if his life depends on it?

"Jaaaiiirrrreeee." Again, I hear my name being called. I follow the voice, hoping to find out who is calling me.

My mind churns, I have so many questions.

Further down the hallway I find a 12-year-old boy rocking back and forth on the bloodied floor. He looks up at me with empty, dark eyes. "You could have stopped him, you know…You're one of his victims too."

My mind spins faster and faster, like a whirlwind out on the plains, out of control. "He needed you, you were important to him…he would not have…you could have stopped him…why didn't you stop him!?"

Am I the tornado, or am I trapped inside one? Is it my fault this happened to all these kids? Could I have done something to prevent it?

"Jaaaiiirrrreeee." From the darkness, a voice calls my name. It's coming from Miss Love's classroom. I feel as if I'm being electrocuted, a burning pulse flowing through my veins. Michael is sitting in the front row before Miss Love's desk. I look around carefully. I don't want her to sneak up on us. I want to be ready for her.

I stop directly in front of him. Like the others, his skin is ashen, and he has dark hollows under his eyes. "Michael, why are you sitting in front of Miss Love's desk?"

Michael's eyes meet mine in a steady gaze. "Jerry. You knew what she was like. You were in her English class. You sat right over there next to the window. She called our language the devil's tongue. You could have warned us about her. I am here because of you."

"You're here because of me? I didn't know I had that kind of power to cause someone to do anything." My ears are ringing, and my head feels like it's being slowly crushed in a vice.

"I will not speak the devil's tongue." Michael indicates the chalkboard with a lift of his chin. I see the scrawl of his words, written out in tiny letters in white chalk against the blackboard. I will not speak the devil's tongue. "She has me writing it out millions and millions of times, or until I learn only to speak English."

I feel a warm breath against the back of my neck, and a familiar voice brings a smile to my face. "I see you have come back, my friend. I missed you very much."

Michael's face goes three shades paler.

"It's…it's…Death." Michael points at Miss Love.

Death? "She's my very close friend. The only one that doesn't blame me for everything that happened here." I take

Miss Love's hand as we walk out of the classroom. Why did the color drain from Michael's face?

Miss Love smiles and touches my arm. "I'll return after I take care of something." I nod okay, and she kisses my cheek. "You're the only one who believes in me," she whispers, disappearing into the fog, heading back in the direction we came from.

Which way now? Left or right? I went right last time, so I choose left. I recall how these halls used to be filled with students, and it's as if the spirit of the school reads my mind. The hallway fills with kids trying to make it to their next class on time. I look at them carefully and recognize some.

The entrance to the gym is across from the main stairs. On either side of the steps are two huge stone columns. I don't remember those being there.

I come within a foot of a pillar and inspect the stone. The rock is pitted and uneven. The more I look, the more it appears as if faces are carved into the surface. The faces of children. I hear them crying. The sound washes over me, hurt building inside me like water behind a dam. I'm certain the pillars are made of the souls of Native children who died in this place.

I turn quickly and down I go into a puddle of blood. The cries of the children grow exponentially. The sound hits me like the blast from an explosion. Niagara Falls white noise. I slide across the slick floor, the force pushing me until I hit a wall. As quickly as it manifests, the sound passes, and the pillars appear to be regular pillars again.

A figure is standing in front of the music room, watching me. I wipe blood from my eyes, and struggle to my feet. I think she was one of my sister's friends. Manitou. Except she has butterfly wings rising from her shoulder blades. I walk toward her.

Manitou smiles. "You are little Jerry, aren't you?"

"Yes," I say, and she hugs me.

"Why are you here?"

"I'm here to help kids with the nightmares. We are all connected in the big circle of life...your Nokomis told you this enough times. Be very careful in this place, there are dark spirits who have waited a long time for you to return."

Nokomis's gentle smile shines in through the window bathing Manitou in soft light. "I will be watching over you. If you ever need me, call out my name. You will know when the time is right. Boy born of the spirit world...we shall meet again." She burst into a cloud of fluttering wings and they curl up into the moonlight like smoke. Outside the window Nokomis is shining brilliantly in the sky. Smiling down upon all her grandchildren.

I step through the doorway of the music room. Musical instruments lay on chairs like their owners just stepped out. There are only two of us in the room, me and Ebah, another one of my sister's friends. She also has butterfly wings rising from her shoulder blades.

I walk around chairs to meet her halfway. "You are a victim like thousands of other native children, but you escape the Walker's grasp. They couldn't trap you like all the others in this damn place. He isn't aware of you right now, but He will soon find out you're here. He will try to bring you under His control. You're the only one that beat him at His own game by walking these halls. And He wants to get even. You hurt Him bad, and He's a real sore loser." Then Ebah bursts into a cloud of fluttering wings that disperse in all directions.

I turn to leave and find my friend Miss Love waiting in the doorway. She smiles and we walk down the hallway. She stops in front of a memorial case that holds pictures of students. We can see our reflection in the glass. A third face appears, all angles and hollows. I look around, but no one else is nearby.

"Who are you, Rat?" Miss Love demands. "Who do you work for?" I stand beside her without fear.

"I am no one." The Rat's reflection's quavers. "And I work for Him. He who walks these halls. He's been here since the 1800s."

"If you tell him about us, I will lock you in the cellars." The face wavers and fades. And then Miss Love fades into the fog, her lips compressed in a thin smile.

My stomach makes a loud grumbling sound. I head to the dining room, hoping to find something to eat. It's been many years since I sat there as a child, but the dining room hasn't changed. It's divided into two large sections; one half where the girls eat, and one half where the boys eat. I was never allowed to talk to, or even look at, my sisters. I close my eyes for a minute and imagine I can hear the sounds of children. Clattering cutlery, scrape of chair legs on floor, and the thrum of voices.

I open my eyes. There before me are the spirits of children sitting at all the tables. Going about their day as if nothing changed. I recognize some of the kids I played with. I remember having a good time with those kids. But I'm also reminded of the bad. Like the time I was caught speaking my Ojibwe language and got punished for it. One boy got caught using sign language to his sister. He was removed from the dining room, and later removed from the school. We never saw him again. I hated those teachers. That very minute I wished Him dead.

I remember feeling all alone, in a room full of Native boys who were just like me, unable to ask the most important question: Why were we being held against our will?

I felt pressure building, like a simmering volcano.

I walk to the spot where I sat as a child. Whatever happened to the boy that sat across from me? I wonder: Is he still alive? Did he get married and have a whole bunch of kids like he said he would? Whatever happened to the kids that sat at my table? Were they still alive?

Blood is oozing down the walls and onto the floor. Is this a sign of what happened to all the boys and girls? I remember what Manitou said. "If you ever need me, call out my name."

My stomach grumbles loudly again, and I remember I brought chocolate bars. I remove one from my backpack and eat it in two big bites. I leave the dining room and step out into a small hallway.

Why the hell is this happening now? Why now of all days?

A boney hand reaches out of the blood-soaked wall as if the bricks were made out of elastic. The hand grabs my arm and pulls me through when the elastic retracts. I feel a stickiness as I pass through. The wall rights itself and I find myself in an empty throne room. On the wall across from a large throne, I see flashes of scenes happening to boys and girls in the school. Walking hallways, sitting in classrooms, standing in the principal's office with heads bowed.

Then I leave the proper way, through an adjoining doorway, and re-enter the dining room. I now see the shadow of death on the boys and girls. Their faces are ashen, with dark circles under their eyes.

A cool breeze dries my blood-grimed face. Screams wash
over me in a wave, like the blast from an H-bomb. I struggle
to stay on my feet, covering my ears to block out the sound.
It is the sound of children screaming.

Is this all my fault? I survived when others did not. Why
did I survive, why?

When the wave passes, I retreat from the dining room.

The hallways are filled with the spirits of children rushing
to class. The principal stands watching the students. I turn
away, and head toward the main stairs. I still can't figure out
where the hell the two pillars came from, they weren't here
when I went to school. I approach them slowly. Is this a big
joke? Back in the day, students were famous for pulling
pranks. But the pillars are not like any I had ever seen before.
The faces of children rise from the rough-hewn surface,
carved in various postures of agony.

I look away. The feelings I've kept bottled up all these
years seem to explode with the force of a sun going nova. I
don't know what to do with my hands. My eyes seem to catch
on fire, they could burn through walls, they could set fire to
this entire building.

I see the Rat who spies for the Walker. I want to strangle
him. His eyes are large dinner plates and he breathes quickly.
"You were born of spirit after your death at birth. Your mother
gave you to the Great Spirit and he gave you life."

How does he know so much about me? I wonder. He
must be a good spy.

"You have been having dreams about the path you're supposed to be on. I'd rather serve you than the Walker. Can I
walk with you?"

My hands still, and the breath rushes out of me.

"You're brave to stand up to the Walker. Walk with me instead?"

We cross the hallway and enter the gym, but it's empty. There isn't a single sound. I remember playing in the gym as a kid. I close my eyes and imagine I hear children. Voices raised in excitement, the squeal of laughter, the squeak of shoes on polished floors. When I open them again, the gym is still empty.

I hear a boy crying at the back of the gym. I head toward the sound and take the few steps up to the stage. A group of children are swallowed by a curl of fog. There is a boy left sitting by himself, he is five or six years old, and he's shaking like leaf. He doesn't take his eyes off the gym door.

I'm about to ask, "What is going on? Are you okay?"

But a short, fat, bald man enters the gym.

"Where the hell are you? You were supposed to meet me in my room."

I look closely at the man's face. It's Mr. Phillips. The scumbag who raped me as well as many other boys.

I walk slowly up to the scumbag. I pull out my knife to slit his throat. I'm about to do all the Native children a big favor, but he fades into the fog.

Standing alone in the empty gym I whisper, "You are one lucky scumbag."

I leave the gym, and head toward the principal's office. The hallways are empty again. A thick fog moves along the corridor at floor level. The walls bleed. Wind blows making the passages moan.

On the Registrar's desk there are files. I pick one up and start to read:

*This Ojibway child is not living up to his full potential. He has ADHD and an overactive imagination. He can't focus on his work, and repeatedly disrupts class. We are changing his assignments to keep him engaged. The last time I inquired why he wasn't doing homework, he said: "I'm saving the universe from creatures from another world bent on conquest. I'm busy gathering a fleet before I leave earth. I'll fly my spaceship beyond the moon and create a wormhole to enter negative space. This way the entire fleet can approach the enemy's world without being observed. Our fleet will drop back to normal space before attacking the planet…"*

Man, this kid is way out there! Who is this kid? I look for his name on the folder, but the lines on the tab are blank. According to the file, the child is "unstable." Seems to me he has a real good imagination, but that doesn't make him crazy. The kid is just a good storyteller.

I put the file in my book bag and enter the principal's office. There are more files in a pile on his desk. I walk over to the window when six Native boys enter the outer office followed by the principal. It's been a long time since I've been this close to Mr. Robertson.

Mr. Robertson points and follows the boys into his office, but turns and stops the sixth Native boy. "You're new to our school, so you don't know our rules yet." Then he calls to his secretary: "Have this young man see the counselor about school rules. I want him to learn them…." – he looks at the calendar – "by the 15th of November, when I will test him."

I'm standing right in front of them, but they don't see me! They don't seem to acknowledge my presence in any way. As if I'm the ghost.

Mr. Robertson closes his office door and pulls the blinds down. "This is your third time getting caught." He takes a leather strap from his desk. "All right, Paul, you're first since you're the oldest and should have known better."

Paul approaches the principal, drops his pants, and bends over the desk exposing his bare bum. Mr. Robertson raises the leather strap in the air and brings it down across Paul's bum. Over and over the leather strap is brought down. Twenty-five lashes.

"Next time you're caught, you'll get 30 lashes, hear me? Now get the hell out of my office." The next three boys also get 25 lashes, but the last boy is the youngest, and he starts to bleed.

Mr. Robertson calls for the doctor to look at little Mark. "You shouldn't hang around with those boys, they will only get you in trouble."

"I can't get this bleeding to stop," the doctor says. "The kid is a bleeder; you'll have to find another way to punish Mark or he'll bleed to death."

Mr. Robertson looks out the window, mere inches from where I'm standing. I try to breath shallowly. He stands there for several minutes but gives no indication that he senses my presence. Then he walks to the outer office and asks the secretary, "Did you find the file on that young Ojibway boy...? You know, the one from Thunder Bay? He has has two sisters here."

The secretary looks through the files on her desk. "I had it here not long ago. It was on top of this pile of files before our meeting with the teachers. I still think we should get other students to help the problem kids learn how to speak English." She adds, "The helpers can earn extra credit."

Frowning, Mr. Robertson walks back into his office.

He takes a deep breath looking directly where I'm standing.

He puts the leather strap in his desk, then walks back to the outer office. "Maybe one of the counselors removed the file? They were asked to come up with a solution for the lad."

While he goes back into his office, I walk out. We come within inches of each other. Though we do not touch I can feel the brush of air at his passing. I follow the secretary down the hallway to the counseling office.

"Did one of the counselors remove a file from my desk?" she asks the secretary.

"None of the counselors have left their offices in a while. They've been dealing with a few students who were being bullied by older boys."

"Mr. Robertson will want to know about these bullies. Are there any other problems the counselors are dealing with?"

"Oh yeah – Mr. Brown needs to see Mr. Robertson about the behavior of six boys that he caught in his back storage room."

"I'll tell him to see Mr. Brown." She headed back to the main office. I follow.

"The counselors don't have the file," she reports. "They've been busy dealing with some bullies who were picking on the smaller boys."

"Have them brought to my office now!"

"Mr. Brown also wants to see you about six boys he caught in his storage room."

He frowns. "There's nothing in that storage room the boys could steal."

The secretary hands Mr. Roberson the note Mr. Brown gave the counselor's secretary.

"Were they caught smoking in the storage room?"

Mr. Robertson unfolds the note. His face turns red. "You got to be kidding. Those boys were doing that? Tell Mr. Brown not to allow anyone in with those six boys, so they stay the way he found them."

Mr. Robertson looks over the names of the six students. "Those are Mr. Phillip's boys…"

Fog fills the room and everything fades. When the fog retreats it leaves behind an empty office.

I head down to the basement where the wood-shop is located. One time there were six boys caught smoking in the back storage room. It was filled with paint, paint thinner, and other flammable things. They could have set the school on fire. I knew where they got the cigarettes, because I was the one who stole them from the root house. And sold them the cigarettes.

In the woodworking shop, Mr. Brown is standing at the doorway to the back storage room. I walk past him and into the room. Six naked boys are having sex with each other. Mr. Brown walks in on them. Once again, everything fades into the fog.

There is a deafening scream. Like thousands of children crying out all at once. I cover my ears with my hands to stop the pain. Oddly, I hear laughter ringing off the walls.

I fall to my knees. "Stop it! Stop it! Stop it! Damn you, stop it right now!"

Everything goes dead quiet.

I get to my feet, dazed. Blood dribbles from my ears. I walk back into the woodworking shop. I remember listening

to Mr. Brown explain how to use many of the tools. I make
my way to the table where I carved my name:

> Jerry
> September 9th
> 1957

That was a real good year. But not for any of the kids at this
school.

I need something to kill this pain.

I leave the workshop and head to the nurse's station.
There's no one on the stairs to slow me down. In the nurse's
station, there are keys on a hook next to the medicine cabinet.
I grab the keys. It's empty. There's nothing to kill the pain.

I get a prickling sensation like there's someone standing
right behind me. I spin around, but there's no one there. It's
the same low-level awareness I've had since entering the
Residential School. I can't shake the suspicion I'm being followed. But why would anyone follow me? I'm not anyone special, just one of the Residential School survivors.

I head down the hallway to the boys' locker room. On the
last locker door there's a towel hanging like an invitation. I
undress from my bloody clothes and step into the shower. The
water is hot. I wash off all the dried blood from my body. I
wash all the blood out of my hair and off my skin. The water
runs red, then pink, as the blood flows down the drain. I shut
off the water, dry off, and put on clean clothes from my backpack.

I leave the locker room, and head for the second floor.

I remember being here alone in the summer. All the other
children went home for the summer, but I stayed at the

school. I helped paint the walls but got more paint on me than on the walls. I thought the painters were the coolest guys because they paid attention to me. One lonely Native child that no one wanted.

On the stairs up to the third floor there's a sick Ojibwe boy throwing up all over the steps. I recognize him. I reach into my backpack and give him some wiikenh root to still his stomach. The boy on the stairs is me. It was me that day. I remember being sick and throwing up all over the stairs.

I step back as a group of boys run past heading up to their dorm. Talking about what they're going to do over the Christmas holidays with their parents.

I make my way up to the fourth floor toward Mr. Phillips' private room. His room is just outside the boys' dorm. I step onto the landing and see a young Ojibwe boy leaning against the railing. Tears flow down his face. No one is coming to see him again this Christmas. He grew to hate Christmas and everything it stands for. I want to reach out to this lonely boy, but I know this lonely boy was me.

I leave the ghost and enter the dorm. There are the rows of bunk beds where we slept each night. I stop at the bunk bed where I slept many years ago.

Hearing the scuffle of feet, I look up to see a few boys enter the dorm. Moments later a short, fat, bald man follows. I see his face, and it feels like I've been hit with a ton of bricks. I remember that scumbag. It is Mr. Phillips, the boys' dorm supervisor. I feel pressure building. That's the scumbag that raped me, and many of the other boys. I clench my fists, ready to punch that jackass out. But once again he fades into the fog.

I turn and see the young boy crying to himself, like he's the only child in the world. My heart aches for him. I lean close and whisper in his ear. "You are not alone. You are going to be all right."

The boy looks directly at me and smiles. He can see me! He mouths the words "Thank you" and fades into the surrounding mist. I feel better as I walk out of the dorm. I hold my shoulders back, as if a weight has been lifted.

I come to a stop. Right in front of Mr. Phillips' room. Then turn and head down the stairs to the main floor. I enter the main hallway and head to the front of the building. The screams of thousands of children fill the air. I cover my ears, trying to make my way to the main door and to the outside world.

"Where the hell do you think you're going, boy?" a booming voice asks.

I know right then, that it is Him. The Walker I've feared all my life. He is the one that haunts my nightmares. The nightmares which caused me to lash out at those around me.

I take a deep, shaky breath. And continue walking toward the main doors, and the outside world. I don't know if I have the strength to make it to the door, I don't know if I have the strength to make it to freedom.

Again, His voice booms. "Where the hell do you think you're going, you little savage. You're all mine! D'you hear me, boy?"

My vision goes dark and my legs feel weak, I am only steps away from freedom, but I can't move forward. I need to let go of my anger and fear, or this place will never stop haunting me. If I can't put down the weight I'm carrying, the nightmare will never end. I can't let this place continue to have power over me. I can't keep feeding energy to this ghostly school, fueling it with my pain.

"Manitou," I whisper. A cloud of butterflies bursts from behind me and they flood out the doors, showing me the way to escape. Suddenly my vision clears and I'm free from whatever chains bound my legs.

"You have no power over me," I say. "I am free of you."

I cross through the door as a boney hand reaches out to grab me. It misses my shoulder by inches.

I step out into sunlight and feel free, for the first time in many years.

Many Native children are held captive by the Walker, forced to relive the hell they lived through over and over again. Or until they manage to break free of Him.

# AHNUNGGOKWAN

## Karen Lee White

If Nokomis saw where that regalia and sacred pipe had ended up she would have disowned her grandson. She had tried to rescue him from the enemy. There was no banishing nowadays. And kids were troubled. Things were upside down in the world. Like Windego was taking over the world with a never-ending tornado. Throwing pieces of people in the air to disappear forever.

If she were standing here and seeing that regalia. If she were standing here seeing that regalia hanging on the wall in the Indian Trading Post. If she were standing here seeing that regalia hanging on the wall in the Indian Trading Post with a price tag on it she would have felt every stab of the needle on her fingers, she would have felt the stiffness of her neck, the ache of her eyes and arthritis from picking up beads, picking up beads so tiny on the sharp fine end of a hairline needle, picking up beads to place each stitch just so on the moose hide. Smoked moose hide with her original designs. Smoked moose hide in her grandson's spirit colors, and she would recall that with each stitch she put her prayers and wishes and hopes and dreams for him. All that his parents had never been able to accomplish, she put that into each stitch. With each bright colored bead, each representing a hope, a dream, a prayer, a wish. That was her hope hanging up there on that wall.

And that pipe in the case, her husband's own prayers in his opwaagan, sitting right there in between all the other sacred pipes. Right out in the open where anyone could see. Hearts are fragile; like pipestone And all that pain would hit her in the heart so that she would hardly be able to breathe. And the dishonor! The bowl attached to the stem! It could break a spirit's heart right in two.

Just standing looking up at it, and then down into the case. It would make her feel the weight of this terribly ugly sad thing. His inability to control his urge, his addiction. The need for money that drained him of power, the need for money that drained him of energy, the need for money that drained him of joy. Hardened him – just like one of those small vampire rocks, vampire rocks wrapped tight in tin foil and hidden in pockets.

How had this happened? There was no one thing she could put a finger on. He sat at her side as she began the project, and checked in on it each day when he came from home from school. "How is it, Granny?" She pinched his chubby cheeks disappearing into a young man's face. She held it up in weakly shaking arms to show him. He was always teasing her: "Is that all you got done? Granny, you should see how much I did in school!" And her response, "G'waaaan, make tea for your old Granny, now."

He had not disappointed her when the regalia was finally completed.

Tears stood in his eyes, and a smile trembled on his handsome face. A face that held more than a trace of her late husband.

If she had been alive to see him at this moment, taking $500 for this beautiful work of art that she had put her last weeks into, she would not have spoken. She would have shaken her head, and walked out, leaning on her cane. Waited silently outside. Wordlessly sat beside him as they drove back to the reserve. As it was, she was dead. All she could do was move her spirit as hard as she could to try to help him feel her, now. In this terrible hour.

Her presence was with him now, as the featherweight of five hundred dollars in bills was counted into his hands. He could smell the dirty, too-many-hands smell of the money, but he smelled her smudge even more clearly. She liked to blend bashkodemashkosiw, asemaa, bashkodejiibik, and giizhikaandagoons with something else, but she would never tell him what. He always thought it was bear-root.

Her voice in his ear: "You are selling your dance outfit? And your pipe? What are you gonna sell next, your spirit name?"

He felt it like a horse kick in the gut. Worse than any craving that ate him from inside; an insatiable rat.

"Can I buy it back if it's not sold?"

"Anyone who is willing to pay $3,000 can have it." The man behind the till was a little sarcastic.

"It's priceless," she said, in Indian, right in his ear, "It's got your name colors on it. Nobody else can have something what I put my prayers into for you. And your Mishomis would die again if he saw what you have done with his pipe."

"I want to raise the money." The shopkeeper looked up.

"What the hell? This isn't a pawnshop. So yeah, going to need to see $3,000. But a collector will get it before you make it back here." The salesman looked him up and down, recognizing the signs; the stink on the boy, the black fingers, and the rapid-fire speech.

"Most times that's who pays for these, that and Europeans. They love the Indian stuff. One guy from Germany paid $5,000 last year. They dance at powwows over there too, you know?"

The boy's mind was far away, beside his Granny, as she hunched over the beadwork, saying, "This is the last one I am ever gonna make, sonny, my eyes aren't so good." He swallowed hard.

When he got into the truck, her kerchief was on the seat beside him. His breath caught. Where did it come from? He picked it up, buried his nose in it to see if it smelled like her hair. Her medicine smudge. It did. His chest tightened, and he could barely get his breath.

He cried all the way to the dealer's house. He cried all the way home. He cried when he loaded the pipe, he cried when he struck the match. These things calmed him. The sound of the fire in the pipe and the sparkling sound. He inhaled the bitter smoke, he held it in. The familiar tearing sensation as his spirit left his body. He traveled now on a runaway crack cocaine railroad, the cars speeding and shaking and rattling along a narrow track.

And then he did not cry anymore. But those in the Ahnunggokwan did, the Star World. And a cold rain began to fall, tears turning to ice as they froze and bounced off of the ground.

# WHERE THEY DWELL

## SARA GENERAL

Imogen dreamed of a cave.

It is the second such dream and each happens the same. The fog. The way the mist hovers amid the autumn leaves, the scent of moss, the trickle of spring water over slick rock before the drop.

It feels like she left something behind. A hat? A scarf?

She can't recall what she wore except the boots.

The boots she remembers: brown rubber that went to her knees, heels caked with mud, wet leaves, and dirt. She steps into a stream, and they filled like cups. She flips them over to empty the water and – somehow – she became cursed.

⁂

She didn't know anything was wrong at first. It was only later that she began to notice things change. Like whatever was affecting her needed time to settle in and take up residence; a strange, spectral visitor.

She lost her appetite. Colors faded. Her relationships soured. The phone rang, but she didn't answer it, and they didn't leave messages. She stopped getting dressed on the weekends – then the weekdays – without bothering to wash between the wearing.

Her chosen uniform: black leggings, black tank top, black sweater. A strip of leather with a pouch filled with red whip. The bark from a dogwood. She couldn't remember where it came from, but it was too much bother to take off, and it was supposed to be a powerful medicine, one that could kill monsters — or so the legends say.

Every now and again she saw flashes of amber brown eyes, and something in her would almost stir to life. But she couldn't muster the energy to figure out what those eyes meant, much less who they belonged to.

Her days became a haze; she did her best to keep up. Sleeping. Waking. Eating. But nothing had been the same since she'd stepped foot in that forest, and as the days wore on even the most mundane tasks became draining.

I'm depressed, she thought, and made a point to go out more.

▲

Going out isn't easy. Her parents are the only ones who still want to spend time with her. Counting herself lucky, she joins them at a dinner party hosted by alumni of the local university.

After dinner, her mother, Lois, told a story she'd heard many times. The kind designed to teach as much as delight, but in her state of mind Imogen didn't enjoy it. She hunched churlishly and watched the other guests.

One man stood out to her. He was ugly, or at least his expression was. The longer Lois spoke, the darker his eyes became, and his mouth twisted in a sneer. When her mother finished, the man lifted his chin. "What do you think of fundamentalism?"

Her mother flushed. The question was designed to knock her down a peg. A woman sitting nearby turned to her mother and said, "I'll take this one, Lois" and lambasted the ugly man with the tone of a woman who is used to standing up to arrogant men. The other guests nodded in approval and tension in the room disintegrated.

But not for Imogen. The scolding barely affected the man. He was still smug. And why not? He'd made his point – her mother wasn't as educated as the other people in the room.

She was better educated.

Her mother knew the stories and ceremonies of the Haudenosaunee. She knew how to treat people.

Imogen wanted to throttle the man. She felt her heart pounding against her chest. Her pulse racing faster and faster as her anger grew.

And – his glass exploded in his hand. Specks of wine flew everywhere and blood welled from the cuts in his fleshy palm.

"Bloody hell!" He leapt out of his seat. Imogen jumped up with him, her heart beating furiously against her chest. Her gaze fell to her hands.

Did I do that? It feels like I caused that…

"I guess that's what you get for being such a jackass, Darren," their host said through lidded eyes, then mopped him up.

That was the end of it – for everyone else. But Imogen could not stop replaying the incident over in her mind, because it was not the first. There was the friend she wished would stop bothering her. Her friend got in a car accident right after dropping her off at home. Then there was the time the lights in her neighbor's house exploded after they refused to turn down their loud music.

Something was happening to her. Her thoughts made manifest. The bad ones, at least.

Darren sent a note months later. His irritation that night spawned from disagreements with his own mother. He only wanted to be an academic for prestige, to prove he was good enough, and resented anyone who found wisdom outside the Ivory Tower.

Including her mother.

"This is why you need to spend time on the land." Lois waved his letter. "To know yourself. To know your heart."

Her mother never spoke of the letter again.

Imogen burned with such righteous indignation she'd caused the man to bleed for it. She might not have been able to prove it, but deep down she knew she was the cause.

▲

She took her mother's advice and booked a cabin on Bear Island.

Temagami is beautiful. Houses stand amongst the islands scattered across the lake. She'd been here once before to photograph a wedding but had never really seen the place. Which was ironic since her work was exactly that – seeing places.

There was a picnic table on the lawn. She sat staring up at the sky, marveling at the great twinkling tapestry. Stars sprawled across the velvety darkness, rolling out a thick cosmic welcome. Trees swayed like giants, and the wind rushed through the tall grass.

It felt like everything was waiting for her to speak.

"I'm a wreck." There was no point denying it anymore.

"Please help me." She could barely squeak out the words.

That night she had a third dream. Caves, and the place where powerful beings go underground – those who both protect and heal. Singing and dancing. A happiness she can't have yet. An enemy in the darkness, waiting to be slain.

At dawn, she packed her bags and took the first boat back to the mainland.

She knew where she had to go.

The border guard squinted at her status card, mouth moving silently.

"That's quite a name," he said. "Is that Indian or something?"

Always be polite, she was taught.

She nodded. "I also go by my English name. Imogen."

The borders aren't real she reminds herself. They are contrived things. This is Turtle Island. It doesn't matter how many laws settlers build over top of it.

Still, she had to suffer these contrivances.

She can tell the guard is trying to decide whether to give her a hard time.

"Destination?"

"Ithaca." It isn't where she's really going. But there's no way she is going to tell him that. Some people just can't be trusted.

"Go ahead." He handed her the card back.

She made a point of wiping it with a sanitizer at the next rest stop. She has no allegiance to the card, not really. It's as much of a construct as the border. But whether she likes it or not, her name is on the card and her mother always told her to take care of her name.

⌖

She left her parked car and set out on the path. There are many well-traveled paths here. The Adirondacks are an ancient place. There was no way to capture the grandeur, the awe, the magnificence of the land on film.

One breath and you can taste pine, oak, sumac, cedar, granite, moss, dirt, clay – and water, the lifeblood of the land. There is magic here. Real magic. It's always been here. Setting foot on the trail is a reminder that the same magic lives inside of her somewhere.

It was six months ago when she came here last, though she can't remember why. She can barely remember anything from the last year.

I used to remember everything. I used to remember my dreams every night.

Sometimes those dreams came true. She once dreamed the happenings of the following day, every night for a week. She knew everything that would happen. There were no sur-prises.

That had been the week leading up to her trip. But some-thing changed, the day she came here. Could it really be some sort of curse?

She steps onto a rock and surveys the forest. Was she foolish to come this far on so little information? To spend her savings crossing the border, renting a hotel in a country increasingly hostile to Indians?

Hostile or not, these are the lands of her ancestors. Her home.

The land sloped, as if to guide her along with ease. With every step, the terrain becomes more familiar. It is spring and everything is thawing. Small streams flooded over.

Limestone gives way to giant granite boulders. Sunlight filters through the trees casting her shadow on the rocks. She follows the slope, down, down, down. Past the waterfall, winding further and further. And stops.

The familiarity is striking. A tingling sensation spreads through her arms to her fingertips. She recognizes this place.

This was where it happened.

"You came back."

She spins around. There's a man, lanky, dark brown hair in a bun at the nape of his neck, chin scruffy with facial hair. He doesn't seem much younger than her – mid-20s, perhaps older. He's leaning, both hands propped atop a walking stick. Behind him, there's a horse and wagon – not something she expected to see here.

"Excuse me?"

"You came back," he said.

She tilted her head to the side. She has never seen this man before and yet there is something familiar about him. "Do we know one another?"

He smiles. "You don't remember me, do you?"

"I don't remember much these days," she admitted.

"I thought so." He takes a step closer. "My name is Marcus."

She doesn't step back.

"You've been bitten by the Adder," he tells her.

"What's that?" she asks, bracing herself.

"It's a snake that eats dreams."

For a split second she remembers coming down the hill. Reaching out to grab hold of a tree. Leaning on it while taking one boot from her foot.

Her eyes fall to her feet, expecting exposed flesh and a painful gash.

"That's not where he bit you."

She looks up and finds him watching her. Marcus has golden eyes like sunlight shining through topaz, like crystallized tree sap.

Slowly, she lifts her right hand.

"That's right," His voice is encouraging.

There are two blood-red marks on her palm. No more than pinpricks, yet it feels like she could disappear into them. How could she have missed them?

"I don't remember being bitten," she says.

"That's probably the first memory it ate."

"I thought you said it ate dreams?"

Marcus chuckled. "What makes you think there's any difference?"

She inspects the wound again. There is a ring of greyish-tinged skin around the bite mark.

Bitten by a snake and possibly cursed. A mysterious stranger. What else happened that she doesn't remember?

She waves her hand at him. "The skin looks like it's dying."

"It is. You're dying. That's an old wound." He paused, all traces of laughter disappearing. "You'll be dead before the end of the day."

She flinches. Dying?

But I'm only just waking up…

"I don't want to die," she says.

"Then you have to kill the snake. Then I can make you an antidote – I have the other ingredients already." He points with his thumb to the wagon behind him. "But I'll need the venom to finish it. And it has to be the snake that bit you. And it has to be gathered by you. That's the only way."

She stares at him. Who is this guy? How does he know all of this?

Not important.

Right now – she needs to focus. "Where do I find it? The Adder Snake."

Marcus points. Water falls from the cliff and pools, before funneling into a cave.

She takes off her coat and bag. "I'm going to trust you with these."

He hands her an empty burlap sack, a small smile on his lips. "That's what you said the last time we met."

She wants to ask him more, but blood rushes from her head and she sways uneasily on her feet.

"You'd better get going. You don't have much time."

She tightens the laces on her boots, steps up onto the rocks and carefully makes her way across the pool of water. The drop off is pitch-black. She shivers looking down.

How big is the Adder Snake? And how am I supposed to kill it?

There is no step to guide her. Legs trembling, she closes her eyes, steps forward, and plummets. The fall is short – her right elbow grazes rock but otherwise, she hits the water unharmed. It is bitingly cold and she regrets not taking off her shoes, now flooded and heavy. She swims, as much as she is able, kicking out like a frog, and reaches a ledge. With immense effort, she pulls herself out of the water.

She collapses against the rock, then pushes herself back on her heels and looks around.

Sunlight filters down through water making the cavern glow with an eerie turquoise light that dances along the cavern walls. Another memory returns. She is peering down into the cave with the flash and whir of her camera.

I came here to take pictures!

Something moves in the corner of her eye. She turns to see a snake's tail slithering out of sight. She freezes. Why hadn't she brought a weapon?

Deeper into the caves she is forced to walk in a stream of water. It's a metre wide and reaches her knees – and it is filled with snakes. They brush up against her legs. Black snakes. Green snakes. Striped and checkered. She's not afraid but suspects that's only because she's not herself. Not fully.

If my dreams return, will I have nightmares about this place?

A short distance, and the tunnel comes to an abrupt fork. There are two ways forward. Only one leads to the Adder. She can sense its presence, like a droning hum in the back of her mind, and she realizes that it has been a phantom in her head for months.

Without hesitation she chooses the cave on the right side of the fork heading toward the drone.

He is waiting for her. An enormous snake –more than ten feet long – with a head the same size as hers. She can see every line of his scales, black as beetles.

"Look who's come back." She hears his voice in her mind.

Her voice is shaky. "I want my memories back. I want my dreams."

"Of course. They're yours, after all. I would be happy to give them."

He's lying. She can hear his thoughts as clearly as her own. He's trying to distract her. Make her lower her guard. Then he can wind himself around her and choke the life out of her.

"Before I do, answer me a question."

Answering would buy her time, time to figure out how to kill him. "All right."

"Did you enjoy it? Using my powers. Being able to punish them? Didn't some good come of it?"

"That's more than one question." She reaches out to balance herself. Her head feels perilously light.

"You're weak. I could make you strong forever."

She can see the memories he's feeding on. Dreams and conversations from the last six months. They do not a pretty picture make. It wasn't just Darren at the party. Her venomous words and actions had pierced her friends, her colleagues. She'd alienated everyone. And the Adder Snake helped her do it.

"They deserved it. You know if felt good to put them in their place."

"No," she said. "It didn't."

And it was true. The satisfaction she got from causing others pain had multiplied her own despair, and fed this snake – made it powerful. She leapt arms outstretched and grabbed him around the neck, fingernails digging into scales.

He shakes her off in one smooth movement and she tumbles away from the water. Her head strikes stone and a jolt of pain flashes through her temples. And just like that – she saw it. The very first memory the snake had taken.

⋏

The bite was flooding her body with poison. Her knees throbbed from where they'd struck the ground and her wrist burned with pain like she'd been stung by an enormous wasp. Her eyes swept the ground, but the snake had already disappeared into the cave.

She heard a man's voice. Saw a pair of beautiful amber-gold eyes, like dripping honeycomb, and a competing warmth flooded her body.

"Stay with me." he said, voice strained.

She sat propped up against a tree, watching him rummage through a wagon.

"Take this." He tied a leather pouch around her neck. "Kill the snake. Then come find me."

She doesn't want to go, but she only has so much time before her first memory is stolen.

"I will," she promised. And then went into the cave.

When she came to the fork, she chose the left tine. By the time she emerged from the tunnel, the snake had eaten her most recent memories. She found her car and thanked the universe she hadn't gotten lost.

⋏

She closed her fingers around the pouch at her neck. It was still there. The only weapon she has, the one she's carried through her darkest days. She tugged the pouch open and shook the contents into her mouth, chewing and swallowing the dried scrapings of bark so quickly she almost choked. It had a pleasant, slightly minty taste.

The Adder Snake wrapped around her leg, dragging her toward the water. She grabbed the rock ledge to keep him from pulling her under. Frustrated, the serpent loosened his grip.

She picked up a rock and hurled it at his arrow-shaped head. He dodged and swooped down at her. He bit her. Two quick jabs. Once on the shoulder and again at her collarbone. The pain was hot and sharp, like she'd been pierced with red-hot pincers.

But she knew she was ready. She'd worn the pouch for the last six months. Worn it in the shower. Worn it to bed. She'd bathed in red whip. A strong medicine, made from the small flowering dogwood tree, in the stories her people tell it is a weapon of defense against all manner of monsters. Her clothes were soaked in it. And now – she'd eaten it.

The Adder's hiss was a shriek filling the entire cavern. The snake recoiled, thrashing against the rock. White foam bubbling from around his mouth. He was shrinking, shrinking, shrinking, until finally he lay on the floor of the cave, nothing but a skeleton husk.

It was over. The snake was defeated.

She drops the sack at Marcus's feet.

"It's done," she says. "The Adder Snake is dead."

He catches her before she hits the ground and helps her over to a tree. Imogen leans against it, sinking to the ground. He steps away and she can barely lift her head. When he returns some time later, he's carrying a clay cup with the antidote he told her he would make out of the snake's venom.

"It's ready," he says. "Drink."

"You already made it?" she asks, eyes wide.

His voice is soft. "I've prepared it every day for the last six months, waiting for the missing ingredient."

She drinks and sets the empty cup on the ground. Her mouth fills with the taste of cinnamon. Heat spreads through her body, warming her chest. She feels her muscles loosen, soothed by the antidote.

Every day for the last six months.

Why would he do a thing like that?

Sleep claims her before she can ask.

There's a fire crackling when she wakes. Marcus is cooking something in the flames but sets it down when he notices her watching.

"Hungry?" He holds out a plate.

It's the best meal she's ever had. Strips of roasted rabbit, sage, and wild carrots. A clump of berries for dessert. Frybread with some kind of seeds sprinkled in. She eats it all, using the frybread to soak up the juices.

He smiles as he watches her enjoy the food.

"Thank you," she smiles. "For everything."

"That was a big risk, letting the Adder Snake bite you like that."

"Our stories always say red whip wards against monsters." She rests her head back and stares up at the moon. "Every last one of them."

The flames cast an orange glow against the trees, their boney arms stretching up to the sky. Soon they would be bursting with leaves. Spring would come. Her dreams would come back, just like her memories.

They hadn't known each other long before the snake separated them, but she could now remember how, in the brief time they'd spent together, he seemed to be the person she'd been waiting for her entire life.

A friend. A companion. Maybe something more.

"A lot can change in six months."

"I made it back, didn't I?"

He doesn't answer right away. "My world is not your world."

He'd told her about his world. The storytellers called it "The Land that Once Was." The place where legends were still alive.

"You'd miss people here," he says. "Your friends. Your family."

"I feel like I might miss you more."

A smile spreads across his face.

"You know I had forgotten this place," she tells him. "I was headed in a different direction."

"What made you remember?"

"The dreams," she says. "But it's strange, because the Adder Snake ate my dreams. So how did I have them?"

"I have certain gifts," He pokes at the fire with a stick. "I can move back and forth across the worlds. When you didn't come back I knew you'd get worse. So I saw a friend – a wizard. He agreed to help. To send a dream powerful enough to cut through the Adder's poison. But not just one dream."

"Three." Three dreams, so she would pay attention. One she might ignore. Two could be a coincidence. Three, she would be less likely to disregard.

"But there was a price."

She shivered, as if cold hands were brushing her skin.

"I can't travel between our worlds anymore. When I go back home – I can never return."

"When?" She pressed her lips together.

"At dawn."

She looked to the sky. It is already beginning to lighten.

"Do you remember what I told you?" he asks.

She can hear her heart beating in her ears. "You said, I could come with you. To your world."

"You can. But you have to decide now."

She wants to go with him. But thinks of her parents, thinks of how she behaved, thinks of everything she put them through while she was cursed. She couldn't leave without saying goodbye .

"I can't expect you to choose me," he says. "It's enough for me that you're alive and well."

"If I stay, can I find you again?" she asks.

He takes her hand, and their fingers intertwine. "The same way we find anything that's lost – through our dreams."

She leans her head against his shoulder. He smells like peppermint and the cool night air.

The morning star steals across the sky, carrying dawn along with it.

"It's almost time." His golden eyes are like flames.

"I'll find a way back to you."

He kisses her hands. "I know."

She closes her eyes, sees a burst of light through her eyelids. When she opens them, she's alone, and her hands are empty.

But she is awake, and she is alive.

She climbs to her feet, kicks dirt on the fire, and walks back to her car. She will stay. She will make amends. And then she will find him again.

In his world.

In her dreams.

# SILK

## Nathan Niigan Noodin Adler

Mushkeg held the strand of spider's silk, glinting silver-blue in the moonlight. The strand swayed ever so slightly in the breeze, fine as thistledown, like the line of a kite. She followed the strand like a pre-schooler holding onto a knotted yellow rope so she wouldn't get lost. The light caught it, just so. It seemed to glow.

She could hear a stream burbling in the distance. Tyner's Creek. A young boy threw stones, adding plopping sounds to the noise the stream made.

"What are you doing here?" Mushkeg crouched, as if approaching a strange dog and worried greater height would only make her presence more threatening.

Couldn't have had more than six or seven winters. Throwing stones into the creek. The stones splashed into the water with a shplunk. Where are his parents? How did he get way out here?

"Waiting for you." The boy's little sausage fingers splayed as they scrabbled at the ground, searching for more stones to throw into the water.

"For me?" That made no sense. "What's your name?"

"Tynuck," the boy said. "But my mom always calls me Oose." The words made the fine hairs on the back of her arms prickle and stand up. Goosebumps. Mushkeg knew the original name for the stream had not been Tyner. The little stream had other names, older names. Before time had stretched and altered its pronunciation and spelling. Perhaps altering the phenomes and morphemes to sounds more pleasing to the English ear, easier for English tongues to shape. Oose was also one of the older Anishinaabe names for the river.

"Where's your mom?"

"Over that way." The boy nodded, slight protuberance of his lips in the general direction of the current. West. Downstream, toward the lake. The cute mannerism was unexpected, yet oh so familiar. Pointing with his lips. It reminded her of her grandfather before he passed. Something from the previous generation. Not something she often saw performed so naturally, so unselfconsciously. Merely mirroring his elders. It made her laugh.

"Let's go find her, shall we?" Mushkeg held out her hand, and Tynuck took it. They set off, following the path of the burbling stream. It was an easy walk. The earth sloping gently all the way down to the lake.

"You know, a river always follows the path of least resistance," the boy skips, swinging their hands back and forth as they walk.

"Now that you mention it, I guess I did know that, yeah." What a weird kid. Too smart for his own good. But it was true, they were like liquid. Gravity drawing them toward the lake. If it wasn't for her heart pumping the blood through her veins, it too would slump, follow the path of least resistance, and congeal at her feet instead of rushing through the conduit of her veins. Eighty per cent water and all that. Ugly bags of mostly water. She always had been a *Star Trek* fan and was tickled by that description of humans by an alien lifeform.

"So what were you really doing out here all alone?" Mush asked.

"Waiting for you."

A gossamer strand of spider's silk caught the light of the moon like a silver thread. Shivering in the breeze, it led in the same direction as the stream. Strange. She looked down and saw that the strand of silk emerged from her belly button like an umbilical cord, exited her body, and disappeared into the murky forest ahead.

"Where are we going?" Mush asked. Suddenly, it no longer felt as if she was leading Tynuck. Instead, it felt as if Tynuck was leading her, and she was merely along for the ride. The little boy leading the grown woman. Blind leading the blind? Or maybe it was the silken thread tugging her forward? That would make her the kite, rather than the kite-string holder.

"To see Nokomis. Grandmother has been waiting."

And Mushkeg nodded, suddenly too fatigued to argue. Her legs felt heavier and heavier with each step. The blood through her veins no longer felt like a river, it felt like mud. Turgid. Slow. Muddling her thought. No flash of silver white scales to relieve the darkness. Finally they came to a stop at the mouth of the river where, at its widest, the Tyner met Ghost Lake.

A confluence. The waters of the lake lapping out, and the current running in, creating swirls and eddies. The light of the moon shimmered on the water, refracting and shattering tri-angular with the peak of each shifting wave. Radio static. Television fuzz. Snow.

"What now?" She arched an eyebrow at the smarty-pants boy. "Swim?"

"This is as far as I go." Tynuck dusted his pudgy little hands. Adorable.

Her gossamer strand of spider's silk arced up and out across the lake, up and up and up into the sky toward the light of the moon, and beyond that, the light of the stars, following the spattering of light where the spiral arm of the Milky Way stretched out across the sky in a band.

"What about you?"

"You have to go the rest of the way on your own." Tynuck's eyes shifted back to the river. A trickle of blood leaked down from his forehead. The red just looked black in the dim light. "I have to stay here."

"Shit, your bleeding!"

Tynuck wiped his temple with one hand, looked down at the molasses-like stickiness, and then wiped his hand on his jeans. "See, all better." When he turned his head again to look back against the current of the river, she could see part of his skull was caved in. His hair matted. How had she not noticed this before?

Again, Tynuck indicated direction with a protuberance of his lips. Adorable little Mshoomis. And the tremulous thread emerging from her solar plexus and up and out to the stars. "You have your course, and I have mine."

Then, as if given permission, Mushkeg was following the silken strand of a spider's web, up and out across the lake, up and out across that band of stars that represented the spiral arm of the Milky Way, up and out past the moon, up into the sky, up into space. Walking at first, then moving faster. Faster than a roller coaster. Faster than the speed of light. Up and out to the stars. But though it was fast, she wasn't scared. It was exhilarating, that speed, the wind blowing through her

hair. Was there wind in space? Cosmic wind? Gawd, couldn't
she just shut off her brain for one second, she wasn't even
watching a movie requiring the suspension of disbelief. She
felt happy and at peace. Rushing toward the arms of her
Nokomis in the sky. Waiting to embrace her.

With vast arms her grandmother enveloped her in
woodsmoke, Mush felt suffused with love, and light. Like
coming home after a long trip. The familiar smells of something cooking; clink of plates and forks; and laughter. She was
coming home. She was home.

Then there was a pull, as though someone was tugging. A
fish on the line. She could hear someone crying. It was her
girlfriend, Eadie. She recognized it. That crying. She'd heard
it enough before, they'd broken up and gotten back together
so many times. But not just crying. She was flat out sobbing.
And saying her name. Mush Mush Mush. You'd think she
was egging a team of sled dogs. It tugged at her. Eadie's sadness. Pulling her away. Drawing her attention away from her
grandmother in the sky.

"It's up to you," Nokomis shrugged. "If you want to go
back. Go. Now that you know your way, just follow the
thread, zenibaanwegin'ikan, and you'll be able to find your
way back again."

"Thank you."

Then Mushkeg was rushing back to earth, rushing back
through the stars, across the spiral arm of the Milky Way, out
across the lake like a zip-line, down to the confluence where
Tyner's Creek met Ghost Lake. Her feet touched land like the
female Gelfling from *The Dark Crystal*, she had wings, and
touched ground light as butterfly. Feeling the grit of stones and
soil beneath her sneakers. She was back home on the Jiibay.

The stars were still out, scattered across the sky in a band. Tynuck was nowhere to be seen, but she could hear the murmur of his creek, so she knew he wasn't far. If she needed him. The trickling sound of the water reminded her of the trickle of blood dripping down from his forehead, and the caved-in section of his skull. She wondered, if she followed the path of the river back to its source, what would she find? Another wound?

She started walking, retracing her path up the creek against the flow of the current, against the pull of gravity. It was all uphill from here, the muscles in her phantom thighs burned with exertion. She was out of shape. The ground was covered in a network of fine gossamer strands, only visible when the threads caught the moonlight just right, like early morning dew caught in a spider's web. The strands were everywhere, the more she looked, the more silver filaments she saw. Stretching between the trees, like a network of interconnections, a physical connection between the web of life.

She stepped more carefully, cautious at first, but realized the silk was made of tougher stuff, and would simply bend or shift aside as she walked. First toward the totem pole, the place where she used to go to field parties. She paused at the firepit, touched the coals getting soot on her fingers. Black ash. The firepit was long since cold. Then out to the old rundown motel that had once belonged to Eadie's Uncle Oogie.

Eadie.

That's whose sobs she heard. Drifting through the trees. The world around her had shifted. The scenery changed. The dilapidated motel was replaced by the boughs of towering trees. Whether she had moved, or the world had moved, she wasn't sure, all she knew she was now in a different place.

She made her way through the interconnected silken strands stretching like webbing throughout the forest and paused at the edge of the clearing where the graveyard began. It was snowing. Though she could have sworn it hadn't been snowing a moment before. Heavy fat flakes fell from a gray sky. Clouds like blankets. Cotton balls muffling the world. A foot deep at least, if not more. The new snow, light and fluffy, lay on top of a hard, chrysalis of ice, and underneath was softer snow. She could feel the harder layer give way underneath her weight; other times, it was strong enough to support her without falling through. When she looked back, the white covering was uninterrupted. No tracks. Only the delicate silken strands, stretched, connecting things here to there.

Eadie knelt before a polished marble headstone, her jeans wet where the heat of her body melted snow, her short blonde hair dyed a shade of electric blue and spiked in all directions. It matched the stud in her pierced nose ring glittering like a sapphire. Her dark under-eye make-up was streaked from tears. The Crow make-up. The headstone in front of her engraved with capital letters that spelled out her name. M-U-S-H-K-E-G.

The scenery shifted again. Blood no longer flowed through her veins, the same rules of physics didn't apply, so why follow them at all if she didn't have to?

Mush stood at the side of the road. It was a hot day. She could feel the sweat on her forehead bead almost instantaneously. There were three wooden crosses. One for her. One for the baby, Jayden. One for her friend, Morrigan. A roadside shrine. They were all dead. And gone except her.

Except she wasn't alone. There were two other women. One wearing black, a black tank top, black cut-off jeans, black sweater tied around her waist. She knelt on the ground before the crosses, the grit of the road grinding against the flesh on her knees, eyes scrunched, hands held to her ears, blood dribbled from her nose as the sequence of events that led to Mushkeg's death played through her head all at once like a movie sped-up. The elk streaking across the road. Momentum carrying them forward as Morrigan slammed on the brakes. The antlers smashing through the windshield to impale her friend on the animal's horns, the kernelling, shattering glass, screech of tires, the car flipping over and over, everything a blur of movement, sensation, centrifugal force, up is down down is up, chaotic, direction made no sense, then the car came to a stop as it slammed into the trunk of a tree with a crushing force. Everything went black. Flashes from the night Mushkeg died.

"Is that how it happened?" The girl on her knees looked up at the other woman who could have been her living mirror, they looked that similar, they must have been sisters, maybe even twins. Her double hovered three inches above the gravel of the roadside, white dress gory with fresh, crimson streaks of blood.

The girl in black wiped the blood from her face on the back of her arm, and stood up, black combat boots crunching on the gravel as she eyed the roadside grave. She reached out and fondled the white MP3 player that had once belonged to Mushkeg. Mush wondered if Eadie had placed it there.

"Take it if you want." Mushkeg shrugged. The girl in black didn't look up from her examination of the device. White earbuds still dangling from the horizontal crossbar. The girl in the bloody white dress turned to look her way. She'd heard.

"Take it," the girl in the bloody white dress said to her sister. "She wants you to have it."

"She's here?" The Goth-girl swiveled her head back and forth, but was unable to see Mushkeg, standing not three feet before her. Shrugging her shoulders she slipped the earbuds into her ears.

"I guess I'm not going to get any better permission," she muttered under her breath, "than from the lips of the dead girl herself," then started walking, black combat boots crunching on the gravel.

⚜

Plop!

Eadie heard an odd sound, like someone casting a stone into a pool of water. Her tears stilled, though she kept sniffling, her face no doubt a mess of salt water and snot. She looked around but nothing looked any different, trees, graves, and the snow falling on everything.

When she looked back at Mushkeg's headstone, she saw it. A delicate tracery of filaments woven across hollows of the engraved letters. A spider's web. When had that gotten there? Had it been there this whole time? The silk so fine it was nearly invisible, like clear fishing line. Maybe she had just missed seeing it?

Eadie remembered the first night they met at a field party, and after Mush had written her name and phone number in red lipstick across the bathroom mirror. And there, written in shivering translucence, was spelled out the last four digits of her phone number.

8706.

"Oh, Mush!" Eadie let out a peal of laughter. "I wish I could phone you." And she had. Many times just to hear her voice again on the answering machine. "Hi, you've reached MUSH!" deep death metal drawl followed by an overly saccharine, "Leave a message!" But eventually the account deactivated and there was nothing but the DOOOOONNNHHH of the dial tone.

This was almost as good. Spiritual telecommunication.

# THE DEATH OF HIM CAME TO ME IN MY DREAMS

## Francine Cunningham

The small trailer holds our bodies. Late into the evening we sip black coffee while picking at stale bannock left by mourners. When Granny speaks, her words crawl out in halting syllables, each break filled with an uncharacteristic silence. We peek up at each other in the ring of light cast by the kitchen's sole lamp. Words dribble from her lips. In the wake of death we are unmoored, two strangers in a tin shelter older than two of my lives stacked together.

"He never wanted to go there, you know."

I nod.

"He never had a choice." She glances at me and then out of the window. Our reflection a murky shadow against the darkness of the woods. Even the stars refuse to shine on this day of death. "Since before time was created his ancestors walked there. But he didn't want to."

Her eyes find mine in the glass. "Every night he would wake up with frost lingering on his skin, mist brought back over from the other side."

I knew that cold. But I didn't speak.

Every morning since you got sick, I wake up gasping, mist wavering above me. A thick layer of frost on glass panes separate me from the day, muting the dawn light.

"He never told me anything other than to sob into my dressing gown. He never wanted to go there."

"Where did he go?" The words hover between us and I slip in a tiny lung full of air as she flicks her eyes to mine.

"I don't know, Jenn." Her hand slams against the cheap plywood table, the dishes rattle and I look away from the sorrow in her eyes. Anger manifests in arthritic fingers, bulging joints which tighten around her mug of lukewarm tea. She straightens her back and hauls herself up. "G'night."

She shuffles past me and into the trailer's dark, narrow hallway. Grief pulling her toward a room empty of you. But filled in other ways. Memories. Stuffed into the cracks of the wall. Pushed under the bed. Hidden away in the folds of clothing hanging in the closest. Fragments of thoughts, smells, touches. Tomorrow we will gather your things, the material of your life – and burn it. Send it to where you wait for us now.

People will be back in the morning. Older women in muted colors, murmuring softly as they take over the kitchen, gradually increasing in volume, until the house is filled with laughter. Until the floor becomes choked with children as they lay staring at the TV. Their parents will come after work. And we will eat. Food to heal. To fill spaces. Food that will linger in our bodies for days. And we will burn a portion for you, sending it on spiraling plumes of smoke laced with tobacco, sweetgrass, and sage. But not until tomorrow. Tonight still belongs to our sadness.

I stumble to the couch and fall back in a whoosh. Too numb for any graceful transition from awake to sleep. I lay in the half-formed thoughts of first sleep and I wish you could hear me, that we could still speak like we used to before you closed yourself off from Granny and me.

I knew. Did you know that? I always knew. That you walked in places no one alive is supposed to walk. You murmured between the ticking of the clock in the afternoons as you kept yourself from drifting into naps. You spoke of mist. Of gray. Of cold. I tried not to listen, but the whole trailer would fill with your frozen dream air during the night. When I caught you in the hallway as I snuck to the bathroom in the grey morning light, you would look at me with eyes filled with mist. And I pretended I didn't see what you saw. I pretended that we weren't the same. Because you never wanted to talk, you just wanted to forget. So I tried to forget too.

The trailer is too quiet. Even though you hardly spoke in the last few months. You still managed to fill the trailer with your presence, the creaks and scrapes of your movement. And now I don't know what to touch, where to move, without stumbling into pockets of silence.

The dream found me as usual, but this time – on the night after your death – it is different. I walk hesitantly down the center line of the bridge in the near gloom of almost morning. Plumes of evaporating salt water greet the ever-lightening sky. The bridge is the same as always, shrouded in fog, so thick the suspension cables seem to stretch endlessly into the sky.

The smell is the same – half rotting, partly digested fish. Whales and otters swimming silently in the murky brown water below. Wind slips itself into the empty spaces in my hair, feeling me, knowing me.

Then it happens. My heart starts racing, my skin feels like it's burning, my lungs constrict as panic overwhelms me. They say that in extreme moments of fear you either run or you fight. I wanted to run. Back to where I came from. But I can't move backwards. I can only stand, listen, sense that something is coming. The only direction I can move is forward. Farther into the mist. Farther away from the calm light, the peaceful forest.

Swirling in the mist around me are shrouded figures. The echoing sound of their feet as they shuffle forward sends bolts of electricity through me every time one gets too close. The sound of waves crashing into the base of the bridge is rhythmic, deep, and powerful.

"Noooooooooo," a cry of anguish from my left.

There you are beside me. A hunched version of who you were in life. Tears slide from your eyes as you stare into the distance. The pressure around me lifts. I can move freely again. Your presence has unglued me from the forward march into darkness.

"Grandpa," I whisper.

You try to look at me, I can see the strain in the tightness around your eyes, but all you can do is move your lips. "My girl."

"Grandpa!" I yell.

Your shoulders slump further into your chest. My eyes meet yours, they are lost, distant, they squint as they try to see me.

"This is where you always came? Isn't it?"

You try to pull your eyes from mine, but I won't let you. Because I'm in control here. As soon as this thought enters my mind, I know it is true. I grab ahold of your arm and squeeze.

"Why am I here?" I yell into your face as I struggle to be heard over the wind.

"Jenn, I'm...sorry." You struggle to form words.

"Why am I here?" I yell again. The trees on either end of the bridge convulse as the wind batters through them; they sway as if they want to uproot and flee. The dark sky is heavy with rain; black and blues swirl in a threatening mix as the mist around us deepens.

"I thought if I didn't teach you...you were a girl. It wasn't supposed to pass on to you. It was supposed to die with me!"

My ears rang, "What wasn't supposed to pass to me?"

"This curse. Shepherding the dead."

Your eyes widen and you let an agonizing cry as a silver flash of lightning passes through your hunched body, splitting through your shoulder and zipping back out into the thickening mist. I brace myself for some kind of shared impact but nothing happens, it was like the bolt was just for you. I scramble to reach out to you but you wave me away as you curl up on yourself.

"I'm okay," you whisper.

A howl from behind us echoes through the mist, I look back and through the haze see the dark shape of something, an animal maybe, approaching. It's too big to be natural. My body shivers; I reach out and grip your hand. It's cold. Too cold. The water thrashes like a churning beast below us, crashing ever higher against the supporting beams of the bridge, whipping itself into white frosted waves, washing over gaping mollusks. Black mouths open to the promise of salt.

Some of the others on the bridge with us are within an arm's reach, I can hear their inhalation of breath, I know they are there even though I can't see them.

When I look back your pupils are like pinpricks mirroring the fear and adrenaline coursing through me. For a second you have lifelike strength as you grab my shoulders and pull me toward you.

"You must walk the path, Jenn. Your task, you must take me over into the darkness. Take us all. But don't…"

A howl from behind us. Whatever creature is behind us is getting closer. A storm brews above us. Wind begins to whip at my small frame. Freezing drops fall onto my face.

I wake with a yelp. Arms stretched out as I reach for you.

Your voice whispers. "Take us, one by one, into the darkness. You must. If you don't, you will stay lost, wither – die."

I clutch at my head, was your voice real? My body convulses in fear, it is covered in a sheen of cold sweat. What did you mean? How would I stay lost? How could I take you, anyone, into the darkness? My fear of what that darkness contains is like its own entity. I feel trapped. I can't breathe. I squeeze my eyes shut. I snap the bracelet on my wrist until it hurts. Because that pain is real and it calms my fear of what isn't. Of the dream.

I sit in the gloom waiting for Granny to come into the kitchen. To pull out the kettle and boil water for her instant coffee. For the sound of the radio as she tunes the dial from one station to the next, looking for the freshest news. Once those rituals are performed, night will officially be over.

The gray light of morning seeps through the trailer's living room window. My eyes find your faded green armchair by the window, and I see you again as you were in the last months of your life. Staring out at the sky, already almost lifeless as me, and Granny kept the trailer warm with the wood stove you installed years ago. And I realize now, you were staring into daylight. Willing away the darkness, willing away the mist, and the ever-rising stench of salt and fish.

We start with your closet. My hands, Granny's hands, both your sisters' hands. With delicate fingertips we brush over the fragments of you, the small things you called your own. We don't speak. Maybe because silence is better, or maybe because your presence is deafening.

Granny holds in her tears for as long as possible before breaking. It starts with a sob. Then a racking cough. Then a fall onto the bed. A gripping of the blanket, that held your smell, pushed into her face. One of your sisters guides her out of the room. And I fall back into the chair beside your bedroom window. Your clothing is piled around me and I can't imagine not having even one shirt of yours left. I start to fold plaid shirts and worn jeans into piles. Your other sister is slowly making her way through your nightstand. Pulling out small things; change, an old pin, a book. As the things start to pile up she hands me a bunch of loose papers. I'm about to toss them into a bag of garbage but notice your scrawl. Tilted letters scratched in a stubborn refusal to ever learn cursive.

I unfold the top paper. The shadow is almost upon me. My time is soon. Good. It will be broken. I set it aside and read through the next one: Nothing is real. All is the mist. All is the field. My heart speeds up. What field? The mist I already knew. My only solace is that it will finally be over. For me. For all of us. I read through each paper. Each says the same thing. You were looking forward to your death. For your escape from the mist. I think back to my dream. You are still there, in the mist. I hear an echo of your strangled cry in my mind, and the papers fall from my hands and scatter on the floor.

"What is it, Jenn?" Auntie's voice is almost a whisper.

"He's…he's trapped. In the mist. On the bridge."

Her deep brown eyes narrow. She flicks her straight gray hair over her shoulder with a hand covered in silver rings and grabs my arm. She hauls me up and pulls me from your room.

"Auntie, what are you doing?"

She doesn't answer or look back. She pulls me through the back door, skirting the women in the kitchen, the watchful eyes of the kids. She only lets go of my arm when we are standing far from the house. The sky is a gray blend of cloud and heavy rain yet to fall. The tree branches still hold the remains of winter. I shift from my left foot to my right as Auntie lights a cigarette. Blackened dead leaves squish.

Auntie looks me up and down as she holds the cigarette up to her face, her other hand thrust into her pocket. "What do you know about the mist?"

My face slackens. Could I lie? Did I want to?

"What do you know about the mist?" I ask instead.

She humphs before settling her weight on a bare fallen log, "I see." She takes another drag from her cigarette, pushing the smoke out through her nose. "You know, your Grandpa never left this territory. Not once in his life. Did you know that?"

I shook my head no.

"He never even went to the Residential School. Nope. He was hidden. By his grandfather. They escaped out into the bush. They lived just them. Until it was safe to go home. Until we were all different people."

"He never talked much," I answer.

"I know, he was..." – she looks at me, her eyebrow cocked up knowingly, like it used to when I was little and she was telling me to behave without speaking – "different."

"How?"

"You know." She pinched her mouth, her eyes squinting as she stared at me with a challenge. When she looked at a person with that look you knew you weren't going to win.

I rub my hand over my face, feel the swelling under my eyes from too many tears on skin. I know I must look terrible. As terrible and sad and lonely as everyone else. "I don't know anything," I challenge.

"You know about the mist though." Her eyes haven't blinked, they've stayed on my face, her mouth only pinching harder.

I give up and look at the ground before collapsing on the log next to her. I wrap my arms around my knees and feel the tears slipping as I lean against her steady weight.

"I don't want to go back there," I whisper. "It killed him."

"No, Jenn. It is death."

"What?"

"I wasn't supposed to know. But I was jealous. My brother was always given different food, given special jobs, given story after story, and song after song. He knew the names of things, the real names of things, and he would talk to these things." She shakes her head and takes a long inhale of breath. "The rest of us were just normal, I guess. But I snuck where I wasn't supposed to sneak. And from our grandfather's lips, I heard about the nature of the mist." The cigarette drops to the damp ground before she grinds it into the mud with her toe. "It's not something to be fearful of." She reaches out and strokes my head. "Your job, the thing you are responsible for now, is to lead."

"Lead who?"

"The dead." She grabs my chin as she says this, looks deep into my eyes. Tears are welled up in them. She doesn't cry. But she feels. I close my eyes against her sadness.

I can see the bridge. I can see the way the mist is curled around the top of the trees. I can hear the scurrying of animals in the distant forest. I can sense the ghosts as they shuffle aimlessly in the darkness. They are lost without a guide through the mist.

My throat feels scratchy. The long days of black-clothed grievers has taken a toll on me. My hands are dry, the moisture sucked out from hands brushing over mine. Neighbors grip my fingers, letting me feel their sorrow at your passing. Dishes need to be washed in the sink after they leave for the night. Granny is too tired at the end of the day to do anything but collapse on the couch in front of the TV.

I want them to just go away. To never come back. I want to be alone. I want to sleep. Curl up in my bed. Close my eyes. Let the darkness come for me. I want to be in the dream because I need to see you.

I let my clothing slide into a pile on the floor. Settle beneath the heavy comforter and sigh into the warmth and safety. I want to believe that my dreams will go back to ordinary, back to how they were before you got sick. But I know that they never will.

The wind howls. The trees bow against it. Waves rise and I can feel the cold sting of the ocean against my face. Rain falls

from the purple sky and lightning cuts open the mist, reveal-
ing the contorted faces of the dead. My screams are drowned
out in their cries. Then you are beside me, your fingers
indenting my wrist.

"GUIDE ME." Your voice louder than everything else. "I
don't know this place. You must."

The bridge is rocking with the force of the storm. I look
ahead at the howling darkness and mist. I don't want to go
there. Only death lurks there. I know that now. I can feel it.

"GUIDE ME." You shake me as you plead.

The moans of the others on the bridge fill me with terror.
Their clawed hands reach for me, desperate in the face of the
storm. I try to back away. Run back into the forest. But my
feet are locked forward. I've lost control over the dream.

Your face distorts in pain as silver flashes pierce your skin.
You let me go as your body spasms. My heartbeat skips errat-
ically. I try to run to the edge of the bridge, I want to leap into
the waters, because anything would be better than this, but I
still can't move.

There is a bear-like growl behind me. As if something is
coming toward me, toward us. I look down at you, writhing in
pain as you beg me to help.

I want to wake up. This dream, this bridge, everything
over here is real, as real as my waking life. You grip the hem
of my pants and my heart stalls. I cough deep and it beats
frantically again. You don't deserve this. I can't hear you; the
wind is stealing your words from my ears but I can see your
mouth forming them as you plead with me. Your eyes, they are
hollow but they are staring into mine, and then I see it – a
flicker of hope, in me. Your fingers let go as another bolt of silver passes through you and you begin to convulse. In a panic,

my own arms trembling as much as yours, I reach down and grip your shoulder. Your body stop shivering. I look ahead. The heart of the storm in front of us. The growling from the woods behind us is growing louder. I crouch down beside you. Pull your body against mine.

"Please." Your voice is almost gone but my whole body hears it. "Lead me."

"How?"

"Just walk."

I grip you under both shoulders, haul you up, drag your weight forward, the more we walk the more you're able to hold yourself up. My feet know the way even if I don't; they lead me through the outstretched hands of the other ghosts.

The closer to the middle of the bridge we get, the higher and closer to the darkness of the storm, and the fainter the moans from the ghosts become, until finally we are out of range. Into the heart of the howling wind and rain and forks of lightning stabbing down, we march across the bridge, ducking our heads against the force of the gale. I keep count of my heartbeats, and one after another we begin to pull through to the other side. At this far end of the bridge the trees stand straighter. The wind calms. But the mist swirls around me as usual. I stare into the maw of the dark forest and my stomach cramps. I don't want to move any closer. Like a rabbit trembling as it's exposed on the top of a hill, I feel exposed and open to that darkness.

"Thank you," you say as you slide away from me. You stand at the edge of the forest and take a few deep breaths. "It won't be long."

"Grandpa." I can hear the tremble of panic in my voice.

"Don't you see?" You point ahead.

And then I do. Through the darkness there is a pinprick of light. When I keep my eyes trained on it, my body stops shaking, my trembling evaporates.

"Am I dead? Why am I here?" I ask.

"You're not dead, Jenn. It's your job, or your curse, or your gift. I thought that because I didn't have a grandson, all of this would disappear. I never imagined you would inherit this. I'm sorry. I should have taught you. I should have…"

"Is this why you never left our territory?"

"Yes."

My stomach flutters as a realization hits me, I can't leave home either then. I try to absorb this. I would be on our land forever. Possibilities of a life in the city, of traveling the world, of anything new – gone. Just like that. My eyes fill with tears and my throat constricts.

"The path I guided was a field. It's different for each of us. My grandfather walked a path across a frozen lake. His grandfather, a beach. You, a bridge."

I pull my eyes from the distant light. It is worth it to look into your eyes one more time. You look different. Lighter. Your shoulders are straight like in that photograph in the living room from when you and Granny are young. Your face is the same one I've always known, kind and thoughtful, except unlined now.

You pull me into a tight hug then release me. "Go, my girl, you can't stay for this part, not until it's your turn to be led."

"What do you mean?"

"As I was dying the path became fainter, until I found myself on your bridge. One day you'll find yourself on some-one else's path. Maybe your grandchild, and hopefully you'll teach them to walk. Not like me. I'm sorry for abandoning you, my girl. But I know you can do this."

I can feel the wind pushing me away from you, back onto the bridge, back into the mist. After one last squeeze of your hand I let myself be pushed, my silent goodbye wishing you well as you step forward into the light.

People here speak of you fondly. They come by with fish, or moose, or for a chat. But nothing we do fills your spaces in the trailer. The bridge won't let me leave; I know that now. I am glued to this land. Like you, and your grandfather, and all the grandfathers. But it's okay. The mist rises off me when I wake, and I go on.

I clean. I cook. I take care of Granny.

She is closing her eyes beside me now. Her chin is dabbing at her chest but she doesn't want to go to her bed. The bed you shared. So I offer her an arm and lead her to the couch instead. It dwarfs her tiny frame as she sinks into the cushions. I pile blankets on her and leave the room with the TV buzzing because you would always speak to her as she drifted off, guiding her to sleep. Quiet voices to let her know she's not alone.

# DREAM MEDICINE

## CHRISTINE MISKONOODINKWE SMITH

Eva's unraveling began when she learned she could speak with spirits.

"It's nothing to be afraid of," her Nokomis had once told her. "In our Anishnaabe culture, it's considered a gift." But that was many years ago.

Eva's friends clomped into her apartment; Jo, was short, fair-haired and bossy, Kat was petite and sleek, and Erin was a curvaceous and bubbly Catholic. Kat carried two eco-friendly bags with Dollarama logos splashed across them.

"What do you have there?" Eva asked.

"Oh, just chips." Kat spoke with a slight Cantonese accent. "Uuunh!" She heaved the bags onto Eva's bed as though they weighed a ton. Eva put her hand to her mouth to suppress a giggle.

Erin also carried a couple bags. "I brought Diet Coke and rum, if you want mix!"

Jo carried something rectangular in a white plastic bag. She pulled out a box and gingerly put it on the floor. The bag had an Apple store logo on it. It was a Ouija board! It seemed like something ancient amidst their tech-savvy world. After all, there isn't an app you can use to conjure the dead.

Eva was curious about her birth father. He'd passed on when she was a child, so if her friends wanted to play Ouija she'd go along with it. She ignored the voice whispering in her head. "Don't do this. Don't do this."

The four girls looked at the board and glanced at each other.

"Should we do this?" Eva whispered.

"We can try to contact lost relatives." Jo swept fingers across a tendril of hair that escaped from behind her ear. Eva nodded. She wanted to contact her dad. Her friends piled their coats on her bed, Jo flicked the light switch, and they all sat in a circle on the hardwood floor. They could barely see each other in the inky darkness, the only light came from a streetlamp filtering through flimsy curtains.

"Cool, that we can do this at your place." Kat patted the floor.

"Yeah," Erin whispered. "If I ever brought a Ouija board into my house, my parents would kill me!"

The other girls still lived with their parents. Eva had lived on her own since she was 17. Orphaned at age 10, she'd lived in foster homes for years. Thankfully she still had contact with her maternal grandmother, Lillian, until her death a few years ago. Though they were the same age, 20, her friends often looked to her for counsel when it came to guys, or problems with their parents. Maybe because Eva had a difficult life, they thought of her as wise beyond her years.

Putting fingertips to the teardrop-shaped planchette, Eva's hands trembled. Butterflies tumbled in her stomach as the planchette stuttered across the board. The spinner seemed to move nonsensically as the girls asked questions. "Who are you?" "Why are you here?" "Who do you want to speak with?"

They all gasped when it moved, gliding from letter to letter.

J...

O...

H...

N...

Her dad's name. Eva felt sick.

"Who's John?"

"Who's John?"

Kat and Jo asked simultaneously.

Eva's breath came raggedly. She felt lightheaded. "It's my dad."

Eva could feel the energies of everyone in the room ripping through her, their tension and anxiety. Eva stuck her tongue out, and the saltiness of tears touched her tongue. The spirit claiming to be her dad seemed to be giving off a palpable negativity. She thought she was going to hurl.

"Calm down, calm down," she told herself. But when she looked up, her friends faces were reflecting her alarm. The planchette continued spelling out:

I...M...H...E...R...E...T...O...H...U...R...T...Y...O...U...

"What the fuck," Kat's voice hoarse.

"Who is that?" Erin whispered.

Eva never told her friends the whole story. How her father died. That her mother committed suicide. "That can't be him."

Memories of her dad flooded Eva's thoughts. She remembered the red plaid shirt he always wore. How upset he'd been with her the day he died. He'd come to give her a hug before work and caught her whispering to someone he couldn't see.

"Who are you talking to?" he asked harshly. His voice was usually so gentle.

She cowered at his raised voice, and he got angry.

"He's just afraid," her Nokomis told her. Lillian had lived with them since her mother died. "Afraid of your abilities to hear spirits, just like your mom before she passed."

It wasn't until later that evening her Nokomis received the phone call that changed their lives forever. Her dad was gone. He'd been killed on his way to work when he tried to intervene in an altercation on the subway.

She recalled words he spoke as he stomped out the front door. "You're too much like your mother. You're going to end up in the loony bin just like her!"

That was the last time she had saw him.

BANG!

There's a thump on Eva's window and a flash of feathers. Erin, Kat, and Jo scream. Eva faints and there is a matching thump as her head hits a table edge and her body hits the floor. Jo, Kat and Erin look from the window to the matching thump. They rush to Eva's crumpled form and gingerly turn her over.

"Should we call someone?" Kat's eyes dart about the room.

"What do we do with the Ouija board?" Erin asks in a shaky voice.

"Worry about it later," Jo says.

Kat stays at Eva's side. Erin rocks back on her heels. Jo flicks the switch. The sudden bath of light is shocking. Blood oozes from where Eva hit her head, and her nose is bleeding. She moans, going in and out of consciousness.

"Don't move." Kat licks her lips. "You…you hit your head pretty hard. We have to call an ambulance." Kat wipes at Eva's nose with a napkin but pulls away when Eva flinches.

Jo punches 911 into her cell phone.

In a fog, Eva can hear Jo speaking in a breathy voice: "Can you send an ambulance to 433 Lesley Street? She hit her head. There's a lot of blood."

After a few minutes they hear sirens approach. Help is on the way. Then there's banging on Eva's door.

A man's gruff voice calls out "Fire Department. EMS."

Jo opens the door. The girls are tiny beside the three men in uniform. One of the paramedics leans down to tend to Eva, his eye catching on the hastily pushed aside Ouija board. Eva is distracted by the nameplate on the left side of his chest. M. Andrews. He is HOT. She tries to hide her loopy grin by wiping her face with her sleeve. Is she a weirdo for thinking such thoughts when she might be bleeding to death?

With a cloth pressed tightly to Eva's injury, Hottie McAndrews looks up at Jo, Kat and Erin. "Tell me what happened." His tone muted, exuding a calmness the girls couldn't gather for themselves.

Eva gripped the EMS's arm tightly with her cold fingers. "He said he was going to hurt us," she mumbled.

"Who's going to hurt you, dear?" the older paramedic asks, checking Eva's vitals. Then Hottie McAndrews gets Eva to sit up. She feels weak, leaning against a leg of the table where she'd fallen. She can see a chunk of her scalp clinging to the edge of the table where she hit her head. The firefighter holds her upright, while the paramedics inspect the wound. Jo broke from the circle the girls formed and passed Eva some Kleenex.

"The spirit... He said he was going to hurt us." Eva felt tears well up in her eyes. The throbbing from her head intensifying as each moment passed. "Don't let him hurt us."

"We're taking you to the hospital," Hottie McAndrews said gently, then frowned at Eva's friends and gestured to the Ouija board. "You shouldn't play with this."

The older paramedic maneuvers a stretcher into the room, they eased Eva to her feet, lay her down, then place a bright orange blanket over her thin shivering frame.

Jo stands with one hand on her hip, Erin is perched on the edge of the sofa, and Kat hangs back shifting nervously from one foot to the other.

"I'm sorry," Eva said tearfully, "I'm so sorry."

They wheeled Eva into the back of the ambulance. One paramedic slammed the door shut, and the other yelled to the driver, "Ready!"

Swaying movement and flashing lights.

"I've been on calls with you before, Eva. And I knew your grandm. She used to mentor youth in our community." It was Hottie McAndrews, which meant he knew her background as a former psych patient. She gave her head a shake. She shouldn't be thinking of him as "hottie." He'd known her Nokomis and the work she did.

"I think I remember, but my Nokomis helped a lot of people." Eva picked at the fabric of the orange blanket.

Andrews gently asked Eva questions:

"How have your moods been lately?"

"Have you been eating properly?"

"What's your sleep been like?"

She didn't answer, but he asked the questions anyways. He was trying to keep Eva preoccupied so she wouldn't sleep.

He said nothing about spirits, probably because he didn't want to agitate her.

Eva didn't want to disclose information to Andrews, someone who knew her, so she burrowed deeper under the thin blanket and turned her head to the wall.

The ambulance ride was quick. The driver pulled into Emergency, and Eva heard the heavy doors creak open. Her stomach lurched as the stretcher hit the ground, and they wheeled her into the hospital.

An hour later, Eva's head wound had been cleaned, stitched up, and wrapped with itchy white gauze. The ER doctor tried to speak to her, but Eva refused to answer. Finally he said, "You're being admitted."

A St. John's orderly brought her up from emergency to the eighth floor. The psych ward. Eva was no stranger to this hospital or to the crazy eighth. Rooms were in high demand but sometimes you could get admitted when another patient ran off and killed themselves, leaving a bed open for another patient to occupy. For the hospital, it was all about numbers, and keeping the ward full. Often, she was the only Native girl on the ward.

Some patients came and went, while others stayed for longer periods of time. Eva wasn't sure which type of patient she was yet, because sometimes her stays were brief while other times she stayed for months. They put her through the usual psychiatric assessment then put her under observation.

"I think you've had a psychotic break." The psychiatrist jotted a prescription. Eva was not thrilled; those kinds of meds made her mind fuzzy. At first, she refused to take them.

"If you don't take them," the orderly said, "we'll mark it on your chart that you're being non-compliant." A note of non-compliance could mean further loss of her freedom, so Eva dry-swallowed the granular pills, refusing to sip from the cup of offered water.

"You won't hear us," the spirits whispered. "You won't be able to help us."

Eva didn't tell anyone that spirits spoke to her, coming in every shape and form possible. The doctors could lock her up for life, stick her in isolation, turn her into a guinea pig for modern medicine. They tried various medicines to silence the "voices" she told them she heard, and the nightmares that hounded her sleep.

Eva fought against sleep, but the spirits weren't always like the Ouija board visitation. Sometimes it felt like an old friend stopping by. But then she remembered Nokomis's stories about Windigo. "They can inhabit vulnerable people. You must be careful which spirits you talk to – they can overtake your spirit, drive you nuts."

Maybe some spirits were windigo in disguise? Having the ability to speak to manidook was draining enough, she believed they were real, but being admitted to the hospital made Eva question her sanity. Were they actually real or was she just losing her mind?

Eva hid under her blankets, dreading the call for her night-time medications. She hated meds but didn't want to be deemed non-compliant. She felt like she was living in two different worlds. The Western world of doctors and science, and the unseen world of spirits.

A nurse would eventually come. "Eva, it's time for your medication."

"Do I have to?" She drew back the blankets, swung her legs over the edge of the bed and shoved her feet into pale blue booties for the trek down to the nurse's station. She shuffled into line with the other waiting patients.

Usually she got a room to herself. Other patients were disturbed by her dreams. She'd scream and cry out at random times through the night. The lights had to be on at all times.

She couldn't believe it had come to this – a night that they were supposed to have fun, and she'd lost it. Eva so badly wanted that rum and Coke now, she thought, and let out a giggle. Her friends on the outside were free to do whatever they wanted, while she felt like a prisoner in the loony bin.

A couple days after she was admitted, Jo, Kat and Erin visited.

"Is there anything we can bring to help you feel better?" Jo asked.

"Not really…Well, maybe."

"What can we do?" Erin stared at the soothing pale blue of the painted wall. Kat delicately patted the soft material of her blanket.

"Bring me a dreamcatcher," Eva asked, even though she knew patients weren't allowed to have personal items. "There's one hanging over my bed in my apartment. My Nokomis gave it to me. I really need it."

After going through the nurses to make sure it was okay, the girls returned with the requested item. Eva lay in bed, head turned to the window.

"Eva?" Jo whispered.

"We're here," Kat shifted on her feet. Erin hovered at the end of Eva's bed.

Eva pushed off her blankets and sat up. "Hey." She tried to smile.

Jo was holding a package in her hands.

"You brought my dreamcatcher?"

Jo handed her the package. Eva unwrapped the tissue paper, her dreamcatcher was nestled inside. "Thank you." Eva caressed the intricate webbing, feeling the dry sinew, the strips of leather wrapped around the ring.

"Your apartment's okay!" Kat blurted out.

Erin's eyes were watery. Eva knew she didn't like hospitals, it wasn't easy for her to be here. "Yeah," Erin finally chirped. "We cleaned up after you left, locked the door. We took the Ouija board away, so you won't see it when you get out."

"Hopefully the dreamcatcher helps," and Jo shifted from one foot to the other.

"We miss hanging out with you on the outside, you know." Kat twisted ringlets in her hair.

"I know." Eva said.

They all looked up and watched as another patient walked by the doorway of Eva's room, an old dude looking into her room as he shuffled down the hallway. Visitors were rare.

"We have to go," said Jo.

"Get out soon, eh?" Erin half-smiled.

"Bye." Kat waved.

A couple of minutes later, Eva mustered enough energy to hang the dreamcatcher above the bed. Maybe bad spirits would keep their distance. The staff noticed that when Eva touched the dreamcatcher before bedtime, she wouldn't make too much of a fuss when it came to turn the lights out. Though she did ask to have her door left open a crack so light from the hallways could spill in.

Other long-term patients complained. "Why does Eva get to keep a dreamcatcher with her, and I don't get to keep any personal items?"

The nurses would shush them and say, "Eva needs this right now."

Every night without fail, Eva would take her protective charm, holding it to her dry, parched lips; tracing her fingers over the sinew, and caressing the feathers. "Please keep me safe again tonight."

"We will come by throughout the night and make sure you're all right," the nurses assured Eva. "No one is going to hurt you."

Though they said this over and over, Eva would still try to stay awake, and the nurses would say, "Come on, Eva, you have to sleep."

When she did sleep, it was tortured. Disembodied voices spoke to her, made her toss and turn. She'd moan and cry out, and a nurse would come and give her another sedative or an anti-anxiety med to calm her down and sleep.

The Blue Scrubbed nurse asked her, "What is so terrifying about sleep?" But Eva just shook her head. She was never able to recall what upset her. But she knew she was haunted by something non-Native doctors and nurses couldn't understand.

How could she tell them spirits visited her from the afterlife? Even before the Ouija board she could see the unseen.

At first, Kat, Jo and Erin often came to visit, but after a month their visits began to dwindle from once a week to every other week, and then even longer. They couldn't handle what was going on with her. She wished they would still drop by but couldn't really blame them.

One night, while curled up in her hospital bed, Eva sensed something in her room. The air felt thick and heavy; a knot bunched in her stomach, and a bitter aftertaste coated her tongue. She had been keeping her eyes closed, so the nurses would think she was sleeping. She let her eyelids slide open slightly.

At the side of her bed was a shadow. She thought it was the Blue Scrubbed nurse, so she reached out to grab the nurse's arm, then yanked her hand back right quick when she realized there was no one there. A gauzy image of her Nokomis Lillian appeared. Eva inhaled sharply through her nose and shook her head to see if the illusion would dissipate. Was this for real?

Then she heard the unmistakeably gentle voice of her Nokomis. "Stay calm, my girl…I've seen what you've been going through. What I don't understand is what you are doing here in this hospital? You don't need to be here. Why are you taking all these medications these Western doctors are giving you?"

"They say I need this medication," Eva whispers. "It's not normal for people to speak to spirits. They can't see."

"Those doctors, they don't understand our culture or your abilities. They are trying to drug you up to mask you from your power."

"Eva! Eva! Who are you talking to?" A Green Scrubbed nurse broke her reverie, causing Lillian's image to dissipate like fog in the early morning dew, but leaving her with the words: "You have a gift, my child, you have a gift. Don't let these doctors take it away from you…"

The Green Scrubbed nurse was standing in the doorway, and Eva turned her head quickly. The nurse peppered her with questions. "Are you all right? Do you need some extra medication? Who in tarnation were you talking to?"

"I wasn't talking to anyone, I swear!" said Eva

"I could hear you in the hallway as I was doing my rounds. Should I tell the doctor you were hearing voices again?" The nurse made her way closer to Eva's bedside.

"No!" Eva said. "I'm fine. I'm not afraid, please don't tell the doctor."

"Who were you talking to then?" asked the Green Scrubbed nurse again.

"No one. I wish you all understood me," Eva answered petulantly.

"Hmmm… Well, tomorrow I'm telling the doctor he must get an Elder in here to speak with you. You're going to talk to someone if you won't talk to us!"

The Green Scrubbed nurse walked away with a self-satisfied sway of her hips, her footsteps receding down the hallway as she continued her rounds. Eva wanted her Nokomis to return, but fighting to keep her eyes open longer was futile.

The next morning, Eva pulled her blanket back and threw her feet over the side of her bed. The coldness hit her feet and made her toes curl, but for once she was excited. Things felt somehow clearer. For the first time she might get to see someone who could actually help her – an Elder. Her Nokomis had been telling her for years that Eva had a gift.

All she needed to do was learn how to discern which spirits were good and which ones were not. If I can do that, Eva thought, maybe I can harness what I see and hear, and I won't have anymore hospitalizations.

She pulled her housecoat around her thin body, holding her shoulders back as she walked out into the hallway.

# THE ROOM WAS CROWDED

## Lee Maracle

Except for the front row, the room is pretty crowded. I am not up to the front row. I spot one empty space in the back row. Once I see that space, I don't bother with the front row or any other, although I am not sure why I don't.

There is a lady up front; she's talking, her voice smooth as butter, lyrical, a song of comfort ringing underneath. She isn't tall, but she's slim. She must be 40, but still svelte, face free of too many age marks; she carries herself like a gracefully aging youth. Settle down, Henry, a woman that pretty is dangerous.

My knee tickles a little. It's an old habit that plagues me. It started the first time I sat in the lunchroom at Saint Mary's Residential School. I was six. I am not sure why the tickle came, but when it did it made me squirm in my seat. Every time I squirmed, one of the brothers would come over and bark, "Sit still, Henry." Henry, it wasn't my name when I got there. I hated that name for a long time, but then one day in 10th grade I was out on the soccer field, someone hollered Hank and I realized that I didn't remember my other name, my original first name and now it is too late to ask my parents. They both died while I was at that school. Damn. I hate this. I am barely in the door and I feel sorry for myself already. Why did I come here?

"You all must be Canadians," the lady quips from the front of the room and the crowd laughs a little. We're Indians, we know there is a punchline coming, but we like laughing beforehand as though we need a laugh. I laugh too. I know I need one. "Did you know that about Canadians?" We laugh again, like we do. We don't. At least I don't.

"Canadians are modest, shy and humble. They fill a room from the back, no one sits up front. Look, the whole first row of seats is empty and there are three people standing against the back wall. What is that?" We roar. It isn't all that funny. Some more people walk in the door as she waves to the people at the back to move to the front. Only the newcomers shuffle to the front obediently while the audience giggles a little.

"Are you American?" she asks. One of them says, "Yes." Now we are totally cracked up.

The tickle crawls down my leg. I cross one leg over the other like that will end the tickle. I close my eyes. I can see a tiny spark of light off in the corner. It's as if I am in a black box and there is some tiny little hole in it where the light outside the box shines through. Christ, pay attention.

"On my right is Vera Manuel, she is going to talk about her experiences at Residential School; on my left we have the United Church pastor and a representative of the Catholic clergy. Oh," she throws her hands up in the air. "Excuse me, gentlemen, you have names…" I stop listening. I don't want to know their names until I can remember my own. Her voice fades.

I open my eyes. There are spots in front of my eyes, light spots that half blind me. My foot shakes not like it's cold, but like it wants to run. The other foot feels like it's nailed to the floor. The lights glare, the glare burns, sparks a scream that invades my ears. Shit, the scream won't stop for a while. The last time it started it went on for days. It didn't stop until I went out and drank myself into a barroom brawl. Please, God. Make it stop.

There's a laugh – like praying ever helped.

"How are you all doing?" We are already on to Vera and I missed the names of the two white guys – serves them right. Jesus, it's not their fault I can't remember my name. The woman at the front is seated. When did that happen? Shut up and listen to Vera. Vera's voice is so gentle, and her accent is so untarnished I can tell she is Shuswap. How long did the other one go on speaking? Shut up. My armpits drip sweat. Why the hell did I come here? Where the hell is George? This was his idea. Bastard didn't even show up.

I can hear someone near the coffee stand stir a spoon in their cup and I smell good coffee, not the kind that comes from the urn at the back, but Starbucks or Second Cup coffee. The seat next to me shifts and someone sits – I look. It's George.

"Did I miss anything?" I can't believe he said this out loud.

"Bother to whisper, eh?" I hiss. Vera is talking about her experience at home and at school.

"No," Vera answers him. We all laugh. "That's the thing about us Indians" she says working the joke. "We arrive at exactly the right time, even when we're late." The crowd laughs some more. The threat the size of the crowd poses diminishes. It feels like we're all one big family sitting around Gramma's kitchen table getting ready for an evening of laughter and reminiscing and not like a bunch of Indians getting ready to talk about the most controversial period in our lives

– Residential School. George has this big goofy grin on his face, tips his cup to her, like some guy would doff his hat. I sink in my chair. My knee stops twitching. The screaming from the light's glare stops too. Maybe I was just nervous about being here without anyone I know. Doesn't matter, I feel better now.

Vera's hair was cut, her body deloused on the first day of school; she didn't recognize the food, finally she was prohibited from speaking her language, all rubber ducky kind of trauma stuff. I almost fall asleep at one point.

My mind drifts as I remember how I got here. Last Friday over a beer I told George that I have a harder and harder time waking up to go to work. We start at eight; I arrived at nine.

"What's up?" George asks. For some reason I want to tell him the truth, so I tell him I go to bed early enough, but I have a hard time getting up.

"This happen often?" His eyes are looking intently at me. I am not sure I like it. My head does a half turn away from his stare.

"Oftener and oftener," I offer, and knock the nearly full beer back in one drain like I am anxious for the buzz. It makes me feel a little self-conscious because George doesn't drink beer or any other sort of alcohol.

"Discharging." He drops it like I knew what it meant. I must have that deer-in-the-headlights-look because he snorts out a chuckle, sips his coffee without taking his eyes off me and says, "Some guys get a wild hair up their ass and they want to sleep, others can't sleep at all. One is called discharging, the other is insomnia. Point is, something's got you by the short and curlies and you're screwed unless you deal with it."

"What would that wild hair be, George?" The sarcasm in my voice is thick.

George grins like he expected it and carries on. "What's bugging you?"

"I don't know. I got a good job. I own a house, could use a wife, maybe. I see my kids every weekend. I don't have too much debt. I don't know. You tell me, what could be the matter?"

"Actually, you do know, 'fact, you are the only one who knows, but for some reason you want to sleep rather than look at it." I crack up. It's funny, bizarre, yet somehow it felt so right.

"There's a conference this weekend, might be the answer to your questions." His voice changed, became solicitous and conspiratorial like he was letting me in on an important and dangerous secret.

"Are you going?"

"Yeah."

"You want to know the answer so bad – you'll go to a conference?" Everyone laughs, clicks glasses. I'm a regular fun guy.

"Yeah, I'm the other guy – insomnia." This bites all the laughter in half. Then I see the bags under his eyes, the sagging skin along the jawbone and the fatigue that bends his shoulders slightly. He cradles his cup like he is at rope's end, like maybe this weekend coming is his last bid for sanity. He needs relief of some kind. Why hadn't I seen that before?

Vera and the priests are finished. Well, only one is a bona fide priest, but I don't know what to call a United Church man "of the cloth" so I call him a priest as well. The crowd scoots their chairs back, strolls to the coffee urn, pours themselves a cup of joe, cliques into clans, tribes or friend groups. George and me stand with our thumbs hooked into our britches and wonder what we should do next.

"Hey, guys, got some room for the moderator?" Her smile lights up the room. Bright even white teeth, big teeth, her lips pulled behind them still looking pretty, not disappearing like some smiles. A guy pulls a team of huskies clear across the Arctic for a smile like that. I am not the only one that feels this way because all three of us jump out of the way. She pretends we are all normal, but we feel like foolish teenagers. She gives us one more smile as she slips away; we watch her walk away. Her walk is as smooth as glass.

"She's so pretty she's dangerous," some guy standing behind us says, which about sums up what George and I are thinking.

"Sam," he offers his name and puts his hand out. We shake hands, exchange names and then sidle to the back wall and slip out the door for a smoke.

"Didn't bother me." Sam says it like he's answering a question we had asked. "Residential School," he finishes – like we asked what?

'You didn't like your parents?" George asks him. I stare at the butts around my feet. Ugly little stubs, dirt clutching them and mucking the white of the paper, half of them flattened by moving feet, all of them wet and leaking old soggy tobacco.

Shit, George, let it be.

"Sure, I like them enough." Sam shifts from one foot to the other, his free fist clenches and his other hand grips the cigarette just a little too tight. He draws a short sharp drag and lets it go noisily.

"I mean you didn't like them enough to want to be at home?" George clarifies. My knee is twitching again. Did I like my parents? Did I want to be at home? A weakness crawls up my leg and I scan the sidewalk for something to lean on, nothing there. If I liked them so much, how come I can't remember the name they gave me? I draw as deep a breath as I can. It catches on the way out. Jeez, I could use a drink and I ain't talking another cup of coffee. If I keep breathing like this, I am going to choke on it. I pull hard on the smoke instead. It settles me down some.

"Well sure, I missed home," Sam says, stamping out a half-smoked cigarette and lighting up another. "But everyone did. We were all in the same boat."

"Long as it was all of us, it wasn't all that bad?" George is needling him. "We aren't a mob of play toys," he finishes and butts out his smoke. That's dangerous, but George is like that, always walking on the cutting edge of things. He is like that at work, volunteers to swing out from the scaffolding to lay the rafters and such. Sweat starts trickling down my armpits again and I know what's coming next, the scream – the fucking scream.

"Didn't go to the same school as me." It dropped out of my mouth before I knew I was saying it. "It was never all of us. Some of us did okay, others got licked every day, some of us saw the dark of the basement, mice and rats, water around the ankles, others got the inside view of a closet, or the confessional that was never intended for the use it got." I was on a roll. I couldn't control my mouth. My voice constricted otherwise I would have just went on and on.

"What happened in that confessional?" Her voice was so serene and slow it rolled out like a smooth clean wave of water barely rippling on the ocean's breast. The sound soothed; my throat relaxed. I closed my eyes and waited for her to say more. I just wanted to hear her voice. "Did you spend a lot of time in the confessional?"

I managed a "Yeah" before I opened my eyes. Her voice brought me back there, back to the confessional. It was as though I felt safe enough to be there because she was there with me. I could see a sliver of light somewhere through the dark of that box shining in my eyes. I turned my head away.

"What are you seeing, Henry? Who is there with you?"

"Fuck," Sam whispers. George leads him away and mutters, "Shush, let them be." What did he mean, "We aren't a mob?"

George's voice dims but I still hear him. "We were so lonely there, Sam. We all wanted to recognize one another as family, so we convinced ourselves that we were all treated the same, that we were the same, that we were family, so we wouldn't miss our real family."

No response from Sam.

"I see a light." All heads flip to look at me.

"What?" George's voice is filled with concern.

"A light, a sliver of light," I answer.

"Does it look far away?" the lady asks.

"Yeah."

"You have a light inside, Henry. Turn it on. Shine it at the light in the distance." She's right. There is this light in my belly and I flash it at the light far away. The distant light comes closer. I swerve. My knees are so week.

"Do you need a chair, Henry? Are you having a hard time standing?" She slips her arms around my waist and leads me away from the sidewalk. My eyes are still closed. My knees are rubbery, and I stumble a little. She tightens her hold. She is strong. For the first time in what seems like forever I relax and lean on someone. Christ, it feels good to just have my fragile flesh held up by someone else, their sinew and hard muscle bearing my weight.

I am seated somewhere. There is a shadow behind the light. She is talking still. I lean my face into my hands and the shadow becomes a face. It is the brother. He has come for me. He is taking me to the confessional. Not this fucking time. I leap. She catches me, holds me. Her voice is more commanding now, but still gentle. "What is he doing?"

"He is taking me to the confessional."

"Is it dark?"

"Yeah, it's the middle of the night."

"Where are you now?"

"Inside the box."

"Is there anyone there with you?"

"Just the brother" drops into the quiet as I watch him approach. "I can hear him unzip his pants." A small "Oh no" high-pitched follows and it sounds so young as it fills my ears. Who is that? Oh my God, it's me. I am just a kid. I must be used to this because I don't resist. I just open my mouth. He grips me by the hair, then slides back and forth. I vomit right there as he comes in my tiny little mouth. I whimper for a while.

"That's good, Henry." I feel her hand on my shoulder. "That's years of old hurt and shame coming up."

My eyes open. George is next to me. He has hold of my hand.

"Good piece of work, bro."

"What was that all about?" I knew. I just had a hard time believing it. Brother James had molested me in that confessional. I wanted to puke again. I wanted to kill someone. I want...my shoulders rock back and forth, my head moves from side to side. I felt so completely tired all of a sudden. I could feel the energy leaving, almost see it slipping away. I wanted to watch it, give it some color, see it dissipate all purple and gold, watch it wash the city block across the street from the Indian Center in its haze.

"You were raped," she uttered the forbidden words quietly, flatly, like she knew all along and had just been waiting for me to see it, to remember it, to feel it.

Across the street there is a woman pushing a baby carriage. She looks like she is in a hurry, trying to get away from something invisible that always seems to follow her. I snort but stop short of laughing and just stare at her walking quickly away.

"What is it?" she asks, looking at the woman hurrying down the street.

"Oh, I'm just busy projecting. That woman with the carriage... I imagine her trying to get away from some invisible beast that never stops following her, but really it's me that's been trying to run from that light. I had a girlfriend. We broke up a few weeks ago. You want to know why? She kept turning on the lights. She liked everything bright. Me, I hate that light. I'd sit in front of the TV in the dark. She would come home from shopping or something – all happy and cheery – flip on the light and I would look for some reason to give her hell. Sometimes it took a while for her to give me one, but in the end she would."

"That's the thing, bro. You can always count on people to be imperfect." The laughter came.. It rose from my belly like thunder, loosened my legs and slowly restored my strength. I got up and we headed back into the building.

At the door, it dawns on me. My name is Bear.

"Bear?" the woman queries? I had no idea I said it out loud.

"My name was Bear. My parents called me Bear before the school changed it to Henry. Do you think that would be on my birth certificate?"

"How old are you?"

"Thirty-seven."

"No. You are too old for them to be allowed to call you that."

"What do you mean?"

"For a long time, it was against the law for us to use names like that – they had to be Christian names and Bear is not a Christian name." She pulled the door gently and it closed quietly behind us.

"You can always change it." It slid out of her mouth like changing your name was so easy.

"I remember my name." She touches my hand as I say it.

"You will remember a lot of things, some of them not so good, but when we forget the past, we forget the good stuff too," and she let go of my hand. I looked at all the people there and for the first time in my life I'm not afraid of the crowd.

"Damn."

# SWORD OF ANTLERS

## RICHARD VAN CAMP

The girl with bound wrists watched as the fat man reloaded his clip. The fat man loved to choke girls and bring them back different. His partner, the skinny one who liked to watch, racked his shotgun. He spit. "What do you think?"

"He's out," the fat one said. X was going to kill his friend after. O had a fungus. O'd lost his toenails. X couldn't stand that O wore sandals. O's toes looked like meatballs. X tried not to look at them, but he did, and winced. Gross. This was their last job, he'd decided. Back of the head. X imagined smoke puffing out O's nostrils as the plates of his skull shattered. He imagined the meatballs of O's feet falling off and rolling under the nearest couch like marbles. He almost giggled at the thought of it: the flash in O's opening mouth. The twitch as O's vagus nerve gave out.

Their mission today was to kill Shinobu and get the sword: the ancient sword capable of cutting through two men at the same time. Japanese soldiers used to practice on prisoners by tying them up and slicing from collarbone to waist. X couldn't wait to hold the sword. He couldn't wait to tie two of his next targets together and do exactly this.

With bound wrists Kendra floated over the abandoned Fort Smith warehouse and watched as the young boy tied the man's leg. It was bleeding. Dark blood.

"Who are those people?" the boy asked.

"Executioners," Shinobu said. "I'm sorry."

Sonny tightened his belt around the man's leg. "What do we do?"

"Draw the sword," the man from Japan said.

The boy did. Sonny drew the sword and it left the sheath in a whisper.

"Hand it to me," Shinobu nodded. "If anything happens," he whispered, "tell my wife and daughter I love them. Tell my father I am sorry. Tell my mother…" He paused to listen and gather himself. "Tell her I should have listened to her. Tell her I love her, too."

The boy watched as the man from Japan pulled himself up and they took a breath together. Sonny saw the brilliant butterfly tattoo flutter on the man's hand: it was the same butterfly on the chest plate on the samurai suit in the library. "The Butterfly Man," Sonny called him the first time they met at the museum.

Shinobu had come to reclaim the samurai sword and suit of armor sent to Fort Smith's museum by mistake. The set was supposed to have been sent to the Fort Smith Museum of History in Arkansas, not the Fort Smith Museum of History in the Northwest Territories of Canada. The katana had a trinity of antlers fused together to hold the curved blade – and it belonged to Shinobu's family, and most importantly it belonged to his baby on the way. A girl. A baby girl set to inherit it.

Sonny's Ehtsi had seen a spirit girl dancing around Shinobu. An unborn daughter. Her brown eyes drifting, following the dance of spirit only she could see. His Ehtsi brought the man back to life after he was beaten half to death by Benny's men. They'd both seen Shinobu's full-body tattoo.

His grandmother's face paled at the sight of the inked demons covering Shinobu's flesh. "Yakuza," Sonny heard Shinobu confess. "I am Yakuza."

Sonny understood that Shinobu was a bad man where he was from, but he also understood that Shinobu was trying to bring honor to his family. He was trying.

Shinobu's eyes shifted toward the sound of the two men on the other side of the wall where they'd taken refuge. Shinobu fixed his grip on his great-grandfather's sword. "Help me," he ordered. "Under this August full moon, help me." Sonny pulled Shinobu into a crouch. Blood streamed down Shinobu's ankle and into his shoe.

"Stay down," Shinobu whispered. "No matter what."

Sonny crouched behind the wall, made himself small. He could hear a plane overhead approaching the runway from the sky. The empty warehouse wasn't far from the airstrip.

A shout grew from the back of Shinobu's throat. Shinobu charged from behind the wall surprising the fat man and the skinny man, the one who called himself X, the other O. As they rose to fire, Shinobu brought his great-grandfather's blade through them in a cleave.

Two skull fragments went flying like Frisbees. There was a thump as two lives became bodies, their souls rising and braiding themselves together in the sky.

Kendra watched in amazement as the souls of X and O rise above as boys. The two assassins held hands and did not look back. She knew now their real names were Philip and Cecil.

She looked down and floated closer to the boy.

If she could, she would have closed his eyes for a while and whispered, "Sonny, don't look don't look don't look..."

But it was too late.

The boy stood to see the dark purple blood pooling farther than the skinny man's hand. It twitched, relaxed.

"Who are you?" Sonny asked the man from Japan who stood trembling. "Who are you really?"

The man from Japan held his bloody hand out for the sheath.

The boy tucked himself down, crouched to gather it. We are no longer friends, he thought. Maybe we never were in the first place.

Shinobu leaned against the wall. His leg pumped blood through his pants freely, despite his belt. The boy handed him the sheath.

The Japanese man felt something in the blade now. A thirst consumed. Lives passing. More blood soaking into the sharkskin of the hilt.

"Who. Are. You?" the boy demanded.

"I am the devil," the man from Japan said. "Your grand-mother was right. Go home."

The boy turned, ran.

Kendra followed him home.

Her wrists no longer bound.

She heard Sonny's breathing

His crying.

Moths danced in a womb of light from the full moon. She looked back only once to see the man from Japan limping his way to the airport, cradling the sheathed sword, his bloody footsteps trailing him. She stepped through the moths, the caress of wings.

Kendra had refused to return to the sky because the fat man choked her while the skinny man watched. But today, she had watched them die. She'd seen them as children. Now she could rest. Now she was free. She could follow them now to the song-filled sky.

# WE ARE
# THE EARTH'S
# DREAMING

WENDY BONE

Office buildings glitter like icebergs as Desma strides down the street swinging her green watering can. With each step, the soil tester stick rattles inside. Her utility belt is full of tools: spray bottle, plant bag, scissors, neem – a natural insecticide from an Indian tree – and a clipboard with the route Guadeloupe assigned her for today. Offices all over the city need their plants cared for, or the newest word for what she does, plantscaping. But most people just call her The Plant Lady.

Her first stop is the Premier's office on the top floor of the Trade and Convention Center with its roof of white sails overlooking the harbor. The elevator doors ping open. A hallway of flags from each Canadian province leads into a narrow inner sanctum. Desma feels the eyes of the security guard on her and tries to smile. The corners of his lips twitch, but his eyes are squinty like he's sure she's going to rob the place. He motions for her to sit on a cedar wood bench to wait for security clearance. They can't have a plant lady go all Mata Hari and discover secrets about some shady land deal – who knows, maybe brokered by her sister's law firm. Desma sits with her watering can and scratches her muscled calf, strong from hauling water and walking around the city.

When the guard finally opens the door, the Premier is at his desk, swiveling back and forth in his executive chair of steel and blond suede, pant cuffs riding up to show skinny ankles in Argyle socks. He's twiddling a pen as he talks on the phone.

"Listen, Joe," he says. "It's not that complicated. That treaty is not constitutionally valid…" On the wall behind the Premier is a tribal mask with fierce red eyes and cedar hair; on his desk an Inuit soapstone carving of a bear. Desma often sees Indigenous art in offices, but the Premier seems to have a special fondness for it. He even has a signed Bill Reid print of an orca leaping through white space.

The guard stands in the corner, eyes trained on Desma. The Premier gives her the side-eye and lowers his voice, swivels to face the mask, rendering Desma invisible. If you appreciate Indigenous art so much, she wants to ask him, why don't you appreciate Indigenous people?

Instead, she keeps her mouth shut and attends to the weeping fig by the window overlooking the harbor. Seaplanes take off and land like buzzing mosquitoes against the backdrop of the North Shore Mountains. Tsleil-Waututh territory. Somewhere in that exclusive neighborhood of river-rock mansions is the house Desma grew up in with her adoptive parents. On the other side of the harbor, on the rough side of town where ships unload their containers and drug dealers oversee their flourishing trade, is her Aunt Hazel's house. Correction: was. Since the accident last year, the house was demolished to make way for an apartment complex.

Desma touches the fig leaves, shaped like tears, glossy and stiff.

"When caring for *ficus benjamina*," Loupe said when she first trained Desma, "you gotta shake it to get all the dead leaves off. Go ahead, try it." Desma gave the weeping fig a timid shake. Loupe humphed. "Don't worry, you're not gonna hurt it. Like this." She shook the tree firmly; with a dry rustle it released a shower of dead leaves. After that, the fig grew a thicker crown of leaves. A tree is more than the sum of its parts. When leaves fall, the tree can still spread its roots, grow stronger.

Desma wraps her hands around the slender, braided trunk of the Premier's weeping fig and gives it a shake. Leaves scatter onto the plush cobalt carpet. The Premier drops the phone into its cradle and swivels around to shoot Desma a withering look, as if she's done something bad to the tree. His tree. Anger wells inside her. You only see me when you think I've done something wrong, she wants to say. Even then, you really don't see me.

But she remains silent. As she bends to scrape up the leaves, something soft brushes her cheek; the feathers of a dreamcatcher hanging from a branch, its web meant to catch all the bad dreams and only let the good ones through.

A few years back, when Desma was 19, she found her birth family through an ad in the paper. In the space of five minutes, she learned two things that would change her life. First, that her birth mother was half Cree. Second, that Desma would never get to meet her because she was dead.

"Prescription antidepressants," her new-found Auntie Hazel said. They were sitting at Desma's kitchen table, sifting through a pile of Polaroids. One was of Auntie and Desma's birth mother, Willow. They stood next to a fallen tree in Stanley Park, their arms around each other. Another showed Desma's grandmother, a dark-skinned woman with black hair and eyes, on a sofa holding an elfin baby. "That's you," Auntie said. "The welfare people wouldn't leave us alone. Kept sniffing around with their questions and clipboards. Then one day when your mom was at school, they took you. She didn't even get to say goodbye."

Though not yet 30, Auntie Hazel made up for lost time. She took Desma everywhere, including her favorite bar. The Rainbow had a faded picture of a rainbow over the doors, ending in two puffy white clouds grey with dirt.

"Hey, guys," she yelled. "You remember my big sister? This is her kid; the one welfare took away." Then she added, like a punchline in a cheesy comedy, "And she just found out she's part Indian." Desma winced and Auntie chortled as if this were the funniest joke she'd heard since forever. Each pair of eyes around the bar, black and grave, studied Desma's face. Then Auntie's friends invited her to sit with them, and told stories about her grandmother, a famous fixture in the downtown scene. One man, big as a grizzly, said, "Your Nana let me stay on her sofa when I first came to the city. A regular Dear Abby when it came to helping people. Too bad she wasn't so good at following her own advice."

Her birth mother's best friend from high school told Desma she had Willow's eyes. "Your mom dreamed of becoming a writer. She wrote original poems on the spot for a dime each."

Auntie took Desma to the cemetery to say hello to her birth mother and grandmother, buried side by side like seeds in the earth. Desma lay on the grass and pressed her ear to the ground, listened for their bones to speak. But she only heard the hum of living soil, the tick of busy insects.

"She couldn't live not knowing where you'd gone," Auntie said, plucking at the grass, the setting sun turning her skin copper. Within a year after Willow's death, Hazel found their mother on the floor with an empty prescription bottle in her hand. The same brand of antidepressants. "Seems we can't live without our daughters in this family," she said, tears tracking down her cheeks.

Desma understood that this sadness was her inheritance, and that whole lifetimes of loss ran in her bones.

Desma reaches into the earth, touches rootlets feeling their way through the dark.

That morning before her route, Loupe inspected her hands. "Fingers like prunes. Grubby nails, too."

Nothing gets past Loupe. She can diagnose a case of spider mites or a broken heart with one glance. She has baby-fine black hair and a constellation of freckles across her nose: Aztec and Norwegian. Mixed, just like Desma and her birth family. Loupe was the only one who took a chance and gave Desma a job.

"Use the tester stick or you're gonna get old lady hands," she warned. But the stick remains in the bottom of Desma's watering can. Feeling the soil connects her to life. Besides, she can detect the conditions better. Her rebellious fingers sift through pebbles, the detritus of dead leaves: sandy when it should be moist, like chocolate cake. The sun has scorched its shade-loving leaves. She takes it from the windowsill and sets it near the armchair, reviving the leaves with mist from her water bottle.

Peace lily, *spathiphyllum*, has long leaves, soft as suede. Together they make an upside-down hula skirt, sending up long-stemmed teardrops of pure white. Desma strokes the tender veins of a leaf, cups a newly opened flower. "Feeling better?" she asks.

Another thing about peace lilies: They don't hide their feelings. When thirsty they collapse and look like they'll never recover. But with the right care they spring right back. Resilient, that's what peace lilies are. She lifts her can and sprinkles a ring of water around the base. The soil sighs, releasing its petrichor scent. Desma breathes in deep. Better than fresh-brewed coffee or woodsmoke in October.

She exhales, finds the accountant peering at her through black-rimmed glasses. She's at her computer, but the rattling of the keyboard has stopped since she started watching Desma tend the peace lily. Plants have this kind of calming effect. Like Loupe says: "Your job is to heal the plants so they can heal people."

The accountant smiles. "Sorry. I thought I was doing it good by putting it in the window."

Desma peels off crispy leaves and puts them in her plant bag. "No problem. It's perked up already." She turns the pot so the flower faces the desk. The accountant's eyes fall to where Desma has pushed up her shirtsleeves, on the tracks of scars running down her forearms. Her smile turns to a frown and her eyes shift back to the screen. Desma's cheeks go prickly and hot. She pulls her sleeves down and forces a smile, "See you next week," she says, but the accountant doesn't respond.

Desma checks her clipboard and sighs. Of all the routes in the city, how could Loupe give her this one? She decides to make a detour and save the next office for last.

⋏

Desma wanted to do everything her Aunt Hazel did. Soon they were holed up in Auntie's decrepit old Victorian with the sweet rush of poppies in their veins.

"I'll never touch prescription pills," Auntie said. "Not in a million years. That shit'll kill ya." Auntie cooked up the golden fluid with a lighter until it bubbled in the bent spoon. Then, with a slip of the needle, the dreams came: lullabies in a language she didn't understand but knew in her bones; pictograms tumbling across snow; a pair of eyes slanted and dark.

*Papaver somniferum* has blowsy, ruffled petals and a silvery pod that bleeds latex if you scratch it. Poppies are a symbol of remembrance when November rains needle the skin. Scattered beneath crosses, they mark the graves of dead soldiers. I can help you remember, the poppy promises. But it's a double agent because the poppy also says, I can help you forget. Like in *The Wizard of Oz* when Dorothy, the scarecrow, the tin man, and the lion stray into a poppy field and fall asleep.

Desma's desire for poppy medicine soon consumed her. If she didn't get it, she'd start retching. Her skin would crawl with an army of bugs. She tried so hard to get rid of them, scratched until her arms bled. But they always marched just below the surface.

*Epipremnum aureum.* Devil's vine. Pothos. The plant with many names is hard to kill, grows with ease from cuttings into green waterfalls.

Sundial Data Systems has a passion for pothos. It hangs from baskets, springs from planters and spills over filing cabinets, making them rust on top. But nobody seems to mind. Without pothos, the office would be sterile as a surgery.

Desma takes scissors from her belt. The pothos is getting a haircut today. She untangles the almost impenetrable mass of heart-shaped leaves marbled white and golden yellow. Some stems are old and woody like ropes, with hardly any leaves. But the ropes are studded with nodes that, given the right conditions, could become roots. She coils them back into their pots and takes a few cuttings, wrapping their base in wet paper towel.

As she works, she looks out the window. On the street below, office workers hurry past two bodies slumped in a doorway. The Sundial building straddles the financial district and the rough side of town. Addicts often gather where the two worlds meet – the city has a growing opiate crisis. Desma feels the old desire crawling under her skin. But she has a new life now, with all kinds of new dreams seeking to take root.

Last night Auntie, her birth mother, and her grandmother came to visit. Wrapped in housecoats, they sat at the kitchen table with cups of tea and a plate of Peak Freens – the kind with red jelly in the center. Desma's favorite. For the past year since Auntie's overdose, they've come in her dreams to advise her, as if helping her practice for a test. Not the kind her adoptive parents helped with when she struggled to get good grades in school. This test was about how to survive. They asked her all kinds of questions, and when she answered they nodded and smiled, their warmth like sunbeams. But when she awoke, she couldn't remember what the questions were, and she'd lost the answers.

Desma runs her fingers over waxy leaves, clears off dust from the cuttings so sunlight can reach their cells.

A worker in a rumpled shirt and tie looks up from his desk. Beneath the stack of lines on his forehead, he gives her a weary smile.

"Aren't they dead?"

She holds up the cuttings, a fountain of greenery spilling from her hand. "Nope. They'll come back to life with a little TLC."

"Really? Mind if I have a bunch?"

Desma hands him the fountain, fetches a glass of water to use as a vase. He smiles gratefully and touches the bits of life curling over his desk.

⁕

Desma arrives at the last office building on her route, her stomach clenched like a fist and an urgent desire for a hit. It would be so easy to just cross the road and make this anxiety go away. But Loupe has given Desma a chance, and she doesn't want to let her down.

The tester stick gives a hollow rattle in the watering can as Desma pushes through the glass doors. In the lobby, workers rush past on important-looking business. The elevator pings open. So far so good: only strangers looking uninterested in their surroundings. As they shoot upward at warp speed – it's one of those ultra-modern elevators – Desma's heart rises, weightless. On the top floor the doors slide open and a receptionist beams from behind her station. "Hello, Plant Lady. Kitchen's down the hall, to the right."

Trying to not rattle the tester stick, Desma pads down the hallway, past planters of English ivy, shelves crammed with case files, and books filled with the convoluted language of law. Quietly, she slips past frosted glass offices and air-conditioned boardrooms where Raphis palms shiver in corners. Plants are like people, Loupe says. They're happier together. Still, clients insist on keeping them apart, since it's more aesetically pleasing. Desma fills her watering can in the sink and grabs the stepladder wedged beside the refrigerator. Softly, she retraces her steps.

"Dessy?"

Her heart flops. Only one person in the world has ever called her that. She takes a breath and turns to face her sister. But the watering can is full and the weight throws her off balance – a splotch of water bloops out of the spout onto the gold carpet. Even more mortifying, the tester stick floats to the top, rattles out of the can, and lands on the toes of her sister's patent leather pumps. With the air of a duchess, Lauren presses her knees together and bends to pick it up.

"Heyyy. Shit. Sorry about that." Desma accepts the tester stick, dismayed that Lauren doesn't flinch at her foul language. Lauren's blonde hair is in a bun and she's perfectly pulled together in a black pencil skirt and blouse. Desma is acutely aware of how slovenly she must look, somewhere between hippy and plumber in her cargo pants, utility belt, and dirt-smudged T-shirt, two skinny braids hanging over her shoulders.

Lauren has always been blessed in the genetic lottery, with good looks and brains. When they were kids she had so many friends she didn't notice her younger adopted sister. They lived in the same house and went to the same school, but they inhabited different worlds. The world that hailed Lauren as prom queen told Desma she looked foreign with her hawk nose and slanted eyes.

Now Lauren is a top corporate lawyer and Desma is just a plant lady. This job has given her purpose and helped save her life, but still, nobody says they want to be a plant lady when they grow up.

"I'll clean the carpet," she offers.

Lauren waves her hand dismissively. "Never mind, it's just water. I'm glad you're here. Can you look at my plant? It's got something wrong with it."

Desma follows Lauren into a big corner office with a wide oak desk and shelves of thick, leather-bound books. She inspects a gilt-framed photo on the wall: Lauren's law team posing with a golf tournament trophy – Lauren holding the trophy, of course. How could their lives have turned out so differently when they were given the same opportunities? Lauren seems to have read her mind because she gives a light laugh, "Oh, it's just a silly tournament."

"Why do you play then?" Desma can hear the sullenness in her voice and hates herself for it. Lauren blinks her saucer eyes and there's an awkward silence. Desma figures Lauren will do what her adoptive family has always done – brush such unpleasantness under the rug. But in a calm, even voice, Lauren says, "I'm not the enemy, you know."

Then she turns to the bookshelf, resuming her pleasant demeanor. "Look at my poor baby." She brings down a copper pot of English ivy with anemic leaves covered in webs. Desma turns one over: tiny eight-legged bugs, relatives of ticks and scorpions, scuttle on its underside, laying eggs and sucking chlorophyll.

"Looks like you've got bad case of spider mites."

"Can you fix it, Dessy? None of the other plant people could."

The plant really is in trouble. Never mind that it's English ivy – *hedera helix* – an invasive species that can choke entire trees to death. Still, it's a plant and needs saving. Desma rolls up her sleeves and unhooks her spray bottle of neem, ready for battle.

"All right, you little fuckers. Time to clear off."

⁂

Under a wheel of stars, Desma and her Aunt Hazel stagger out of The Rainbow, back to the decrepit Victorian to cook up with some friends. With a slip of the needle the walls fall away, and after comfortably floating awhile, Desma lands in a circle of trees. Within the trees is another circle, a circle of relatives she's never met but knows in her bones – aunties, uncles, grandmothers, and grandfathers – dancing to the drum of her heart. What are they celebrating? Auntie. With her laugh that charms everyone, Auntie Hazel dances a little jig as Desma's birth mother and grandmother come forward to embrace her.

It's a family reunion, the one Desma has longed for since she was a little girl. Except that Desma isn't included. She's outside the circle, aching to join but unable to move. She stands rooted to the spot, abandoned. Alone.

"Auntie!" Desma shouts. "Don't leave me."

The beat falls silent. The shadow dancers stop dancing and turn their eyes to Desma. Her Auntie, birth mother, and grandmother – all her ancestors – look into her so deeply that Desma knows they can see every part of her, even down to her tiniest, most horrifying flaws. But instead of looking away, their eyes hold her. They tell her she is loved. They say they will guide her, even when she is blind. And they will accompany her when she is alone. From the circle, words arise in a collective voice she hears not with her ears but with her heart.

"We are the earth's dreaming," the voices say. But what does it mean?

She awakens, gasping in a world of loud voices and spinning red and blue lights. A circle of faces is bent over her, but they are not her ancestors. And though dressed in white, they're no angels either. Desma realizes she's lying on the floor, on a layer of ash and cigarette butts. She turns her head.

Auntie is lying next to her, surrounded by paramedics. Her face a mask, still and calm.

⟁

The tester stick spins, knocking a rhythm in the bucket of swirling water. The scent of damp soil rises. Spider mites slide off leaves, tiny legs waving as she jets them with water. Her fingers pluck dead leaves and aerate the soil, bringing life back into the plant.

As she works she falls into a daydream and becomes a seed. The darkness that once threatened to consume her is the soil that nurtures her. Rain penetrates the soil, each drop softening her tough, protective coat until she splits. She may be invisible, but she is not destroyed. With all her strength, she reaches to stretch in opposite directions – one half unfurling to push up toward the light, the other sending roots down to find anchor and nourishment in the darkness – both sides of her guided by ancient, unerring instinct.

When she breaks the surface, what will she be? Whatever she becomes, it doesn't matter that she is not her sister.

On the way down in the elevator, Desma catches her reflection in the glass. She may be dishevelled and sweaty, but her cheeks have filled in and the light is back in her eyes.

The elevator stops on the sixth floor – a methadone clinic. Desma chose to go cold turkey instead, enduring the army of bugs under her skin and days of retching until she was finally free. A skinny teenager gets on. He's got sores on his face and his pupils are pinpricks, like his soul has curled up in a ball. But she can see it there inside him. She smiles, reaches for the hidden seed as words surface: "We are the earth's dreaming, all of us. Grow, grow."

The boy smiles back. "You have a great day." The doors ping open and he lopes across the street. Desma goes the opposite way, toward the city center. She takes the wide stone steps up to the art gallery two at a time, tester stick rattling, and sits with her clipboard to complete her report. Peace lily OK. Weeping fig happy. Pothos trimmed. Spider mites under control. She wants to be meticulous so she won't let Loupe down. Correction: so she won't let herself down. Desma turns her face west, feels the warmth of the late afternoon sun on her skin. At the bottom of the steps, kids play hacky-sack in a circle and an artist at an easel sketches the portrait of a young woman. Desma soaks up the life around her, feels her loved ones near, anchoring her between the worlds.

# ISHWAASE

## AFTERWORD

I like to think of Indigenous People as "resilient and relent-less" a phrase coined by Indigenous youth in Toronto, emblazoned on T-shirts created from the ENAGB initiative out of the NCCT, the Native Canadian Centre of Toronto. The NCCT played a pivotal role in my twenties and how I came about processing my Indigenous identity. I was a Sixties Scoop survivor taken from my biological family and adopted into a non-Indigenous family. Writing and the very function of stories, the way they are told and written, paved a way for me to begin healing. Stories help shape and form our identity, and our sense of cultural belonging.

It was an honor to be asked to co edit this anthology by my fellow writer and friend Nathan Niigan Noodin Adler. This anthology *Bawaajigan* (dreams) has been a labor of love from the minute we announced it, did the call out, and saw the submissions trickle in. Picking the stories to be included was difficult because I wanted to see everyone who submitted get a chance to be published, but I'm very pleased with the final selections we compiled. We considered putting together a glossary to translate the various languages represented throughout the anthology, but in the end we decided against it. We felt that if we were to include a glossary, the onus to educate would be on us. We felt that this wasn't fair, because as editors we hope these stories will encourage Indigenous and non-Indigenous people to seek out resources to learn more about these cultures and languages.

Indigenous Peoples from Canada and around the world have unique, vibrant cultures. No matter how much governments try to eradicate our voices, we have storytellers like Lee Maracle, Richard Van Camp, Joanne Arnott and others who continue to blaze a path for Indigenous writers to be heard.

Since time immemorial, stories have defined how we govern ourselves and interact with each other. Dreams are also important because they complement many of the teachings we receive from our Elders. Our stories serve many functions, coming from various nations and various teachings. They also help us to see and interpret a worldview that is different from the Western perspective.

We are full of stories waiting to be given an audience. Cherokee writer Thomas King famously says, "The truth about stories is that's all we are." There is a lot of diversity in the lives of Indigenous Peoples and it is important for our stories to have a platform for that diversity of experience to be reflected. It is thanks to Michael Callaghan, and the teamwork of Exile Editions, for seeing the importance in this project, and helping us go beyond dreaming to see this anthology become a reality.

Dreams are our unconscious way of processing experiences. In the same way stories vary in form, sleep has various stages; there is non-REM sleep (Stages 1, 2, and 3) and a fourth stage known as REM, our deepest sleep where dreams often occur. Without sleep, without dreams, without enough REM, people lose their grip on sanity, and on reality. Without enough of the stuff of which our dreams are made, without enough unreality where anything is possible, we lose our grasp on reality. Dream worlds and the real world are intimately connected. The stories in *Bawaajigan* are like our dreams, they are central to the way we process experiences. Dreams give us power, because without our dreams, we lose our realities, and our ability to imagine our futures.

Christine Miskonoodinkwe Smith

# ABOUT THE AUTHORS

**Nathan Adler** is the author of *Wrist*, an Indigenous monster story written from the monster's perspective. He is a writer and artist who works in many different mediums, including audio and video, drawing and painting, as well as glass. He is an M.F.A. candidate for Creative Writing from UBC, first-place winner of the 2010 Aboriginal Writing Challenge, and a recipient of the 2017 Hnatyshyn Foundation's REVEAL Indigenous Art Award. He has a short story forthcoming in *Love After the End*, and has published in the magazines *Redwire, Canada's History, Shtetl, Kimiwan Zine, Shameless, Event, Prairie Fire/CV2*, as well as in various blogs and anthologies. He is Anishinaabe and Jewish, a member of Lac Des Mille Lacs First Nation, and currently splits his time between Mono, Ontario, and Vancouver, British Columbia.

**Joanne Arnott** of Métis/mixed-blood was born in Winnipeg and now lives in British Columbia. She has received the League of Canadian Poets' Gerald Lampert Award (1992) and the Vancouver Mayor's Arts Award for Literary Arts (2017). Joanne has published primarily poetry and essays, most recently *Pensive & beyond*, and a co-edited collection, *Honouring the Strength of Indian Women: Plays, Stories and Poetry by Vera Manuel*.

**Yugcetun Anderson** of Vancouver is an Inuit (Inupiaq and Yup'ik) as well as Malemiut, Holicachuk, Black, and Seminole. She completed her Indigenous Film-making Bachelor of Arts at the University of Alaska Fairbanks and her Creative Writing Master of Fine Arts from the University of British Columbia. Originally from Alaska, she wanders about the North American continent writing Indigenous content. Her short film *Yugumalleq* debuted in 2018 on U.S. television. She's had a myriad of plays produced in Vancouver and Alaska, including *Something in the Living Room* – a multimedia play about an assassin's bad day – and *Get Samantha*, her first multimedia work using Twitter to engage with the audience in a play about infertility in the wilds of Alaska.                    @SnowGigglesAK

Autumn Bernhardt has appeared in two anthologies: *Blood, Water, Wind, & Stone* and *Grazing the Fire*. She currently teaches social and environmental justice courses at Colorado State University. More work can be found in *Red Rising Magazine, The Tulane Journal of Law & Sexuality, Prism International*, as well as a number of other academic and literary publications. Autumn is a Colorado native of mixed Lakota descent (non-citizen) and is wičhákte.

Wendy Bone is Métis and a Sixties Scoop survivor whose family is originally from Northern Alberta. Her most recent work has appeared in *River Teeth* journal, *Creative Nonfiction, Lunch Ticket, Prism,* and Exile Edition's anthology *Cli-Fi: Canadian Tales of Climate Change*. A graduate of the University of British Columbia's Creative Writing M.F.A. program, Wendy has recently completed a book about her travels through the Indonesian rainforest.

@wendyboneabroad   www.wendyboneabroad.com

Francine Cunningham is an award-winning Indigenous writer, artist and educator originally from Calgary, Alberta, but currently resides in Vancouver. She is a graduate of the UBC Creative Writing M.F.A. program, and a recent winner of the Indigenous Voices Award in the 2019 Unpublished Prose Category and of the Hnatyshyn Foundation's REVEAL Indigenous Art Award. Her fiction has appeared in *Grain* as the 2018 Short Prose Award winner, on the *Malahat Review's* Far Horizon's Prose shortlist, *Joyland, The Puritan* and more. Her debut book of poetry is titled *ON/Me*.   www.francinecunningham.ca

David Geary writes fiction, film, theatre, and haiku on Twitter @gearsgeary. He's originally from New Zealand of Māori and Pakeha/ Settler blood, enjoys creating Trickster/Shapeshifter stories, and teaching in the prestigious IIDF Indigenous Filmmaking program at Capilano University. Two of his short stories feature in *Purakau: Maori Myths Retold by Maori Writers* (2019), but "Jumpers on Both Bridges" is based firmly on the traffic jams outside his home in North Vancouver. His short play *OWN NOW!* was produced around the world as part of Climate Change Theatre Action in 2019.

**Gord Grisenthwaite** from Lytton, British Columbia, is a member of the Lytton First Nation and resides in Kingsville, Ontario. He will graduate from the University of Windsor with a M.A. in English Literature and Creative Writing in spring 2020. His stories and poems have appeared in *ndncountry, Offset17, The Antigonish Review,* and *Prism International*, among others. Some of them have earned prizes and awards, including the 2014 John Kenneth Galbraith Literary Award and the 2007 *Prism International* short story prize. Palimpsest Press has scheduled a fall 2020 release of his first novel, *The Wrong Woman Blues*.

**Sara General** belongs to the Turtle Clan and the Mohawk Nation. She lives in Six Nations of the Grand River, a First Nation community located in Southern Ontario on Turtle Island, with her husband and daughters. She is a writer, an artist, a language learner, and a researcher. Sara holds a Doctor of Education from Western University and works at the Deyohahá:ge: Indigenous Knowledge Centre.

www.sarageneral.com

**Brittany Johnson** is a Ph.D. student in English and Film Studies at the University of Alberta, residing in the Edmonton area. She is Métis and also a member of Beaver First Nation. Brittany was recently published in *ndncountry* and was a finalist for the Indigenous Voices Awards 2019.

**Lee Maracle** is the author of a number of critically acclaimed works, including *Ravensong; Bobbi Lee; Daughters Are Forever* and *Celia's Song,* which was longlisted for Canada Reads and shortlisted for the ReLit Award. She is also the co-editor of the award winning *My Home As I Remember,* and *Conversations with Canadians* which was short-listed for the Toronto Book Award, and continues to be a best-selling non-fiction book. Her latest work is *Hope Matters,* co-written with her daughters, Columpa Bobb and Tania Carter. Maracle has served as Distinguished Visiting Scholar at the Universities of Toronto, Waterloo, and Western Washington. Lee received the J.T. Stewart award, the Premier's Award for excellence in the arts, the Blue

Metropolis First Nation's literary award, International Festival of Authors award, and the Anne Green award. She received an Honorary Doctor of Letters from St. Thomas University, an Honorary Doctor of Laws from University of Waterloo, the Queen's Diamond Jubilee medal, and is an Officer of the Order of Canada. Lee was one of the global finalists for the Neustadt Prize in the United States, often referred to as the American Nobel Prize. She currently teaches at the University of Toronto.

**Gerald Silliker Pisim Maskwa** (Sun Bear) lives in Calgary, and was born in Thunder Bay, Ontario. He has a B.F.A. in Drama and a B.A. in Canadian studies from the University of Calgary, as well as a diploma in Addiction Studies: Aboriginal Focus Program from Bow Valley college. A play of his was aired on CBC radio.

**Christine Miskonoodinkwe Smith** is Saulteaux from Peguis First Nation. She is an editor, writer and journalist who graduated from the University of Toronto with a specialization in Aborig-inal Studies, and went on to receive her Master's in Education in Social Justice in June 2017. Her first non-fiction story, "Choosing the Path to Healing," appeared in the 2006 anthology *Growing Up Girl: An Anthology of Voices from Marginalized Spaces*. She has written for the *Native Canadian, Anishinabek News, Windspeaker, FNH* magazine, *New Tribe* magazine, *Muskrat* magazine, and the Piker Press.

**Katie-Jo Rabbit/Naatowaapistoaakii** is a member of the Blood Tribe, a freelance writer, and a sporadic spoken word artist. As an aspiring author and part of a small group of authentic Blackfoot writers, Katie-Jo is currently working on her first novel that strives to put into perspective the female Blackfoot experience and dismantle the typi-cal stereotypes of Indigenous womyn. Katie-Jo finds herself writing in Lethbridge, Alberta, where she was the columnist for "Aboriginal Voices" for the *Lethbridge Journal*. You will now find her published in various columns and Indigenous magazines throughout Southern Alberta. Katie-Jo strives to increase the voice of the modern Blackfoot womyn through art and writing, as there are many stories left to tell.

**Cathy Smith** is a Mohawk from Six Nations of the Grand in Ontario. She is a co-winner of the 2016 Indigenous Futurism contest for her story "The Mindchanger." You can follow her latest projects at:
Wordpress: bit.ly/2e41qWT
Facebook: bit.ly/2dP3rXd
Twitter: @khiatons
Instagram: cathy2891
Tumblr: bit.ly/2G3dEjo

**Délani Valin** is a Cree-Métis writer living on Vancouver Island's Snuneymuxw traditional territory, in British Columbia. She holds a B.A. in Creative Writing from Vancouver Island University. Her poetry has been awarded *The Malahat Review's* Long Poem Prize, *subTerrain's* Lush Triumphant Award, and she was nominated for a National Magazine Award in 2018. She has read for *Room's* Indigenous Brilliance series, and her work has also appeared in Exile Editions' *Those Who Make Us*, as well as *Adbusters*, *Soliloquies Anthol-ogy*, and *Portal*, among others.                    @delanivalin

**Richard Van Camp** is a Tlicho Dene from Fort Smith, N.W.T. He has 23 books out these past 23 years in just about every genre. Visit him on Facebook, Twitter, Instagram, www.richardvancamp.com

**Karen Lee White** is Northern Salish, Tuscarora, Chippewa, and Scots from Vancouver Island, British Columbia. Adopted into the Daklaweidi Wolf Clan of the Interior Tlingit/Tagish people, on whose land her first novel, *The Silence* (2018 Exile Editions), unfolds – it went into a second printing within six weeks of release. In 2018, Karen was commissioned by the Banff Centre to produce a story for the *Fables for the 21st Century*, special edition. In 2017, Karen was awarded an Indigenous Art Award for Writing by the Hnatyshyn Founda-tion's REVEAL Indigenous Art Award. Her work has appeared in Exile Editions' *That Damned Beaver* anthology, *EXILE*, *Impact: Colonialism in Canada*, and other literary journals. A play-wright, she has been commissioned by theatres in Vancouver and Victoria.

# ANTHOLOGIES IN THE SERIES

AND SOME PREVIOUS PRAISE

"*Bawaajigan* is the Anishinaabemowin word for dream, but the struggles and, as the title also suggests, forces of power narrativized in this anthology are very present in waking life too... In each story, the author's unique prose lays bare the complex time frames of violence, events, and wisdom – the long, long course of things. It's a tough but refreshing look at the different way spiritual and cultural power can adapt and surprise, even in the echoes of the darkest struggles." —*Broken Pencil*

"*Those Who Make Us*, an all-Canadian anthology of fantastical stories, featuring emerging writers alongside award-winning novelists, poets, and playwrights, is original, elegant, often poetic, sometimes funny, always thought-provoking, and a must for lovers of short fiction."
—*Publishers Weekly*, starred review

"*New Canadian Noir* is largely successful in its goals. The quality of prose is universally high...and as a whole works well as a progressive, more Canadian take on the broad umbrella of noir, as what one contributor calls 'a tone, an overlay, a mood.' It's worth purchasing for several stories alone..." —*Publishers Weekly*

"In *Dead North* we see deadheads, shamblers, jiang shi, and Shark Throats invading such home and native settings as the Bay of Fundy's Hopewell Rocks, Alberta's tar sands, Toronto's Mount Pleasant Cemetery, and a Vancouver Island grow-op. Throw in the last poutine truck on Earth driving across Saskatchewan and some 'mutant demon zombie cows devouring Montreal' (honest!) and what you've got is a fun and eclectic mix of zombie fiction..." —*Toronto Star*

"*Cli-fi* is a relatively new sub-genre of speculative fiction imagining the long-term effects of climate change [and] collects 17 widely varied stories that nevertheless share several themes: Water; Oil; Conflict... this collection, presents an urgent, imagined message from the future."
—*Globe and Mail*

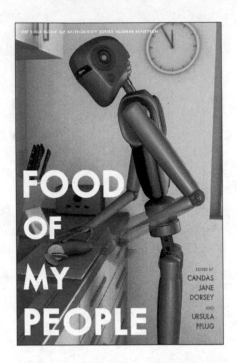

## FOOD OF MY PEOPLE

### CO-EDITED BY CANDAS JANE DORSEY AND URSULA PFLUG

"Food, culture, and magic are deeply interlinked: geography and climate and trade routes determine ingredients, traditions transmit recipes, recipes are linked to folk beliefs, and ultimately the things we consume shape us. We are what we eat, and what we believe about the things we eat says something about us. Eating is a necessary act, and so there's magic in it, varying with culture and ingredients…

"The range of different cultures – Indigenous, settler, and other – is notable because in each story we see the linkage of culture and food. And, often, a link to myth or traditional story. The concreteness of food becomes a way to embody the abstract idea of culture, and to embody the structure of a familiar story. You could argue that the food's a kind of objective correlative for myth, a tangible symbol that gets across meaning. Or you could say that a recipe is a kind of story, with a fixed structure that produces something a little different every time you tell it. Then again, you could also say a recipe's like a ritual, that (hopefully) ends with the miraculous production of something tasty and nutritious… Or say this: the stories here use myth as an ingredient, but blend tastes to make a rich meal…"

—*Blackgate/Adventures in Fantasy Literature*

Richard Van Camp, Autumn Bernhardt, Brittany Johnson, Gord Grisenthwaite, Joanne Arnott, Délani Valin, Cathy Smith, David Geary, Yugcetun Anderson, Gerald Silliker Pisim Maskwa, Karen Lee White, Sara General, Nathan Niigan Noodin Adler, Francine Cunningham, Christine Miskonoodinkwe Smith, Lee Maracle, Katie-Jo Rabbit, Wendy Bone.

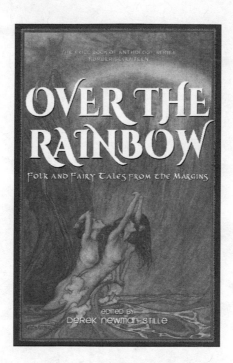

The Exile Book of Anthology Series
Number Seventeen

OVER THE RAINBOW
FOLK AND FAIRY TALES FROM THE MARGINS

Edited by
Derek Newman-Stille

# OVER THE RAINBOW:
# FOLK AND FAIRY TALES FROM THE MARGINS
## EDITED BY DEREK NEWMAN-STILLE

Fairy tales tell us the stories we need to hear, the truths we need to be aware of. This is a collection of adult stories that invite us to imagine new possibilities for our contemporary times. Collected by nine-time Prix Aurora Award-winner Derek Newman-Stille, these are edgy stories, tales that invite us to walk out of our comfort zone and see what resides at the margins. *Over the Rainbow* is a gathering of modern literature that brings together views and perspectives of the underrepresented, from the fringe, those whose narratives are at the core of today's conversations – voices that we all need to hear.

Nathan Caro Fréchette, Fiona Patton, Rati Mehrotra, Ace Jordyn, Robert Dawson, Richard Keelan, Nicole Lavigne, Liz Westbrook-Trenholm, Kate Heartfield, Evelyn Deshane, Lisa Cai, Tamara Vardomskaya, Chadwick Ginther, Quinn McGlade-Ferentzy, Karin Lowachee, Kate Story, Ursula Pflug, and Sean Moreland

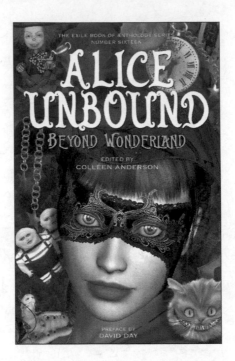

# ALICE UNBOUND:
# BEYOND WONDERLAND
## EDITED BY COLLEEN ANDERSON

"This tremendously entertaining anthology…will delight both lovers of Carroll's works and fans of inventive genre fiction." —*Publishers Weekly,* starred review

A collection of twenty-first century speculative fiction stories that is inspired by *Alice's Adventures in Wonderland, Alice Through the Looking Glass, The Hunting of the Snark,* and to some degree, aspects of the life of the author, Charles Dodgson (Lewis Carroll), and the real-life Alice (Liddell). Enjoy a wonderful and wild ride down and back up out of the rabbit hole!

Patrick Bollivar, Mark Charke, Christine Daigle, Robert Dawson, Linda DeMeulemeester, Pat Flewwelling, Geoff Gander and Fiona Plunkett, Cait Gordon, Costi Gurgu, Kate Heartfield, Elizabeth Hosang, Nicole Iversen, J.Y.T. Kennedy, Danica Lorer, Catherine MacLeod, Bruce Meyer, Dominik Parisien, Alexandra Renwick, Andrew Robertson, Lisa Smedman, Sara C. Walker and James Wood.

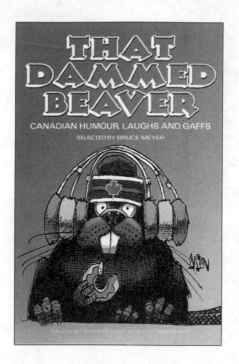

# THAT DAMMED BEAVER:
# CANADIAN HUMOUR, LAUGHS AND GAFFS

### EDITED BY BRUCE MEYER

"What exactly makes Canadians funny? This effort from long-standing
independent press Exile Editions takes a wry look at what makes us laugh
and what makes us laughable." —*Toronto Star*

Margaret Atwood, Austin Clarke, Leon Rooke, Priscila Uppal, Jonathan Goldstein, Paul
Quarrington, Morley Callaghan, Jacques Ferron, Marsha Boulton, Joe Rosenblatt, Barry
Callaghan, Linda Rogers, Steven Hayward, Andrew Borkowski, Helen Marshall, Gloria Sawai,
David McFadden, Myna Wallin, Gail Prussky, Louise Maheux-Forcher, Shannon Bramer, James
Dewar, Bob Armstrong, Jamie Feldman, Claire Dé, Christine Miscione, Larry Zolf, Anne
Dandurand, Julie Roorda, Mark Paterson, Karen Lee White, Heather J. Wood, Marty Gervais,
Matt Shaw, Alexandre Amprimoz, Darren Gluckman, Gustave Morin, and the country's
greatest cartoonist, Aislin.

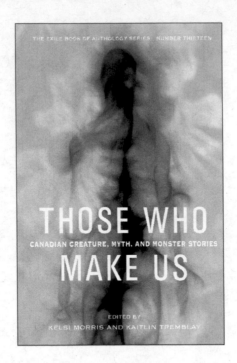

## THOSE WHO MAKE US: CANADIAN CREATURE, MYTH, AND MONSTER STORIES

### EDITED BY KELSI MORRIS AND KAITLIN TREMBLAY

What resides beneath the blankets of snow, under the ripples of water, within the whispers of the wind, and between the husks of trees all across Canada? Creatures, myths and monsters are everywhere…even if we don't always see them.

Canadians from all backgrounds and cultures look to identify with their surroundings through stories. Herein, speculative and literary fiction provides unique takes on what being Canadian is about.

"Kelsi Morris and Kaitlin Tremblay did not set out to create a traditional anthology of monster stories… This unconventional anthology lives up to the challenge, the stories show tremendous openness and compassion in the face of the world's darkness, unfairness, and indifference." —*Quill & Quire*

Featuring stories by Helen Marshall, Renée Sarojini Saklikar, Nathan Adler, Kate Story, Braydon Beaulieu, Chadwick Ginther, Dominik Parisien, Stephen Michell, Andrew Wilmot, Rati Mehrotra, Rebecca Schaeffer, Délani Valin, Corey Redekop, Angeline Woon, Michal Wojcik, Andrea Bradley, Andrew F. Sullivan and Alexandra Camille Renwick.

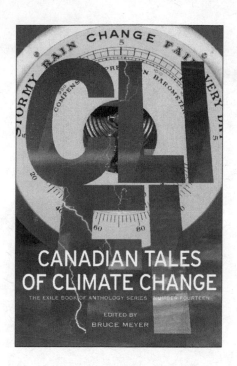

# CLI FI:
# CANADIAN TALES OF CLIMATE CHANGE

## EDITED BY BRUCE MEYER

In his introduction to this all-original set of (at times barely) futuristic tales, Meyer warns readers, "[The] imaginings of today could well become the cold, hard facts of tomorrow." Meyer (*Testing the Elements*) has gathered an eclectic variety of eco-fictions from some of Canada's top genre writers, each of which, he writes, reminds readers that "the world is speaking to us and that it is our duty, if not a covenant, to listen to what it has to say." In these pages, scientists work desperately against human ignorance, pockets of civilization fight to balance morality and survival, and corporations cruelly control access to basic needs such as water....The anthology may be inescapably dark, but it is a necessary read, a clarion call to take action rather than, as a character in Seán Virgo's "My Atlantis" describes it, "waiting unknowingly for the plague, the hive collapse, the entropic thunderbolt." Luckily, it's also vastly entertaining. It appears there's nothing like catastrophe to bring the best out in authors in describing the worst of humankind. —*Publishers Weekly*

George McWhirter, Richard Van Camp, Holly Schofield, Linda Rogers, Seán Virgo, Rati Mehrotra, Geoffrey W. Cole, Phil Dwyer, Kate Story, Leslie Goodreid, Nina Munteanu, Halli Villegas, John Oughton, Frank Westcott, Wendy Bone, Peter Timmerman, Lynn Hutchinson Lee, with an afterword by internationally acclaimed writer and filmmaker, Dan Bloom.

The Exile Book of Anthology Series
Number Eleven

playground of LOST toys

Edited by Colleen Anderson and Ursula Pflug

# PLAYGROUND OF LOST TOYS

## EDITED BY COLLEEN ANDERSON AND URSULA PFLUG

A dynamic collection of stories that explore the mystery, awe and dread that we may have felt as children when encountering a special toy. But it goes further, to the edges of space, where games are for keeps and where the mind plays its own games. We enter a world where the magic may not have been lost, where a toy or computers or gods vie for the upper hand. Wooden games of skill, ancient artifacts misinterpreted, dolls, stuffed animals, wand items that seek a life or even revenge – these lost toys and games bring tales of companionship, loss, revenge, hope, murder, cunning, and love, to be unearthed in the sandbox.

Featuring stories by Chris Kuriata, Joe Davies, Catherine MacLeod, Kate Story, Meagan Whan, Candas Jane Dorsey, Rati Mehrotra, Nathan Adler, Rhonda Eikamp, Robert Runté, Linda DeMeulemeester, Kevin Cockle, Claude Lalumière, Dominik Parisien, dvsduncan, Christine Daigle, Melissa Yuan-Innes, Shane Simmons, Lisa Carreiro, Karen Abrahamson, Geoffrey W. Cole and Alexandra Camille Renwick. Afterword by Derek Newman-Stille.

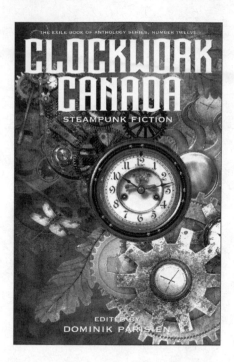

# CLOCKWORK CANADA: STEAMPUNK FICTION

## EDITED BY DOMINIK PARISIEN

Welcome to an alternate Canada, where steam technology and the wonders and horrors of the mechanical age have reshaped the past into something both wholly familiar yet compellingly different.

"These stories of clockworks, airships, mechanical limbs, automata, and steam are, overall, an unfettered delight to read." —*Quill & Quire*

"[*Clockwork Canada*] is a true delight that hits on my favorite things in fiction – curious worldbuilding, magic, and tough women taking charge. It's a carefully curated adventure in short fiction that stays true to a particular vision while seeking and achieving nuance."

—*Tor.com*

"…inventive and transgressive…these stories rethink even the fundamentals of what we usually mean by steampunk." —*The Toronto Star*

Featuring stories by Colleen Anderson, Karin Lowachee, Brent Nichols, Charlotte Ashley, Chantal Boudreau, Rhea Rose, Kate Story, Terri Favro, Kate Heartfield, Claire Humphrey, Rati Mehrotra, Tony Pi, Holly Schofield, Harold R. Thompson and Michal Wojcik.

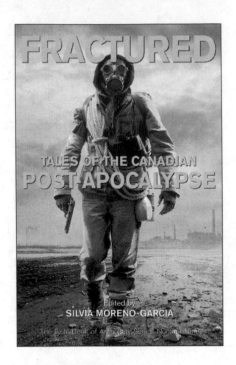

# FRACTURED:
# TALES OF THE CANADIAN POST-APOCALYPSE

### EDITED BY SILVIA MORENO-GARCIA

"The 23 stories in *Fractured* cover incredible breadth, from the last man alive in Haida Gwaii to a dying Matthew waiting for his Anne in PEI. All the usual apocalyptic suspects are here – climate change, disease, alien invasion – alongside less familiar scenarios such as a ghost apocalypse and an invasion of shadows. Stories range from the immediate aftermath of society's collapse to distant futures in which humanity has been significantly reduced, but the same sense of struggle and survival against the odds permeates most of the pieces in the collection… What *Fractured* really drives home is how perfect Canada is as a setting for the post-apocalypse. Vast tracts of wilderness, intense weather, and the potentially sinister consequences of environmental devastation provide ample inspiration for imagining both humanity's destruction and its rugged survival." —*Quill & Quire*

Featuring stories by T.S. Bazelli, GMB Chomichuk, A.M. Dellamonica, dvsduncan, Geoff Gander, Orrin Grey, David Huebert, John Jantunen, H.N. Janzen, Arun Jiwa, Claude Lalumière, Jamie Mason, Michael Matheson, Christine Ottoni, Miriam Oudin, Michael S. Pack, Morgan M. Page, Steve Stanton, Amanda M. Taylor, E. Catherine Tobler, Jean-Louis Trudel, Frank Westcott and A.C. Wise.

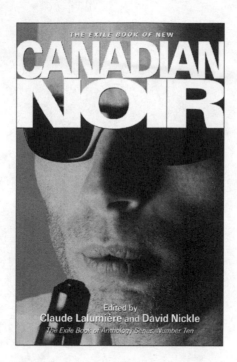

## NEW CANADIAN NOIR

### EDITED BY CLAUDE LALUMIÈRE AND DAVID NICKLE

"Everything is in the title. These are all new stories – no novel extracts – selected by Claude Lalumière and David Nickle from an open call. They're Canadian-authored, but this is not an invitation for national introspection. Some Canadian locales get the noir treatment, which is fun, since, as Nickle notes in his afterword, noir, with its regard for the underbelly, seems like an un-Canadian thing to write. But the main question *New Canadian Noir* asks isn't "Where is here?" it's "What can noir be?" These stories push past the formulaic to explore noir's far reaches as a mood and aesthetic. In Nickle's words, "Noir is a state of mind – an exploration of corruptibility, ultimately an expression of humanity in all its terrible frailty." The resulting literary alchemy – from horror to fantasy, science fiction to literary realism, romance to, yes, crime – spanning the darkly funny to the stomach-queasy horrific, provides consistently entertaining rewards." —*Globe and Mail*

Featuring stories by Corey Redekop, Joel Thomas Hynes, Silvia Moreno-Garcia, Chadwick Ginther, Michael Mirolla, Simon Strantzas, Steve Vernon, Kevin Cockle, Colleen Anderson, Shane Simmons, Laird Long, Dale L. Sproule, Alex C. Renwick, Ada Hoffmann, Kieth Cadieux, Michael S. Chong, Rich Larson, Kelly Robson, Edward McDermott, Hermine Robinson, David Menear and Patrick Fleming.

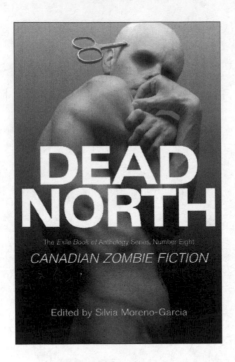

# DEAD NORTH:
# CANADIAN ZOMBIE FICTION

### EDITED BY SILVIA MORENO-GARCIA

"*Dead North* suggests zombies may be thought of as native to this country, their presence going back to Indigenous myths and legends…we see deadheads, shamblers, jiang shi, and Shark Throats invading such home and native settings as the Bay of Fundy's Hopewell Rocks, Alberta's tar sands, Toronto's Mount Pleasant Cemetery, and a Vancouver Island grow-op. Throw in the last poutine truck on Earth driving across Saskatchewan and some "mutant demon zombie cows devouring Montreal" (honest!) and what you've got is a fun and eclectic mix of zombie fiction…" —*Toronto Star*

"Every time I listen to the yearly edition of *Canada Reads* on CBC, so much attention seems to be drawn to the fact that the author is Canadian, that being Canadian becomes a gimmick. *Dead North*, a collection of zombie short stories by exclusively Canadian authors, is the first of its kind that I've seen to buck this trend, using the diverse cultural mythology of the Great White North to put a number of unique spins on an otherwise over-saturated genre."—*Bookshelf Reviews*

Featuring stories by Chantal Boudreau, Tessa J. Brown, Richard Van Camp, Kevin Cockle, Jacques L. Condor, Carrie-Lea Côté, Linda DeMeulemeester, Brian Dolton, Gemma Files, Ada Hoffmann, Tyler Keevil, Claude Lalumière, Jamie Mason, Michael Matheson, Ursula Pflug, Rhea Rose, Simon Strantzas, E. Catherine Tobler, Beth Wodzinski and Melissa Yuan-Ines.

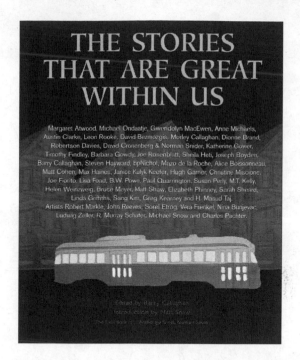

# THE STORIES THAT ARE GREAT WITHIN US

## EDITED BY BARRY CALLAGHAN

"[This is a] large book, one to be sat on the lap and not held up, one to be savoured piece by piece and heard as much as read as the great sidewalk rolls out…This is the infrastructure of Toronto, its deep language and various truths." —*Pacific Rim Review of Books*

Among the 50-plus contributors are Margaret Atwood, Michael Ondaatje, Gwendolyn MacEwen, Anne Michaels, Austin Clarke, Leon Rooke, David Bezmozgis, Morley Callaghan, Dionne Brand, Robertson Davies, Katherine Govier, Timothy Findley, Barbara Gowdy, Joseph Boyden, bpNichol, Hugh Garner, Joe Fiorito, Paul Quarrington, and Janice Kulyk Keefer, along with artists Sorel Etrog, Vera Frenkel, Nina Bunjevac, Michael Snow, and Charles Pachter.

"Bringing together an ensemble of Canada's best-known, mid-career, and emerging writers…this anthology stands as the perfect gateway to discovering the city of Toronto. With a diverse range of content, the book focuses on the stories that have taken the city, in just six decades, from a narrow wryly praised as a city of churches to a brassy, gauche, imposing metropolis that is the fourth largest in North America. With an introduction from award-winning author Matt Shaw, this blends a cacophony of voices to encapsulate the vibrant city of Toronto." —*Toronto Star*

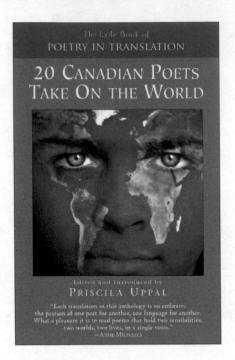

# 20 CANADIAN POETS TAKE ON THE WORLD

## EDITED BY PRISCILA UPPAL

A groundbreaking multilingual collection promoting a global poetic consciousness, this volume presents the works of 20 international poets, all in their original languages, alongside English translations by some of Canada's most esteemed poets. Spanning several time periods and more than a dozen nations, this compendium paints a truly unique portrait of cultures, nationalities, and eras."

Canadian poets featured are Oana Avasilichioaei, Ken Babstock, Christian Bök, Dionne Brand, Nicole Brossard, Barry Callaghan, George Elliott Clarke, Geoffrey Cook, Rishma Dunlop, Steven Heighton, Christopher Doda, Andréa Jarmai, Evan Jones, Sonnet L'Abbé, A.F. Moritz, Erín Moure, Goran Simić, Priscila Uppal, Paul Vermeersch, and Darren Wershler, translating the works of Nobel laureates, classic favourites, and more, including Jan-Willem Anker, Herman de Coninck, María Elena Cruz Varela, Kiki Dimoula, George Faludy, Horace, Juan Ramón Jiménez, Pablo Neruda, Chus Pato, Ezra Pound, Alexander Pushkin, Rainer Maria Rilke, Arthur Rimbaud, Elisa Sampedrín, Leopold Staff, Nichita Stănescu, Stevan Tontić, Ko Un, and Andrei Voznesensky. Each translating poet provides an introduction to their work.

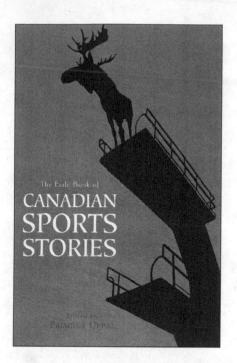

# CANADIAN SPORTS STORIES

## EDITED BY PRISCILA UPPAL

"This anthology collects a wide range of Canada's literary imaginations, telling great stories about the wild and fascinating world of sport... Written by both men and women, the generations of insights provided in this collection expose some of the most intimate details of sports and sporting life – the hard-earned victories, and the sometimes inevitable tragedies. You will get to know those who play the game, as well as those who watch it, coach it, write about it, dream about it, live and die by it."

"Most of the stories weren't so much about sports per se than they were a study of personalities and how they react to or deal with extreme situations...all were worth reading"
—goodreads.com

Clarke Blaise, George Bowering, Dionne Brand, Barry Callaghan, Morley Callaghan, Roch Carrier, Matt Cohen, Craig Davidson, Brian Fawcett, Katherine Govier, Steven Heighton, Mark Jarman, W.P. Kinsella, Stephen Leacock, L.M. Montgomery, Susanna Moodie, Marguerite Pigeon, Mordecai Richler, Priscila Uppal, Guy Vanderhaeghe, and more.

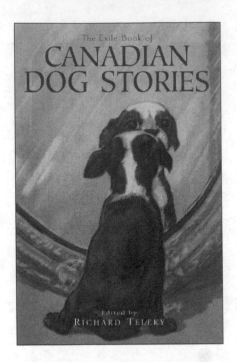

## CANADIAN DOG STORIES

### EDITED BY RICHARD TELEKY

Spanning from the 1800s to 2005, and featuring exceptional short stories from 28 of Canada's most prominent fiction writers, this unique anthology explores the nature of the human-dog bond through writing from both the nation's earliest storytellerssuch as Ernest Thompson Seton, L. M. Montgomery, and Stephen Leacock, as well as a younger generation that includes Lynn Coady and Matt Shaw. Not simply sentimental tales about noble dogs doing heroic deeds, these stories represent the rich, complex, and mysterious bond between dogs and humans. Adventure and drama, heartfelt encounters and nostalgia, sharp-edged satire, and even fantasy make up the genres in this memorable collection.

"Twenty-eight exceptional dog tales by some of Canada's most notable fiction writers... The stories run the breadth of adventure, drama, satire, and even fantasy, and will appeal to dog lovers on both sides of the [Canada/U.S.] border." —*Modern Dog Magazine*

Marie-Claire Blais, Barry Callaghan, Morley Callaghan, Lynn Coady, Mazo de la Roche, Jacques Ferron, Mavis Gallant, Douglas Glover, Katherine Govier, Kenneth J. Harvey, E. Pauline Johnson, Janice Kulyk Keefer, Alistair Macleod, L.M. Montgomery, P.K. Page, Charles G.D. Roberts, Leon Rooke, Jane Rule, Duncan Campbell Scott, Timothy Taylor, Sheila Watson, Ethel Wilson, and more.

The Exile Book of
NATIVE CANADIAN
FICTION AND DRAMA
Edited by
DANIEL DAVID MOSES AND BARRY CALLAGHAN

# NATIVE CANADIAN FICTION AND DRAMA

## EDITED BY DANIEL DAVID MOSES

The work of men and women of many tribal affiliations, this collection is a wide-ranging anthology of contemporary Native Canadian literature. Deep emotions and life-shaking crises converge and display Indigenous concerns regarding various topics, including identity, family, community, caste, gender, nature, betrayal, and war. A fascinating compilation of stories and plays, this account fosters cross-cultural understanding and presents the Native Canadian writers reinvention of traditional material and their invention of a modern life that is authentic. It is perfect for courses on short fiction or general symposium teaching material.

Tomson Highway, Lauren B. Davis, Niigaanwewidam James Sinclair, Joseph Boyden, Joseph A. Dandurand, Alootook Ipellie, Thomas King, Yvette Nolan, Richard Van Camp, Floyd Favel, Robert Arthur Alexie, Daniel David Moses, Katherena Vermette.

"A strong addition to the ever shifting Canadian literary canon, effectively presenting the depth and artistry of the work by Aboriginal writers in Canada today."

—*Canadian Journal of Native Studies*

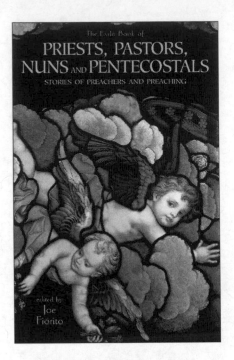

# PRIESTS, PASTORS,
# NUNS AND PENTECOSTALS

## EDITED BY JOE FIORITO

A literary approach to the Word of the Lord, this collection of short fiction deals within one way or another the overarching concept of redemption. This anthology demonstrates how God appears again and again in the lives of priest, pastors, nuns, and Pentecostals. However He appears, He appears again and again in the lives of priests, nuns, and Pentecostals in these great stories of a kind never collected before.

Mary Frances Coady, Barry Callaghan, Leon Rooke, Roch Carrier, Jacques Ferron, Seán Virgo, Marie-Claire Blais, Hugh Hood, Morley Callaghan, Hugh Garner, Diane Keating, Alexandre Amprimoz, Gloria Sawai, Eric McCormack, Yves Thériault, Margaret Laurence, Alice Munro.

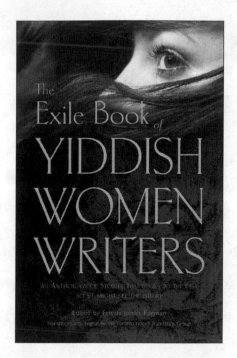

## YIDDISH WOMEN WRITERS

### EDITED BY FRIEDA JOHLES FOREMAN

Presenting a comprehensive collection of influential Yiddish women writers with new translations, this anthology explores the major transformations and upheavals of the 20th century. Short stories, excerpts, and personal essays are included from 13 writers, and focus on such subjects as family life; sexual awakening; longings for independence, education, and creative expression; the life in Europe surrounding the Holocaust and its aftermath; immigration; and the conflicted entry of Jewish women into the modern world with the restrictions of traditional life and roles. These powerful accounts provide a vital link to understanding the Jewish experience at a time of conflict and tumultuous change.

"This continuity…of Yiddish, of women, and of Canadian writers does not simply add a missing piece to an existing puzzle; instead it invites us to rethink the narrative of Yiddish literary history at large… Even for Yiddish readers, the anthology is a site of discovery, offering harder-to-find works that the translators collected from the Canadian Yiddish press and published books from Israel, France, Canada, and the U.S."
—*Studies in American Jewish Literature*, Volume 33, Number 2, 2014

"Yiddish Women Writers did what a small percentage of events at a good literary festival [Blue Metropolis] should: it exposed the curious to a corner of history, both literary and social, that they might never have otherwise considered." —*Montreal Gazette*